Jury
of One

Charlie Cochrane

RIPTIDE
PUBLISHING

Riptide Publishing
PO Box 1537
Burnsville, NC 28714
www.riptidepublishing.com

Jury of One

Cover art: L.C. Chase, lcchase.com/design.htm
Editor: Carole-ann Galloway
Layout: L.C. Chase, lcchase.com/design.htm

ISBN: 978-1-62649-377-3

First edition
March, 2016

Also available in ebook:
ISBN: 978-1-62649-376-6

Jury
of One

Charlie Cochrane

RIPTIDE
PUBLISHING

To all the authors of all the mysteries I've read over the years, who inspired me to take up my pen and write.

Table
of Contents

Chapter One

Robin Bright wiped the residual shaving cream from his face and grinned at his reflection in the mirror. Life tasted good, better than it had in a long time. Work was going well, with a promotion to detective chief inspector on the cards, but that wasn't the only thing making him so happy. He had plenty of blessings in his private life, and if he was counting them, the number one was at present down in the kitchen, clattering about. And Robin's second-best blessing was probably sitting in his basket, chewing on dog biscuits and hoping somebody might throw the end of a sausage in his direction.

Was it only a year ago that he'd have woken on a Saturday morning with nothing more to look forward to than the delights of washing and ironing, accompanied by the radio commentary of Spurs getting thrashed by the Arsenal? He used to hope the phone would go, calling him in to work because a gang of little scrotes had misbehaved on Friday night. How things had changed.

"Are you going to be in there forever?" Adam Matthews's voice sounded from downstairs. "Your tea's going to get cold."

"I'll be down soon. Got to get my shirt on."

"Yeah. You don't want to scare the postwoman again." The sound of footsteps and the *thud* of the kitchen door indicated that Adam had gone back to making breakfast.

Robin took a final glance at the mirror, decided he'd do, and went off to find his favourite T-shirt. Hopefully his phone would keep silent today so a proper shirt and tie wouldn't be needed; surely a man deserved his relaxation time? In the meantime he should get his backside downstairs before Adam sent Campbell, the huge black

Newfoundland that shared their lives—when he couldn't share their bed—to fetch him.

"Smells good." Robin soaked up the delicious aromas as he came into the kitchen.

"Me or the crepes?" Adam expertly flipped a pancake. "Can you let himself into the garden? I suspect he's bursting."

"He probably doesn't want to go out in case he misses a crumb falling on the floor." Robin opened the back door and eased the dog outside, with a promise that they'd keep him some of their breakfast.

The radio was on, the relentlessly cheerful tones of the Monkees forming a standard part of Radio 2's Saturday morning fodder. Adam's well-nigh tuneless tones competed with Davy Jones's much more melodious ones as they encouraged Sleepy Jean to cheer up.

"Just as well you didn't sing for those kids." Robin let Campbell back in. "You'd never have got the job."

Adam had recently been interviewed—successfully—for a deputy headship that he'd be taking up at the start of the next term. The recruitment ordeal had included being grilled by the school council, who'd insisted that each candidate sing them a song. Adam, being a smart cookie, had managed to persuade the kids to do the singing instead, and they'd loved him for it.

"Look at me ignoring that." Adam produced a stack of pancakes from the oven, where they'd obviously been keeping warm. "Get some of those inside you. Busy day."

More than busy. Lunch with Adam's mum, followed by a bit of shopping, trying to navigate the tricky issue of what Robin's mother might want for her birthday. What do you get for the woman who insists that all she wants is for you not to be at work so you can share her birthday dinner?

"I just hope the bloody phone doesn't go."

"So do I. Can't you put it onto divert and make the call go through to Anderson?"

"He'd kill me if I did." There was another blessing, Anderson still being on Robin's team, making snarky remarks and useful leaps of deduction. "Or at least put laxative in my coffee."

Adam sniggered. "You need to make the most of him. He won't be with you forever."

"True." Anderson's promotion was on the horizon, as well. He'd proved himself a bloody good copper, as Robin had.

"Even Campbell likes him, and that dog's no fool."

"He's an excellent judge of character." Robin stirred his tea. "I wish there were more like Anderson in the force. People who don't think themselves above being civil and pleasant to the old salts who'll be walking the beat until their retirement."

"More clones of you, then?"

"Why not?" Robin didn't like to boast, but he knew he did his job well. He'd won plenty of friends on the way up, and when they neared retirement, he'd be on his way to becoming superintendent. "It's not hard to do the job. Keep nicking people, keep your nose clean, and keep your paperwork up to date."

"Yes, sah!" Adam saluted, then tucked in to his breakfast.

Robin had put away his third pancake and was eyeing a fourth when his mobile phone sounded. Adam made his eye-rolling "I hope that's not work" face, although the bloke was getting used to being at the beck and call of Stanebridge police headquarters. You couldn't expect anything else when you'd hitched up to a rozzer.

Robin grabbed the phone. "Robin Bright speaking."

"Cowdrey here." His boss's not-so-dulcet tones came down the line. "Sorry to interrupt your Saturday morning, Robin, but we've got a tricky one. Bloke got killed last night, a stone's throw from the Florentine restaurant, in Abbotston. Bit off our patch, but the local superintendent's a friend of mine and wants us to handle things. His team's tied up with those attacks."

Abbotston, fifteen miles away, was twice the size of Stanebridge, with a crime rate four times as high, and its very own ongoing crisis. "The Abbotston Slasher," the papers had christened whoever was making the knife attacks, although that title smacked more of *Carry On* films than the terrifying reality: three young women stabbed these last three months, each on the eve of the new moon, and one of them had died of her wounds. The moon would be new again tonight; Robin guessed leave had been cancelled and any unexplained death not related to the case would be an unwelcome distraction.

"Never rains but it pours, does it, sir?"

"Pours? It's bloody torrential. There's the cup tie, as well."

"Oh hell, I'd forgotten about that." Millwall hitting the town, to play non-league Abbotston Alexandra. Even their cleaning lady was going to the match. Robin mouthed *Sorry* at Adam, then grabbed a pen and notepad.

"What do we know about the murder, sir?"

"It happened about three o'clock this morning. A couple of passers-by found the victim alive, just, although unconscious, and they called an ambulance. He didn't make it beyond the operating theatre. Died at six o'clock. " Cowdrey sounded short of breath; he was corpulent, asthmatic but as hard as nails. "Stabbed four times at least."

"Any leads?" Robin, while making notes, was already building up a picture. The Florentine was an upmarket kind of a restaurant to get stabbed near, the sort nominally run by an up-and-coming television personality chef. It attracted punters from across the Home Counties. Perhaps, he thought—irreverently and guiltily—the dead man was one of the waiters and the murderer had been a customer incensed at the size of the bill?

Whatever was going on, there was a guarded edge to the chief superintendent's voice as he continued. "The men who found him reckoned he'd been drinking at a local bar earlier, and got himself into a fight there in the process. We got called in with the ambulance and managed to start taking statements at the club concerned. One of these all-night-opening places." The slight hesitation in Cowdrey's voice made Robin stiffen; he could guess what was coming.

"Which bar was this, sir?"

"The Desdemona."

The Desdemona. Robin had been there once or twice, back when he was single; it wasn't a bad sort of a place. It was on the pricey side, but the decor was tasteful, and there were neither slot machines nor TV screens to ruin the atmosphere. It was about two hundred yards from the Florentine, both of them in the posh part of Abbotston. And the bar flew a rainbow flag outside, which was presumably one of the reasons why *he* was being put onto the case when the local boys needed a hand.

"Homophobic element, sir?" Might as well ask the obvious.

"Too early to say." Cowdrey exhaled, loudly. "Sorry, but I think your Saturday's ruined. I'll call Anderson and get him to meet you at the scene."

"Thanks. I'll be there in half an hour or so. Less if the traffic's kind." Robin ended the call, looked longingly at the fourth pancake, and decided to snaffle it now. It could be a while before he got anything else to eat today. At least Lindenshaw, where Adam lived, was the right side of Stanebridge for getting to Abbotston quickly.

"A case?" Adam said in the supportive tones—supportive but with an edge of resignation—he used on these occasions.

"Yeah. A bloke's been murdered. Stabbing," Robin said between mouthfuls.

"Blimey. It's getting like Morse's Oxford round here." Adam half filled Robin's mug. "Here, wash those pancakes down."

"Thanks. And this is hardly Morse country. It's only the second murder investigation I've led on."

"That's two too many." Adam patted Robin's hand. "Sorry. I shouldn't be so tetchy."

"I should be the one apologising. For buggering up the weekend."

"It's not your fault, it's your job. Like marking a ton of books is mine." Adam smiled. "And it's best part of a year since the last one, so I shouldn't complain, even though I probably will. Where did it happen?"

"It's not our patch, thank goodness. Abbotston." Robin let his guilt subside under the details of the case. "Near that posh restaurant with the Michelin star."

"The one we could never afford to eat at?" Adam's eyebrows shot up.

"That's the one. Don't think the victim ate there either. He'd been at the Desdemona, earlier."

"The Desdemona? Did they bring you in because . . .?" Adam finished the question with another lift of his eyebrows.

"Because I'm a bloody good copper?" Robin grinned, then swigged down the tea before going over to give Adam a kiss. "No. My boss is bosom buddies with the local detective superintendent, so it was a case of helping out an old mate. The local guys are up to their eyeballs with these attacks on women, and if whoever's doing it plays to form, there's likely to be another tonight."

"I know. Sally at the school lives over there, and she won't go out after dark." Adam gave Robin's cheek a squeeze. "You look after yourself, right? I don't want *you* getting stabbed."

"Yes, Mother." Robin swiped an apple from the fruit bowl, on the principle that it might be as much lunch as he'd get, then legged it upstairs to put on that bloody shirt and tie.

Abbotston wasn't the kind of place Robin could warm to. The posh parts were much posher than anything Stanebridge had to offer, but it lacked character, except in some of the outlying areas where villages had been absorbed. The centre had been bombed during the war, and the rebuilding programme had been typically 1950s: utilitarian and horribly ugly. Part of it had seen recent redevelopment, and the Florentine was located there.

The telltale blue-and-white police tape surrounded a piece of concreted hardstanding behind an estate agent's office next to the restaurant—probably where he or she parked their big, swanky car. The area was partially hidden from the street and not likely to be well lit at night, so you'd avoid it if you were female and the new moon was about to appear. Within its boundaries, a solitary crime scene investigator was finishing off his painstaking task.

Robin noted the groups of people gathered on the pavement, who stood for a while watching, then went about their normal Saturday morning business with the added bonus of a mystery to speculate about. *Who, why, when?* The word would soon get around. The local news was probably already carrying it, and people would watch, wonder, and just as soon forget. Robin wouldn't be able to do that until the culprit had been brought to book.

According to Cowdrey, who'd briefed Robin on arrival at the scene, the victim had left the Desdemona, turned east, and headed up the main road, towards the smart new block of flats about a mile away, which, according to the business cards the CSI had found on his body, was the contact address he gave. It also turned out to be where the man lived. That was a mystery in itself, not because it was so unusual to work from home, but because he'd have had to double back to get to this end of town.

Thomas Hatton, Tax Consultant.

They'd found the victim's wallet seemingly intact, so robbery didn't appear to have been the motive. Hatton's keys had been in his pocket too, and, once the CSI had finished at the scene, the police were going to have to work through the dead man's flat, trying to build up a picture of him.

Four stab wounds indicated to Robin that hatred or some other deep passion had been involved. Though the police couldn't rule out a random attack from somebody who was so drunk or drugged up that they didn't know what they were doing.

He looked up and down the road. If Hatton had initially been heading home, why had he taken a detour and ended up here? Had he met someone en route and been walking with them? The early reports were that he'd left the club alone.

"Surprised nobody saw him being attacked, sir." Sergeant Anderson's voice at his shoulder made Robin jump.

"Must you creep up on people?"

Anderson grinned. "Reconstruction. I've proved the victim could have been crept up on. Assuming he hadn't come along here voluntarily with his killer. Into a dark car park for a bit of slap and tickle, perhaps?"

"I'm not sure why anybody would have come up here." Robin shrugged. It might be as simple as a few minutes of fun gone horribly wrong. "Hardly Lovers' Lane."

"Some people appreciate the sleazy aspect. I wonder why he wasn't heard, either. Did he shout out? Or did he know whoever killed him, and get taken off guard?"

Robin nodded. Certainly children were most at risk from people they knew and trusted, family and friends being more dangerous statistically than strangers were. The same applied, if to a lesser extent, to adults. "Does it get that busy round here in the middle of the night? That you'd not be seen or heard?"

"Fridays and Saturdays, yes, or so my mates say. Clubs and bars turning out. The men who found him had been drinking not far from here. Not one of your haunts?"

"No," Robin replied, coldly. "I can't help wondering if these local drinkers are so universally sloshed that they wouldn't notice somebody running away covered in blood? This would have got messy for the killer."

"Some of the people who roll out of clubs are so far gone they wouldn't notice if aliens invaded." Anderson rolled his eyes. "Point taken, though."

"I suppose if you had a big enough coat, one that you discarded for the attack and then put on again, you could have hidden a multitude of sins." Especially under street lighting that would have been hazy at best. "If the killer made his or her way off into the residential area, they could have easily gone to ground. That's supposed to be a complete rabbit warren."

"You don't like Abbotston, do you?"

"No."

"Not even the football team?" Anderson didn't wait for a response. "I wouldn't have minded getting called in for cup tie duty."

"You enjoy aggro?" Abbotston Alexandra's stunning progress through the early rounds of the FA Cup was about to be put to an end by a Millwall team who were having a great league run and whose supporters had a nasty reputation. All in all, Abbotston wasn't a nice place to be at present.

Anderson made a face. "It would make more sense to escape up by the apartment blocks than to go along the main road. Unless you had a car waiting for you, then you'd slip in and Bob's your uncle." And a car wouldn't have necessarily attracted attention at chucking-out time if things did get that busy, because there'd have been taxis milling around and people getting lifts home.

"That lack of noise bothers me. Even if Hatton was attacked suddenly by somebody he knew, he was stabbed time and again, so why didn't he call out?"

"Maybe he did and the noise got swallowed up among the traffic. Or it coincided with some rowdy mob coming out of the Indian restaurant." Anderson gestured vaguely along the road.

"Or, if he knew his attacker, that line of thought may be irrelevant because he could have let them get close enough to put a hand over his mouth." Robin shook his head. Too much speculation and no proper evidence to go on, yet.

Robin glanced towards the pavement, the other side of the tape, where Cowdrey was talking to Wendy May, a young, tired-looking WPC, who'd been called the previous night to help take statements from the people at the Desdemona. Whose idea had it been to send a female, black officer into the club to accompany the white, male, local officers? Had someone seen the rainbow flag—or known of the establishment's clientele—and decided that if they couldn't find a gay officer, then some other minority member would have to do?

He wasn't being fair, and he shouldn't make snap judgements. WPC May was described as an excellent copper, but he'd always been sensitive to outbreaks of political correctness. It was a weakness he found hard to overcome. People said a gay copper would have opportunities galore to get on the force if he displayed any talent. And possibly if he didn't; the powers that be wanted minority officers to hold up as examples of the constabulary's open-mindedness.

It grated. Somehow being condescended to in such a way was as bad as coming up against rampant discrimination. Adam felt the same.

"Inspector Bright. Sergeant Anderson." Cowdrey called them over. "WPC May has been updating me on the statements she took with Inspector Root. He's gone to get a couple of hours' sleep before this evening." They all nodded.

"Is there anything to follow up, sir?" Robin liked presenting the superintendent with opportunities to show off his knowledge. It made the man happy and by some reverse psychology seemed to give Cowdrey the impression that Robin was a particularly bright spark.

"Hatton was involved in a scuffle inside the Desdemona club. He and the other man were ejected at about twelve forty-five. The doorman made sure they went off in opposite directions."

Twelve forty-five. That left the best part of two hours unaccounted for.

"Do we know who the other man was?" Anderson asked the superintendent.

Cowdrey shook his head. "Seems like no one had seen him there before. Someone called him Radar, but that wound him up, so it's not a lot of use."

Radar? That was a character in a show they ran on the classic-comedy channel; maybe he was a fan? Or an air traffic controller, or one of a hundred other things. "I suppose it would have been easy enough for this 'Radar' to double back or go around the block and meet up with the victim again? How long would that take, May?"

"To get here? About four times as much as going direct. It wouldn't take two hours, though." The constable stifled a yawn.

Cowdrey adopted a paternally encouraging expression. "You've done a good job here, given us a start. Before you get some rest, can we pick your brains? Who would *you* follow up first out of the people you spoke to? You met them; we didn't."

May nodded. "As I said previously, sir, there was only one I think needs further questioning at the moment, and I've put his statement at the top of the pile. Max Worsley. I know it's only a gut feeling, but I'm certain he knew more than he was saying."

"Thank you. Go and put your feet up." Cowdrey turned to Robin, handing him a dossier stuffed with paper. "There you are, Bright. Not often you get a murder to keep you two out of mischief."

"Thank God for that, sir."

"Think of it as good for your careers." Cowdrey nodded at Anderson, then left, ushering May with him.

"Good for our careers?" Anderson snorted. "Only if we don't make a pig's ear of it."

"Too true." Robin looked at the dossier, glanced at where the murder had happened, then puffed out his cheeks. "I'm assuming we rule out a link to the Slasher?"

"Don't you always tell me never to assume?" Anderson flashed his cheeky grin. "Can't make an obvious connection, though. Victim's the wrong sex; wounds aren't in the same places."

"That's what I thought." It would, however, be unwise to dismiss a connection entirely; last night had seen the appropriate phase of the moon. He noted the address on the statement. "Right. Get your phone and find out where Sandy Street is. Let's see if this Worsley bloke has surfaced this morning."

Sandy Street was in the part of Abbotston that had been developed back in Victorian times, when the railway arrived, best part of a mile from where Hatton had been found. The quality of the properties shot up a notch as they turned the corner in Worsley's road.

"Number twenty-one will be on the left side." Robin peered at the numbers. "Looks like you should be lucky with a parking space."

They drew up outside an elegant town house; the column of names and bell pushes showed it had been divided into flats, though the facade was well maintained and there wasn't the air of seediness there usually was about such conversions. They rang, gave their names and purpose over the intercom, were let in, and went up to the top floor. Worsley—a muscular bloke with two days of stubble and a gorgeous smile—was waiting for them at the turn of the stairs.

"It's about last night." Anderson dutifully flashed his warrant card. "One or two things we need to clarify."

"Come in, I was just making myself some coffee. Bit of a late night. Want some?"

"I wouldn't say no." Anderson looked at Robin hopefully.

"Count me in as well."

Worsley ushered them into a little dining area, set in a corner of the lounge, with a view of the local rooftops. A vase of flowers on the table and another on the bookshelves helped fill the place with colour. Worsley soon appeared, bearing coffee-filled china mugs, leaving the policemen to juggle with drinks, notebooks, and pens.

"Did you see either of the men who were in the scuffle at any other part of the evening?"

"Not really. I was too busy drinking and chatting with friends."

Drinking with friends? Robin was trying to find a subtle way to phrase the natural follow-up question when Anderson cut in with, "Do you go to the Desdemona a lot?"

"As often as I can. Even my straight pals hang out at the place. I assume the question actually meant 'am I gay?'" Worsley grinned.

"Not at all." Anderson, if he'd been wrong-footed, made a swift recovery. "I was trying to establish if you were a regular there, in case you could tell us whether Hatton or the man he fought with had been at the club before."

"My apologies. And no, I've never seen them there before. Not that I remember, anyway."

Robin took a swig of coffee, earning some thinking time. What had May picked up that made her think Worsley had more to say? They couldn't ignore the fact that he lived relatively close to the scene of the crime, and it was possible that he could have left the club, done the deed, run home to clean himself up, and returned to the Desdemona later, bold as brass.

"Have there ever been similar incidents near the Desdemona? Or the Florentine?" Anderson—eyes darting about—was clearly taking in the flat, maybe searching for clues. "Not necessarily stabbings, but trouble of any sort."

"Not that I remember. The Desdemona's a pretty staid place. Matches the area. Very quiet part of Abbotston. Safe." Worsley shrugged and drank his coffee.

"And is there anything else, however small or insignificant it might seem, that you can add to what you told WPC May last night?" Robin was on the verge of closing his notebook and leaving.

Worsley's face became guarded, as if he was weighing his options. "What do you know about Hatton? Come to think of it, what do you know about me?"

Well spotted, WPC May. Looks like you were *right about him knowing more than he'd let on. Adam would be giving you a house point if you were in his class.*

Robin shared a wary glance with his sergeant before replying. "Very little. Hatton's business card says he was a tax consultant . . ."

"Tax consultant? I suppose he might have been by now, assuming he'd left GCHQ."

"GCHQ?" Alarm bells started to go off in Robin's head. "Do you mean Hatton was involved with the secret services? How on earth do you know that?"

"The answers to those are, in order, 'yes,' 'he used to be,' and 'I did some computer work for them and saw him there.'" Worsley grinned again, the sort of grin that made Robin uncomfortable around the collar. If he didn't know better, he'd say he was being flirted with.

You're not my type, dear. And anyway, I'm already spoken for.

"Let me get this right," Anderson said. "You saw him there? How long ago was that?"

"Oh . . ." Worsley wrinkled his brow. "Three years?"

"Three years and you remembered him?"

"Yes. I have a photographic memory for faces, especially handsome ones, and he was a real silver fox. How I hadn't clocked him in the bar before the fight, I don't know. Maybe because it was crazy busy."

Maybe. If he was telling the truth.

"I'm bloody useless with names, unfortunately." Worsley carried on, oblivious. "I must have seen him around and about GCHQ perhaps half a dozen times over the course of a month, even though I wasn't working in his department."

"I suppose you can't tell us what you were doing there?" Anderson asked.

"Afraid not. Official Secrets Act and all that, although I'm sure you can verify my security clearance and the like, if you need to make sure I'm a good, reliable boy."

"We will, believe me." Anderson had clearly taken a dislike to this particular witness. "Did you notice anybody else you recognised from GCHQ while you were at the club?"

"No. Should I have?" Worsley appeared to be equally disenchanted with the sergeant.

"Please. We're only trying to find out who killed Hatton," Robin reminded them both. "You work in computing?"

"Yeah, part of a consultancy. Helping to put in new systems or troubleshooting old ones." Worsley ran his finger round the rim of his mug. "And in answer to an earlier question, I have no idea if he was gay. He certainly didn't give the impression of being on the pull last night."

Robin nodded, but he'd keep an open mind on that point for the moment. "You said you saw Hatton half a dozen times. Ever speak to him?"

"Not back at GCHQ."

"Last night?"

Worsley shrugged. "No."

"What about the other guy in the fight?" Anderson asked. "Did you interact with him? You said you'd 'not really' seen either of them. Is that a yes or a no?"

"It's a qualified no. Unless you count me saying 'thank you' when he held the door to the men's toilets open. And for the record," he added, with a sharp glance at Anderson, "nothing goes on in those toilets."

"I never said anything." Anderson raised his hands in a gesture of innocence that clearly fooled nobody. "I don't suppose there's any point in us trying the old 'do you know of anyone who had a grudge against Hatton' question? Or whether you've got any further bombshells to drop?"

"No, I'm sorry." Worsley's regret sounded genuine enough. "Although if that changes, I'll get back to you. Have you a contact number?"

Robin produced a card with the relevant details on it. "This is the Stanebridge police station number, but someone there can make sure I get any message; I'll ring you back."

"Okie dokie." Worsley took the card, studied it, then put it in his wallet. "Just as well I've got this, because I'll never remember your names."

"Don't put yourself out remembering mine." Anderson pushed back his chair, signalling that the interview was finished.

Robin made an apologetic face, smoothing over the awkwardness with some platitudes, before getting Anderson through the door. They were halfway down the stairs and out of earshot before he asked, "What rattled your cage?"

"Him. He put my back up." Anderson made a face, as though even referring to Worsley left a bad taste in his mouth. "We should keep an eye on him."

"And is that based on anything other than the fact he narked you?"

Anderson grinned. "Call it instinct. Anyway, if Hatton *was* still involved with GCHQ when he died, this is likely to get messy."

Robin nodded. Murder wasn't something he had a broad experience of, with the exception—the wonderful exception—of the case that had brought Adam across his path. Terrorism was outside his experience entirely. Of course, Hatton might have been acting as nothing more than a tax consultant at the time of his death, or that could be a cover story; they'd have to wait for further information.

"We'll get back to the station and plough through the rest of the statements first." They'd reached the car, although Robin stopped and took a deep breath before getting in. "And we'll get Davis to work her usual magic on the background stuff."

"Sounds good. She'll love you for spoiling her weekend." Anderson grimaced.

"She can join the club. Your Helen won't have been happy at you getting called in."

Anderson shrugged. "She's got a hen do tonight, so she's glad to have me out from under her feet."

"I'll volunteer you for more Saturday jobs, then." Adam wouldn't be so glad. He accepted the long hours as part of a policeman's lot, in the same way *he* worked every hour God sent at times, but they'd got used to having their weekends together. Robin was ready to go, but Anderson seemed to be lost in thought. "Are you thinking about the earache you'll get if I keep screwing up your weekends?"

"No. I'm trying to work out why *he* bugs me." Anderson jerked his thumb towards the house. "He'll be trouble. Mark my words."

"I will." Robin started up the engine. Trouble? Robin couldn't work out how. But the nagging voice in his head reminded him that Anderson had been right about this kind of thing before.

Chapter Two

Adam and Campbell took advantage of having time on their own by taking a Saturday morning run. Since Robin had moved in, they'd had to adapt to a new routine, and while Adam wasn't complaining—a change of habits was far preferable to an empty space in his heart—sometimes it was nice to slip back into bachelor ways. Campbell clearly appreciated the opportunity as well, straining at his lead to urge Adam on to faster speeds.

Mum would be sad not to see Robin at lunch, though, given her soft spot for him, and Campbell couldn't take his place at the restaurant, no matter how much he'd have relished the chance. She often said she was lucky she got to see Robin at all; in fact, it seemed like a miracle that *he* and Robin got to spend any time together, given the hours they both put in. Thank God the Stanebridge crime rate wasn't soaring, particularly in the school holidays when there wasn't quite so much work to call on Adam's time.

"Slow down, Campbell." Adam pulled on the lead, trying to restrain the dog's enthusiasm. "I've got a lot to do today, and you'll wear me out before I've even started."

And he'd have to do it on his own, given that Robin wasn't likely to be back until late. Murder or child abduction took priority over everything else, as did this Abbotston Slasher business. Sally, one of the learning support assistants in the infants' part of the school, wasn't the type to panic, being used to dealing with children with bodily fluids coming out of every orifice at once. She was kind but formidable; Adam wouldn't have liked to meet her in a dark alleyway if she bore him a grudge. Even so, she was locking her door in the evening and never going out alone at night, if only to put the bins on the pavement, irrespective of the phase of the moon. Apparently her neighbours were similarly edgy. It didn't help that she knew one of the victims.

"Murder's never nice, is it, Campbell?" Adam hadn't intended to voice his thoughts, but they'd come out anyway. Just as well there was nobody but the dog within earshot.

The repercussions spread wider than the victim and his or her family; Adam knew that from experience. Those in the vicinity of the crime, witnesses to it, and those who ended up under suspicion all suffered. And the poor bloody rozzers, as Robin kept reminding him, had to mop up the mess while juggling too many balls, not least the interest of the media. What chance of the national press keeping away if there turned out to be a link to the Florentine and its celebrity chef? Adam had gone through that once before, when the media had invaded Lindenshaw on the heels of the murder at the school. He envied no one the experience.

Adam shivered, a sudden wave of cold sweeping over him as he recalled those days. "Come on." He and Campbell broke into a run, which might both warm him up and make the unpleasant memories go away.

Hopefully Robin would get home at a reasonable time that evening, so Adam could fuss over him, feed him up, and get a bit of a debrief. Not that a mere schoolteacher would be able to offer anything in the way of insight to the average police problem, but Robin said having to explain the case to somebody not involved helped *him* to get things clear in his mind. Not only that: when Adam asked for clarification or needed points explained, Robin said he sometimes began to view matters afresh, get a new angle on things, and cut through the dross. It helped.

The first batch of dross came with the late afternoon local news on the telly, the stabbing taking precedence even over the FA Cup game. Adam, curled up on the sofa with Campbell, both content from lunch and a postprandial nap, watched with interest.

"A man was found dead with stab wounds early this morning in Abbotston," the reporter said, in a piece that must have been filmed earlier that day.

"No sight of himself," Adam said, scratching Campbell's ear. "He'll be avoiding the cameras, I guess."

"Police are appealing for witnesses, particularly anyone who saw a fight in the Desdemona club in Abbotston last night." The reporter finished her piece and the feed went back to the studio, where talk turned to the gutsy but ultimately losing performance by Abbotston Alexandra.

The football fans had behaved themselves, miracle of miracles. Maybe it had been the result—or the unexpected sunshine—that had tempered things.

"Perhaps the police got the catering staff to put something in the half-time Bovrils, to take the edge off their aggression. Like you need when you see that big moggy from up the road." Adam grinned at the dog's expression. "Only joking. With any luck, your favourite person will be back to tuck you up in bed."

Adam's hope came true, but only just. The clock was striking nine when Robin came through the door, tie undone, looking desperately tired. They'd worked out a routine for such occasions, one that got sporadically reversed when Adam was late back from a governors' meeting or a school parents' evening. Robin kicked off his shoes and slumped on the settee with Campbell while his better half performed the kitchen duties, rustling up a hot drink and a bite to eat, waiting for it to be wolfed down before getting into any proper conversation. Feeding the body before he exercised the brain.

"We saw your case on the news, although I doubt we got the real story." Adam settled himself on the sofa once the dishes were put away. "Campbell doesn't believe anything he sees on the telly anymore."

"He's always had a lot of sense, that dog."

"He won't grill you if you'd rather clear your mind."

"Nah. I'd rather keep you up to date." Robin gave Adam an outline of some of the things the media didn't yet know, including what the police had found out about the dead man, which admittedly wasn't a lot at present. "Every indication is that he genuinely was working as a tax consultant, so the witness we had who saw him at GCHQ either made a mistake or Davis hasn't managed to trace things back far enough. We'll come at it fresh tomorrow. Sorry to spoil the weekend. I never even asked how your mum is."

"She's blooming. Kept going on about her new bridge partner. I might be getting a new *dad*, the way she talks." Adam rubbed his partner's arm. "And don't worry about tomorrow. Now I can't feel guilty at the pile of marking and planning I have to do. I suspect you've got the better deal."

Robin stifled a yawn. "Sez you. Right. Bed. I could sleep for a week."

"I'll set the alarm to make sure you don't. Come on, boy," Adam encouraged Campbell to come with him to the kitchen. "You go up, Robin, while I get this lump settled for the night."

By the time Adam had made sure the dog emptied his bladder and was happy in his basket, and got himself ready for bed, Robin was out for the count. Adam watched over him for a while, concerned at how tired the bloke appeared, upset that he'd been deprived of his well-deserved weekend of rest. He supposed this would always come with the territory.

Adam just hoped that this case would get sorted out as soon as possible, and normal—or what passed for normal—life could resume. He also hoped it wouldn't veer quite as close to home as the previous murder case had.

Sunday morning brought rain, so the prospect of having to work—marking or investigating—wasn't too unpleasant. Robin, looking refreshed, wolfed down his breakfast and talked murders.

"There are various possibilities, but you need to start with the obvious," he said, waving a slice of toast and driving Campbell mad in the process. "I'd always go down the line of nearest and dearest, because they're the people you're most at risk from."

"Charming. Still, I suppose you're right. Who were Hatton's nearest and dearest?"

Robin shrugged. "Not sure yet. Both parents are dead. No wife, no live-in girlfriend—or boyfriend. Nothing much on social media and very little evidence in his flat of any relationships, apart from some packets of condoms, so possibly he always played away from home and kept it casual."

"Possibly." Somebody must have known the man, though. "But it could have been the person he got into that fight with, couldn't it? Was that an unhappy client who'd found out Hatton had been swindling him?"

"That's for us to find out. Mind you, given the GCHQ angle, the attack might have been about something distinctly nasty."

Adam shuddered. "The Slasher is bad enough. Can you imagine terrorists loose in Abbotston? My mum would have kittens. Campbell would have kittens."

The Newfoundland frowned, looking suitably offended.

"Did *he* strike last night, by the way?" Adam asked.

"Not that I've heard, but I've been wrapped up in my own case. Anything on the news?"

"Not a dickie bird. This Hatton couldn't have been *him*? Somebody found out and got their retaliation in first?" The timings were remarkably coincidental if there wasn't a link.

"We *did* think of that, you know, Superintendent Matthews." Robin slapped Adam's arm. "Nothing to suggest a connection in his flat, although we're keeping an open mind. Okay. Let's go and see what the new day brings. Not sure when I'll be home, I'm afraid. I'll text you, but it could be late. Sorry."

"I'll make a cottage pie or a casserole or something. Easy enough to heat up when you do get back."

"You spoil me. God knows what it would have been like if this case had cropped up before I met you."

"You wouldn't have eaten properly, for a start," Adam said, avoiding anything emotional. This wasn't the time or the place; best leave it for when the case was wrapped up and they could wrap themselves up in the duvet in their big, comfy bed. Which might be a while off, but it was a more enticing prospect than the pile of marking on Adam's desk.

Stanebridge police station in the rain wasn't exactly the world's nicest place; a damp odour hung about it, mingling with the smell of disinfectant from where one of the Saturday night drunks had disgraced himself. *Or herself. We are an equal opportunity puking facility.*

Davis was hovering outside his office.

"Here's what we've got sir." She waggled a file.

"Have you been here all night?"

"No. Not quite, anyway. I can get forty winks this afternoon. If you let me," she added, with a smile at Anderson, who had appeared in the doorway. "It's useful living in Abbotston. I called in to Hatton's block of flats on my way here and helped his next-door neighbour put out her recycling. Little old lady. Great source of information."

"Aren't they always?" Anderson settled behind his desk. "What did she say?"

"That Hatton was one for the women. He left at least two of them to mourn him, one in Abbotston and one here in Stanebridge. A shop girl for weekdays and a bit of posh totty for high days and holidays."

Robin flinched. He would have rapped Anderson's knuckles for talking like that; he couldn't decide whether Davis needed the same. What was sauce for the goose . . .

If Anderson had noticed Robin's reaction, he didn't show it. "Blimey. Got any names?"

"Not surnames. Beryl and Sandra, which is why the woman remembered them. Characters off some old TV programme, she said." Davis shrugged. "Anyway, I'll have a shufti through his address books. Mrs. Cowan, that's my friend with the recycling, says she'd expect Beryl the shop girl to be heartbroken and Sandra the posh one to be pretty philosophical."

Anderson would have said that put to bed the question of whether Hatton was gay, but that was being too simplistic.

"And what's that observation based on? How the Liver Birds would react?" Robin ignored Anderson's quickly suppressed chuckle. So what if he'd gone and outed himself as a fan of TV reruns? He'd been indoctrinated in British comedy classics at his mother's knee.

"Not with you, sir." Davis frowned. When elucidation wasn't forthcoming, she cracked on. "Anyway, she's met Sandra, and wasn't particularly impressed. The other woman she'd just heard about."

"Good work. Which would be even better if you got their addresses." Robin tried his most persuasive smile.

"I'm on it, sir." Davis waggled what must have been Hatton's mobile phone. "I'll get May on the case, too, when she comes in."

"Excellent. She struck us as being perceptive."

Davis rolled her eyes. "She is. Workwise. Wouldn't trust her choice in blokes; she's had a few dodgy fellers. Now she goes out with a dog handler." She smiled, then left them to contemplate Hatton's complicated love life.

"Sounds like Hatton got himself in the old eternal triangle, sir. What's the chance that one of the girls got overcome by the green-eyed monster and took her revenge on the love rat?"

"Must you talk like you're a tabloid journalist? Some offices have swear boxes—you need a cliché box." Robin shook his head, although Anderson was quite right. Was one of these women the deadly "nearest and dearest" he'd been talking to Adam about? The sudden reappearance of Davis, still clutching the mobile phone and wearing a superior smile, suggested he wouldn't have long to wait to find out.

"Beryl's rung. She had a hell of a shock to hear a female voice on the end of the line."

"I bet she thought you were Sandra." Anderson said.

"I'm not posh enough for that!" Davis laid on the Welsh accent good and thick. "Anyway, she's been away for a few days and heard the news on the radio when she came back. She was hoping against hope it was about another bloke called Hatton."

Robin nodded. It was one of the parts of the job he loathed intensely, telling people that their loved one wouldn't be coming home. "How is she?"

"Devastated, like Mrs. Cowan said she would be. She wants to talk to you, though. As soon as is convenient."

"We'll get round there now." Robin picked up his car keys from the desk where he'd not long since laid them down. Chances were it would be late that evening before they lay in their usual place in the hallway.

Why was it so tempting to make assumptions, based on nothing more than a name? Robin had got it into his mind they'd be meeting some Barbara Windsor type, all bleach, brass, and bling. But Beryl Simmonds was a quiet, well-dressed brunette who worked, or so she told them, at a posh boutique where the mothers-in-law-to-be of the local area went to get their wedding clobber.

"I can't believe he's gone," she said once they were ensconced in the lounge of her edge-of-Abbotston flat. "I only saw him four evenings ago, before I went away."

"Business trip?" Anderson asked.

"Yes, looking at some new Italian lines we're hoping to stock." She sniffed and blew her nose, the redness around the eyes a clear indication of how hard this must have hit her. "I hear he'd got in a fight? Was that with the person who killed him?"

"That's what we're trying to establish. Anything you can help us with would be much appreciated." Robin leaned forward; this was another bit he hated, having to pose this particular question when he was pretty sure the person he was asking it of was innocent. "I'm sorry to have to do this, but it's a question we put to everyone. Can you give us the details of your whereabouts yesterday and the day before?"

"Oh, of course. Yes, I know you have to do your jobs." Beryl reached for her handbag, to fish out both a clean tissue and a folded piece of paper. "This is the bill for the hotel we were staying at, so you can check with them I was there. I'll give you my boss's details too. We can vouch for each other, I suppose. Flights and everything," she added, before bursting into tears.

Anderson offered her yet another tissue and asked if he should go and make them all a cup of tea. Both offers were gratefully received.

"Take your time. We don't need to rush this," Robin assured her, against a soundtrack of sobs and the sergeant clanking about in an unfamiliar kitchen.

"I can't think of anyone I know who'd have wanted to hurt him," Beryl murmured once the tears had dried. "Unless it was to do with his work. It was a bit hush-hush."

"He'd worked at GCHQ, we understand."

"He continued to do so. Oh, thank you." She managed a smile for Anderson as he came in with the much-needed refreshments. "He wouldn't talk about his job. Wasn't allowed to, to be honest."

Robin blew on his tea and nodded. Continued to work for GCHQ? Not according to what Davis had found so far; they'd have to pursue that line.

"It's a fair old hack across to Cheltenham, further than the normal commuter journey." Anderson stirred his tea.

"Yes, but I don't think he was based there all the time." Beryl sipped her drink. "This is nice, thank you."

"My mum taught me well." Anderson beamed.

"Tom couldn't make a cup of tea to save his—" Beryl stopped, sniffed, then continued. "He had to go away sometimes, for a few days. On business. I asked him about it, but he said the less I knew, the better."

"Quite right," Anderson said, although he gave Robin a roll of the eyes. Was he too wondering whether these "business trips" were occasions when Hatton was getting together with Sandra? "You wouldn't be able to give us the dates for any of those, would you? It could be very helpful."

Beryl frowned. "I'm not sure. I mean, I didn't make a note, but if I look back through my diary, I might be able to give you a rough idea." She reached for her handbag, but Robin put his hand out to forestall her.

"That can wait until later. How long have—sorry, had—you and Thomas Hatton been dating?"

"About a year. I met him at Ascot races, in a queue for a bookmaker, believe it or not. We got talking and were amazed we both lived in Abbotston. Quite a coincidence." She took a sip of tea.

"Coincidences happen." Anderson frowned. They both knew what question had to be asked. "This is a bit delicate, but—like that thing about your whereabouts—we have to ask it. Did Hatton have any other girlfriends?"

"No. Although there was someone who'd liked to have been." Beryl narrowed her eyes.

"Sorry?"

"Sarah. Sandra. Something like that. We were in a restaurant once and she came over, making trouble."

Anderson inclined his head sympathetically. "What did Hatton do? When she tried to horn her way in on your date?"

"Told her he was busy. That he'd talk to her later." She took another, longer draught of tea. "He said they'd met through work. That she kept bothering him and he'd have to tell her to push off, but he wasn't going to lower himself to her level by having a scene at a restaurant."

It would be interesting to get Sandra's version of the story.

"It couldn't have been her that killed him, surely? Because she couldn't have him, nobody was going to?" Beryl began to well up again.

"If it was, then we'll do our utmost to bring her to book," Anderson said soothingly. "Whoever did it, we'll be chasing them down."

"Thank you." Beryl rummaged in her bag, producing yet another tissue. "I said I'd give you those dates."

"If you could, please." Robin noted her hands shaking as she brought out a diary. "Do you know anyone with the nickname 'Radar'?"

She looked blank. "No, I don't think so. Is it important?"

"We don't know as yet." Time to work up to another question Robin dreaded. "Do you have someone to keep you company?"

She nodded. "Mum's on the way down from London. She'll be here later this morning. Don't worry, I'll be all right. I simply need to keep my mind off it."

Robin took a deep breath. "I've got a further request. We need to have Mr. Hatton's body formally identified. If you'd rather not, do you know if there's a member of his family we should ask instead?"

Beryl, face paler than ever, shook her head. "He was an only child, and both his parents are dead. There's a grandmother in a nursing home somewhere, but the shock would kill her. I'll do it. When Mum gets here. She can vouch for him as well." She stopped, closing her eyes for a moment. "Will it be horrific?"

"No. If you just look at his face, you'll be fine. As fine as you can be. I realise this is a terrible burden." Robin tried to appear reassuring. "Thank you for doing this. Let us know when would be convenient."

"This afternoon. Then it's over and done and I won't have to worry about it."

"Very wise." It was a task that Robin didn't envy anyone.

"It *is* him, isn't it? I mean there's no chance I'll get there and find it's been a dreadful mistake?" Beryl's voice was so full of hope it seemed heartbreaking to have to reply in the negative. Robin made a quick mental list—the phone, the identification on the body, the evidence at the flat that had included at least one photo of the dead man—then shook his head. "Not unless somebody tried to take over his identity, which I suppose is possible. You'd better prepare for the worst."

"There isn't a chance that it's a case of identity swopping?" Anderson asked once they were back at the car. "If Hatton was still with the security services, weird stuff might be going on."

Weird stuff? Anderson always had an interesting way of talking, although this time he had a valid point.

"We'll have to wait until Davis or one of her merry men works their magic on that, too."

Davis must have had not only her magic wand at hand, but her crystal ball, as well. Robin had no sooner got out his car keys to drive them back to the station when his mobile rang, and her chirpy Welsh tones came down the line.

"I've run Sandra to ground, sir. He had her listed under 'Booty girl.'"

"Charming." Robin's impression of Hatton continued to plummet. "Have you spoken to her?"

"Yes. She already knew about his death from the press reports, but she didn't seem that bothered. Not like Beryl."

"Your informant Mrs. Cowan could be right, then." Or that might be the way she handled grief. Some people refused to let their feelings show.

"If you can get over there now, she'll be able to talk to you. She says she's got plans for the afternoon. Plans that can't be changed." Davis gave a disdainful little snort. "I'll text the address to you."

"Okay. Any news about whether Hatton remained with GCHQ? Beryl thinks he did, although he might have spun her a line. I've got her to come in and identify the body this afternoon, by the way. We'll try to be there, but..."

"I understand. I'll get them to call me if you're not around."

"Thank you. And make sure you go home afterwards. I need your brain fresh, all right?" Robin was certain he wouldn't be able to call on Davis's abilities much longer. The girl was too bright and too efficient not to be made up to sergeant soon. They'd need to make best use of her while they had the chance.

"Noted, sir. See you later." She rang off, no doubt to get back to her information gathering, a terrier down the rabbit holes of the local lowlife.

"What next?"

"Off to catch Sandra, once— Ah, here it is." Robin opened the text message, then passed his phone to his sergeant. "You can navigate."

"I get all the fun jobs." Anderson frowned. "Well, we really are going up in the world. She lives in Kine's Lea. Dead posh out there."

As he drove, Robin recalled a discussion he'd had with Adam about the way some villages were as upwardly mobile as the people who occupied them, although they'd never actually reached a conclusion as to which of the two things was the driver. It would have been useful to have Adam in the car with them, given his extensive knowledge of the local villages and their gossip, but while calling on his local knowledge had been justifiable—in Robin's head, anyway— in the Lindenshaw case, there wasn't a viable connection to him this time round.

Kine's Lea St. Mary's, the village school, had amalgamated with the one in the next village maybe ten years back, owing to falling numbers. Almost every child in Kine's Lea—and there weren't that many to start with—went to a private school. The original buildings of St. Mary's had been converted into a pair of smart cottages, and it was in the smartest of these that Thomas Hatton's other woman lived.

They knocked on the door, heard a cry of, "Coming. Let me put the dog out the back," then waited to be admitted.

"Sandra Williams?" Anderson asked as a tall, elegant woman with jet-black hair opened the door.

"*Zandra* Williams, yes."

Robin was glad the acid (if cut-glass) tones used to say "Zandra" hadn't been aimed directly at him. Mrs. Cowan had either misheard the name or had made a Liver Birds-influenced assumption.

"You must be the police." She gave them a withering look up and down. "I'd better see your identification."

Anderson handed his warrant card over, sheepishly, while Robin flashed his. They'd had better starts to interviews.

"Come in." She ushered them into an immaculately decorated hallway and through to a pristine lounge. She offered them a seat, which Robin accepted gingerly, worried that he'd somehow dirty the spotless upholstery. Anderson appeared to be trying to hover, half seated, half standing, in mid-air. "Please sit down. You make me nervous dithering like that."

Anderson shot into his seat as though propelled on rockets; Robin had never seen the man quite so biddable.

"You'll understand that we have a job to do," Robin began, "and questions we have to ask of everybody close to Thomas Hatton."

"Like where I was on Friday night?" Zandra fixed Robin with a stony glare. "I was with my mother, in the casualty department. I got a call during a meeting at the office that she was in agony. She's not a woman to make a fuss over nothing."

Like mother, like daughter?

"My mother's exactly the same." Robin smiled sympathetically.

"It turned out she had a perforated appendix with a risk of peritonitis. They removed it yesterday."

"I'm glad they got it sorted." And that should be an easy alibi to check.

"That's why Tom was on his own Friday evening. We had a dinner date planned, but family have to come first." A crack appeared in the icy veneer. "You probably think I'm a proper bitch, but losing Tom didn't hit me half as hard as nearly losing my mother."

Robin nodded. "So would you say that you and Hatton were very close or just . . ." He struggled for the correct term, one that wasn't indelicate.

"Just people who enjoyed going to bed together?" Zandra seemed amused at Robin's discomfort. "The latter. Tom had other women. Whether he was more attached to any of them, I don't know."

"How attached was he to Beryl?" Anderson cut in.

"Beryl?" Zandra laughed. "Oh, bless."

Robin narrowed his eyes and tried not to write "superior, supercilious cow."

"Why do you say that?" Anderson asked.

"Because she's not the brightest button in the box. I'm not sure what Tom told her about him and me, but it won't have been anything like the truth." Zandra's smile disappeared. "She'll miss him."

"And you won't?" Anderson clearly couldn't resist the barb.

"Of course I will." She adjusted herself in her chair, looking down her nose at him. "But I was never in love with Tom, like she was."

The jealousy motive was out of the window, then, unless she was hiding it well. And unless her alibi was broken. Robin changed tack. "Was he still working at GCHQ?"

"Don't you know the answer to that?" That annoying, knowing, Mona Lisa half smile was back on her face.

"Nobody's being straightforward with us." That was as near the truth as Robin wanted to go.

Zandra raised her eyebrows. "He didn't talk much about his work, but I think his days with the spooks set were long gone. As far as I could tell, he was a bog-standard, boring accountant." She loaded the word "boring" with a lascivious grin, but Robin wasn't going to ask what Hatton hadn't been boring at.

"Have you any idea who might have wanted to hurt him?" he asked.

"If I did, I'd tell you. I know I must appear pretty heartless, but I'm not. Tom was a good friend to me, even if we weren't Romeo and Juliet. Whoever killed him needs to be found and punished. I'll come and cheer at the trial when they send the toerag down." Sharp peaks of colour blazed on Zandra's cheeks.

"Nobody had threatened him or anything like that?" Robin pressed on. "I can imagine if you work for the spooks, as you call them, you can make yourself enemies."

Zandra frowned. "He did mention something, but it's from years back. How he fell foul of some ex-IRA bloke who said he'd get his own back. Tom didn't seem to take it seriously."

IRA? If they were getting into those waters, they'd be in murky depths.

"Perhaps he should have," Anderson said, tapping his notepad. "What did he tell you about it?"

"Not a lot. Something about his being in the wrong place at the wrong time." Zandra suddenly seemed to be fascinated by something outside the window.

Robin nodded, calmly waiting; she'd turn back eventually. "Go on."

"Tom had been having a drink with one of his colleagues, who'd been working out in Belfast. Could have been undercover, I don't know. Anyway, some Irish chap, accent thick as Ulster peat, came in the pub and started slagging off Tom's workmate. Something to do with him getting the Irish guy's brother killed. They got the police to chuck the troublemaker out, but not before he'd threatened to get even. With Tom as well as his mate."

Anderson whistled. "Any idea what this mate was called? Or the pub?"

"No, sorry. As I said, Tom didn't appear worried, and I didn't press him if it was about his work. He said it was completely under control. That was an end to the discussion."

"The nickname Radar didn't crop up at any point?"

Zandra hesitated then said, "No. If it had, I would have remembered."

Robin glanced at Anderson, then shrugged. They'd need to go searching for answers on that one elsewhere. Time to change tack. "You said you were planning to go out for dinner. Where to?"

"The Florentine, of course," Zandra said with a touch of condescension, then looked from the sergeant to Robin and back again. "Wasn't he attacked near there?"

"Yes. We thought it was odd he was in the area at all." Anderson leaned forward, clearly noticing something of interest. "I wouldn't have thought it would be on his route home from the Desdemona. And why was he *there* in the first place?"

"Why not? Because it's a gay bar, doesn't mean it's off limits to straight people. Straight doesn't mean peculiar, does it?" Zandra sounded even more patronizing and slightly disparaging. Despite his earlier wish, Robin was pleased Adam wasn't there to hear her; he had little patience for such snarkiness. "It's a nice place and the food's good. We used to go there together sometimes. But as to why he went so far out of his way home . . ." She shrugged. "Maybe he'd picked up a girl."

"He doesn't seem to have done that in the club, according to the statements we've got. Left on his own." Unless he'd picked somebody up pretty damn quickly afterwards—that missing two hours had to be accounted for somehow.

"Is it the sort of thing he would do?" Anderson cut in. "If he had Beryl and you already?"

Zandra laughed. "Beryl was away last weekend, which is why Tom and I had a date booked. I wouldn't have put it past him to find a bit of company for the evening, even if it was simply to have a drink with. He didn't like being alone."

Robin looked up sharply from his note taking. "Was there a reason for that? His dislike of being on his own?"

"It wasn't a case of safety in numbers, if that's what you're thinking. He was an only child, and he hated that. He wanted companionship." A swell of emotion sounded in her voice. "Can I see him one last time? To say goodbye."

"I'm sure that could be arranged. I'll have a member of our family liaison team get in touch. Although you might want to avoid this afternoon." Robin raised an eyebrow. "We've got Beryl and her mother coming in to identify the body."

Zandra nodded. "Good point. We wouldn't want a scene in the mortuary. Beryl doesn't like me. She doesn't understand what the arrangement was between me and Tom."

"It doesn't look like he ever explained it to her. She thinks you were after him and he didn't like it," Anderson said waspishly. "She reckons he was going to tell you to clear off."

"The cheek!" She grinned. "Not her. Tom. I can imagine him stringing her along with some tale. I almost feel sorry for her now."

Almost? That was damning with faint praise, or whatever the equivalent was in this situation.

"Was he fond of telling tales? Or telling lies, should I say?"

Zandra gave Anderson another of her withering glances. "Tom never lied to me about anything, as far as I know. There would have been no need. And if you believe his embroidering the truth may have led to his death, I suggest you ask those he may have embroidered the truth for."

With that, Zandra left her seat and made her way to the door to show them out. Robin wasn't going to argue, not until he'd checked that alibi.

"Bloody hell, she was a tough cookie," Anderson said when they were back in the car.

"She reminded me of one of those hard-boiled women in a film noir." Robin started the engine, keen to get away and get his head clear. Murder cases always came as such a tangled knot, one that needed to be picked apart before it could be put together again. And this one didn't have the advantage—if it was advantage—of a handsome teacher to make some of the interviews bearable.

"Film noir?"

"Eh?" Robin realised he'd been daydreaming about that first time he'd questioned Adam, in the library at the school. "You know. Sam Spade. Philip Marlowe." The puzzled expression on Anderson's face made Robin swiftly change the subject. "If Tom Hatton liked telling porky-pies, perhaps he told them to the wrong person."

Anderson nodded. "Yeah. When I first heard he had two women in tow, I wondered if this would turn out to be nothing more than the old green-eyed monster gone wild. Easy to forget who you've told what. But it sounds like it's more than that. If he's been stringing along the IRA . . ."

"Wild speculation, Sergeant." Even if Robin's thoughts had gone down those lines as well.

Before Anderson could reply, his mobile went off, and Davis, who'd clearly added mind reading to her many skills, reported in. Although Robin couldn't make out the words, those Welsh tones were unmistakable, and—from hearing Anderson's half of the conversation—what she was saying must be significant.

"What's the news?" he asked once the call was ended, pleased that they were on a straight, quiet stretch of road where he could concentrate on what Anderson had to tell him.

"Davis says Hatton is supposed to have left GCHQ a year ago, and since then he's been running a legitimate financial consultancy." Anderson wrinkled his nose. "Mind you, I'd like that bit about him having left to be corroborated. You can't trust these people as far as you can throw them."

"We'll get Cowdrey on it. He can pull rank."

Anderson nodded. "Davis also said the people she spoke to weren't overly twitchy about Hatton, although she didn't know about the IRA element then. This mysterious Radar might have worked for them."

Back to that; Anderson was getting a typical bee in his bonnet about the terrorist connection. Yes, they had to explore it, but it was one of many potential angles.

"He might equally well have worked for GCHQ, for that matter. Davis can follow it up when we've confirmed that Beryl and Sandra—Zandra—were exactly where they said they were in the wee small hours."

"You always rate the domestic side first and foremost, don't you?" Anderson didn't sound reproachful.

"It's the natural place to start. And did you see Zandra's nails?"

"I didn't particularly look at them. She's the kind of woman that makes me keep my head down."

Robin smiled; it was always good when the opposite sex got one over on his sergeant.

"Two of them on the left hand were bitten. The rest were flawless, but she'd not had time to repair those others."

"Which signifies?"

"I've no idea. Except the conclusion that she's been worrying about something."

"It might simply be grief, sir. She doesn't want to let it show, so she gnaws it away, literally. My Helen does the same thing."

"You could be right." Amateur psychology wasn't likely to get them anywhere. It was too easy to read too much into any little sign when you were on a case. Maybe Zandra was giving up smoking, and biting her nails instead was the lesser of two evils. The mundane rather than the sinister. "Any news from the house-to-house enquiries round the Florentine?"

"You'll have to ask Davis that one yourself." Anderson grinned. "You need to do some of the work."

"Cheeky sod. I'll do that very thing."

He did, as soon as they were back at the station. Davis was bleary-eyed, as bleary as WPC May had been the previous day, but she proved equally efficient.

"There's not a lot come back yet from the area, but the team are still out, working their way towards the Desdemona. Most of the Florentine-end-of-town shops and restaurants were shut by that time of night. Although somebody thought they'd seen Hatton walking past their shop window as they locked up. One of those open-all-hours-type corner-shop places, along the road."

"Open-all-hours corner shops? Do they have them in that part of Abbotston?" Anderson rolled his eyes.

"Apparently. The shop's supposed to be just as upmarket as the rest of the businesses round there. More Châteauneuf-du-Pape and emergency supplies of pesto than a can of Newcastle Brown and a packet of Rizlas." Davis waved her handful of papers. "Anyway, Hatton peered in through the window, as though he might come inside to buy something, so the shopkeeper waited, but then he walked on."

"Alone?"

"Alone. And in the direction of where he was killed."

"When was this?"

"About one o'clock in the morning."

"Right." Robin drew out a large map of the area that they'd printed earlier. God bless Google.

"Let me do that, sir." Anderson loved charts and diagrams and the whole business of who was where and when. He started to mark Hatton's travels on it.

"You go and get some shut-eye, Davis." Robin jerked his thumb towards the door. "Your way with information is key to us getting this solved. You're no use to us knackered."

"Yes, sir!" Davis saluted, grinned cheekily, and left.

"So where was he those missing couple of hours?" Anderson traced Hatton's supposed route with his finger. "This end of town, unless he spent the entire time yo-yoing about."

"But where could he have gone?" Robin stared at the map—this was a real needle-in-a-haystack job. The telephone's insistent tones put an end to his speculation. "Better pick this up. Hello? Robin Bright speaking."

"Cowdrey here." The boss sounded as tired as Davis had looked. "Any news?"

"Not as much as I'd like." Robin gave a summary of what they'd found out so far, which was frustratingly little, apart from the terrorist element. "It would be good if you followed up on the GCHQ bit. You know what these places are like for fobbing us off. We need to know if he continued to work for them, if he'd had dealings with the IRA, and whether they were aware of any threats made on his life."

"Okay. I'll get on it. Once I've been wheeled out in front of the cameras. I'm going down to the press conference now."

"Hope that goes well." Nobody particularly liked having to address the media, but Cowdrey accepted it as part of the job and was better than most at the art. He had a special knack of asking for the public's input, one that got results, rather than encouraging every crackpot to crawl out from under the skirting boards.

"I'll need it. Keep me informed."

"I will." If he ever got anything decent to keep the boss informed about. He went back to peering at the map but got interrupted again, this time by Anderson's phone.

"Beryl's here to do the identification," the sergeant said once he'd put the phone down. "Want me to handle it?"

"Please. I'll go through all the witness statements once more, just in case we've missed anything."

"Right. Good luck."

Robin made a face. Usually sheer, dogged, boring legwork brought results, but he had a feeling this would be one of those cases where serendipity would play a part. He took a deep breath and began ploughing through the statements, stopping only to watch Cowdrey live on the local news and to text Adam to say he'd likely be home late. Again.

Getting the information from the estate agent would have to wait until Monday, when they reopened, although it was extremely unlikely that anyone had been working there in the wee small hours. The feedback from the Florentine was more interesting. They shut their doors at eleven o'clock, and everybody had been cleared and out by midnight, except the chef on duty—not the celebrity one—who'd had some stuff to do before he went on holiday. Robin checked his watch; the bloke would be on a plane to Barcelona right this minute. Convenient coincidence that he'd had this holiday planned.

Anderson soon came back to his desk, unusually solemn.

"Want a cup of tea?" Robin offered.

"No thanks. How did Cowdrey get on with the press?"

"Usual star performance. Rather him than me, though. Made a good appeal for witnesses."

"I think I'd have preferred to face the press than that." Anderson jerked his thumb over his shoulder. "It went as well as these things do, but I still hate this business. Beryl says it's definitely Hatton."

"How did she take it?"

"Like a trooper. Her mother helped her keep calm, even though they were both sobbing as they left." Anderson stared at the desk. "Sometimes I loathe this job."

"I know. That's why we've got to run the scrote who did this to ground. Any sign of the forensics?"

"No, but that looks like Davis steaming along the corridor."

Robin hadn't appreciated the makeover Stanebridge police station had undergone the last few months, even though the glass partitions had made it easier to spot who was approaching. Not every visitor was as welcome as this one.

"I thought you'd gone home?" Robin asked as she came through the door.

"No point. I found a quiet corner and had a nap." She fingered a pile of notes. "I thought you'd want to know this. Don't get too excited, though."

"Go on."

"Beryl's alibi checks out. As does Zandra's. Beryl's boss could be covering for her, of course, but the hotel receptionist would have to be in on the act. And Zandra would have to have not only her mother telling porkies, but the staff at the hospital. Every indication is that she was being a very devoted daughter."

And with their distinctive good looks, both women would have been memorable to the average heterosexual male.

"Thanks. I think." Robin curled his lip.

"Sounds like we can put the girls out of the frame." Anderson scooped up and tidied away a pile of paper clips, clearly reconfiguring his thoughts. "Unless they got somebody to do the deed for them."

"It's possible. Blokes will do stupid things to impress women."

"Don't forget they'll do stupid things to impress other blokes as well." Davis grinned. "Murder's an equal opportunities crime."

"Less of your sauce." Robin laughed, then struck a dramatic pose. "Will nobody bring me forensics?"

"I heard they were on their way, sir." Davis backed towards the door. "I'll go and chase them."

"She's too good to be true at times." Robin observed her nipping down the corridor. "She'll outrank us all in ten years."

"Really? I thought you'd be chief constable by then?"

"Shut up and go and get that cup of tea."

By the time the brew arrived, so had the preliminary forensic report. Hatton had been attacked with a sharp, straight-edged knife that had gone in—and come out—easily. They'd found some "alien" fibres on the body: black suede, possibly from gloves worn by the attacker; and camel-coloured wool, good quality, perhaps from an overcoat. Not a scrap of DNA that didn't belong to Hatton, so he hadn't been getting his oats in those missing two hours. He *had* been indulging in a glass or three of red wine, though.

"Chefs have knives." Anderson might have been reading Robin's thoughts.

"They do. Even if anybody can buy a pretty fierce cook's knife down at John Lewis." Adam, for one, had a spectacular collection of blades for every food and function.

"Yes. But it's suspicious that—" Anderson checked the report "—Jim Phillips left on a plane today."

Robin tapped the desk. "He has means, the knife, and opportunity, given that he was in the area. But we have no idea what his motive would have been. Or even if he knew Hatton."

"Don't forget Hatton and Zandra were due to be dining at the Florentine."

"Okay. Have we got a mobile number for Phillips?"

"Yep." Anderson fished it out.

Robin had dialled for the third time, with no response so far, and was wondering how much evidence the Spanish police would need to go round to Phillips's hotel, when a deep male voice answered.

"Yes?"

"Jim Phillips?"

"No. I'm afraid not. Who is that?"

"The police. We want to talk to Mr. Phillips about a murder that happened near where he works."

"You'll have to wait. He's just gone down to theatre."

"I'm sorry? He's supposed to be in Spain." Robin tried to gather his wits.

"Yes, so I believe. He never made it. Didn't even get home after work. His car got hit by a lorry. I'm the nurse on his ward."

"Is he all right?"

"He's in a serious condition, but we're pretty confident his injuries aren't life threatening. If you want to interview him, you'll have to wait a day or two. Hold on." The nurse consulted his colleague, muffled words that made Robin itch with curiosity. "Hello? Is he in any danger?"

"Not that we're aware."

"Is he a danger to anyone else?"

"We don't know as yet. We need to talk to him as a potential witness. He's not going anywhere, is he?"

"Not for the foreseeable future, no. Not least because his leg's in traction."

As their suspicions were based on what might be simple coincidence, and they didn't even have enough proper evidence to get a warrant to search either the restaurant or Phillip's home, there wasn't a lot else to be done. Robin took the ward's contact number and some details about where the accident had happened, put down his phone, then updated Anderson.

"Bugger that."

"Couldn't have put it better myself." Robin had reached the point where he couldn't put two sensible thoughts together unless he got a decent meal inside him and a decent night's sleep. "Right. I'm going home, and you should too. They can ring us if anything new comes in."

They didn't need to ring. Davis caught him in the doorway, just as he'd got one arm into his coat.

"Superintendent Cowdrey's come up trumps as usual." She beamed. "Want a hand with that?"

"I'm not a pensioner yet." Robin slipped the other arm into its sleeve. Whatever the news, he guessed he'd be leaving the office, whether homebound or out to interview a witness.

"He doesn't get his official-issue Zimmer frame until next week," Anderson quipped. "What have you got?"

"A member of the public rang in to say she'd seen the lights on at the Florentine around half past two on Saturday morning. The lads at the desk put her through to me."

"Why not to us?" Anderson asked.

"You'll see in a minute. She particularly wanted to talk to a female officer, and she was in a bit of a rush." Davis wore a secretive little grin.

"Stop torturing us." Robin usually had plenty of time for banter, but he was too tired for games now.

"She's been in that posh private maternity unit on the London Road. Thought she was in labour but it was a false alarm, and she's only just surfaced today. Missed all the hoo-ha yesterday."

"Where does she live?"

"In the apartments opposite the Florentine. She was up on Friday night, having what she thought were contractions."

Anderson's face screwed up in distaste, but Davis ploughed on.

"Her husband dashed her off to hospital at that point. Before Hatton was attacked, I guess, because she says she didn't even realise there'd been a stabbing until she saw the local news. She says she'll make a proper statement when she can."

"Why can't we go and take that now? She might have spotted something on Saturday morning and not appreciated its importance." It happened. Careful questioning could get a lot more from witnesses than they realised they knew.

"I'm not sure that's going to work, sir. She rang us on her mobile, heading back to the maternity unit."

"Perhaps it'll only be another false alarm?" Anderson sounded hopeful.

"Doubt it." Davis shook her head. "Her waters have broken."

Robin held up his hand. "Spare us the gory details. It can wait." He fished out his car keys, fiddling with them as he gathered his thoughts. "Do we know where Phillips lives?"

"Byfield, I think. I'll check." Though the check probably wasn't necessary—Davis had a memory that catalogued everything. "Why?"

"There's something that's bugging me." Robin returned to his desk, unlocked the drawer, and took out the information he'd got from the hospital. "Phillips had his accident on the dual carriageway near the Abbotston industrial estate. That's the other side of town from Byfield, and not that near the Florentine, either."

He looked up, exchanged glances with his colleagues. "Doctor's orders or not, we're going to get down to the hospital and talk to Phillips tomorrow. I don't like people acting illogically."

On such small discrepancies, investigations could succeed or fail.

Adam had completed his marking, finished his preparation for the week ahead, walked Campbell, made a casserole, then sat down with a beer and the Sunday afternoon football. Still no sign of his favourite policeman, although that was to be expected. Funny how Adam felt like he'd spent more time with Robin back in the days of the Lindenshaw murder case, when Robin had come round to pick a local brain as often as he could and more than he should have.

Getting involved with Robin had been a bit of a minefield. Probably against all rules, given that Adam had been a witness in a murder case—and at one point a suspect—so they'd played it as cautiously as they could. Life had got so much better when the killer was run to earth, even though it had involved an act of heroics from Campbell to preserve Robin's life.

Alas, real life wasn't like a dating site; you couldn't choose the person you fell in love with based on their career choices. If Robin had a nine-to-five job, he'd be here now—although maybe *he'd* be the one moaning at Adam's work intruding on their weekend. And Robin not in the police force wouldn't be the guy he'd fallen for, or the guy who'd moved in.

There was a whole other problem. Robin's flat lay empty, waiting to be put on the market, although progress on that front seemed to be slow, if not non-existent. Pressure of work, of course, and his wanting to spend spare time with Adam, not with estate agents, Robin kept saying, but that line was wearing thin. A particularly violent trailer for a cop show, shown during half-time, brought the chilling reality of their new life into focus. If there was more than one person going round Abbotston with a knife and a grudge, then that grudge might hit close to home.

Campbell, preferring rugby to football, had soon bored of the round-ball game and fallen asleep in the middle of the floor. His distressed whimpers and twitches suggested something in his dream must be petrifying, but he soon settled once more. Possibly he was reliving that first series of murders too, and the starring role he'd had in the final scenes.

Please God the Newfoundland wouldn't be needed in a similar role ever again.

Chapter Three

Monday morning, back to work routine, but the talk in the staffroom wasn't the usual Lindenshaw St. Crispin's school lunchtime discussion of what had been on the telly over the weekend or who'd seen what on Facebook. The staff fascination with local crime had resurfaced.

Their prurience had received a reality check when murder struck the school itself, because something so close to home hadn't been gossip fodder, but people had short memories, and once more murder was on the rumour-mongering menu.

This time, inevitably, Adam found himself being subtly questioned to see what he'd let drop, even though people knew better than to pump him directly for inside information. Chinese whispers were running riot throughout the county, and the resulting stories about Hatton's murder—added to the fact the Abbotston Slasher *hadn't* struck on Saturday night—were moving away from what Adam understood to be the truth. He kept his mouth shut; just one of the challenges of living with a policeman.

He'd not fully come out at work until the Lindenshaw murders. Doing so had been forced on him, the pair of them having been spotted, walking arm in arm down by the river towpath, by another teacher. Adam had made a declaration at the staff meeting the following Monday afternoon. To his surprise, nobody had really batted an eyelid. Three people had come up to him afterwards saying he shouldn't have been so worried about coming out, when everybody had guessed, and the vicar had given him a tremendous hug at the governors' meeting two days later. News travelled fast around Lindenshaw, even if it didn't always travel accurately.

He'd need to dispel one or two of the wilder rumours about the Abbotston case. For a group who should have been good at analysing facts and coming to sensible conclusions, the teaching staff were circulating a stupid amount of pointless tittle-tattle.

"My sister lives in Abbotston," Mandy—the most opinionated of the learning support assistants—said as she sat down with a mug of tea. "She's heard that the bloke who got stabbed was with three other men at a lap-dancing club." Mandy had always allegedly come across a weird version of events.

Adam had no idea where that particular story had come from. One of the tabloids, probably—the *Daily Mail* had featured Hatton's stabbing on page five and would likely have embroidered the tale with one of its current obsessions. Today they were apparently considering if he'd been the Slasher, given that the pattern of attacks had been broken.

Adam shook his head. "I don't know where your sister gets her information, but she needs to find a better source. No lap-dancing club."

Mandy opened her mouth but was beaten to it by Luke, the newest member on the teaching team.

"Your Robin not heard anything?"

"He's got the case." There was no point in trying to hide the fact; Adam had never been an efficient liar. "Which means I'm going to discuss it even less than usual, so don't ask me if Hatton was the Slasher, because in the unlikely case that I had an inkling, I wouldn't tell you. All I'll say—because it's been on the local news—is that the dead bloke *is* called Hatton and he *did* get in an argument, although it was probably over nothing more than a spilt drink and a stained shirt. Same old Friday night stuff."

"The papers say he was in the ga—Desdemona." Luke stuck his nose in his coffee cup, not quickly enough to hide his flushed cheeks.

"That's where he got in the argument."

"Have you been there, Adam?" Mandy asked.

"Not my sort of place." Adam sidestepped the question. "It's got a bit of a reputation." He watched Luke out of the corner of his eye. The poor bloke had gone a lovely shade of pink.

"Really?" Mandy winked at one of the other women. "Tell us more."

"Well . . ." Adam leaned forward, confidentially. "You wouldn't want to take your husband there. You see . . . the beer's overpriced."

"Oh, you." Everyone laughed at Mandy's mock outrage, before comparing prices at their favourite restaurants.

Adam picked up his coffee and a pile of books, then left. At least he couldn't be grilled if he had his head down over some marking. Five minutes later, the door to Adam's classroom flew open and Luke's head appeared round it. Adam hadn't bargained for him being quite so persistent.

"You'd think people would have more sense, nattering like a load of old biddies. It can't be easy for you not to give something away inadvertently." Luke's face displayed a mixture of concern and discomfort. His condemnation was ironic, given his own chatter earlier on. And given that his brother was a copper at Stanebridge, on the team of dog handlers who'd been called across for duty for the Millwall match, he must know what it was like to be regarded as a fount of inside police knowledge.

"You've got it in one. I guess the only thing that could be worse would be going out with a doctor, because then people would want to discuss their symptoms with you." Adam wrinkled his nose. "I never asked how your Sam got on at the weekend. No heads kicked in, I hope."

"Not as far as I know. Everybody behaved themselves. Even Inky." Inky was the Alsatian Sam worked with. According to Luke, it was the brains of the partnership.

"That dog and Campbell could run the country." Adam paused as Luke dithered in the doorway, as though he wanted to say something. It could be about work, Adam being Luke's official mentor. The lad had shaped up well so far, but you never knew. He'd had to put an unhappy childhood behind him, as had his brother. A chequered history of their being fostered out of a troubled, violent family into the care of the Brunning family, eventually being adopted by them. It was a life story that might make or break somebody.

Adam held up one of the pupils' books. "This new marking scheme seems to help the kids, doesn't it?"

"Yeah. I'm impressed. It's certainly making a difference to my lot."

"You should have been here before Chris came. Or maybe not."

"Was it that bad?" Luke continued to dither, neither in nor out of the room.

"Worse. He's made a world of difference to us."

"Here! That's one for my buzzword bingo card. 'Making a difference.'" Luke grinned. "You were lucky to get him."

"Tell me about it. He relocated down from Manchester because he wanted to be near his parents. They're getting on a bit." Adam tidied the books into a neat pile. "And yes, before you ask, we did have to go through three rounds of recruitment before we were successful."

"So I heard. People are cagey talking about it, though."

"It wasn't an easy time."

"Yeah. You don't expect a murder at a school, do you?"

"No." Adam shivered, despite the warmth of the room. He should remember that if it hadn't happened, Adam wouldn't have run into Robin, so some good had come from it. Thank God for small mercies. "Made a big impact on us."

"Making an impact. Another clutch of buzzwords!" Luke cackled. "They're breeding."

"Leave before I throw these books at you." Adam shook his head as Luke went out the door. Buzzword bingo. He'd been thinking of that very thing the day he and Robin met. "Small mercies. And big ones," he muttered, and got on with the marking.

Abbotston Hospital was large and modern, a superficially attractive building when the sun was shining and grim as death when it rained. Today was drizzly, so the place wore a dreary and unwelcoming countenance. As they made their way through seemingly interminable corridors, Robin checked his phone, finding a message from Adam reassuring him that dinner would be available whatever time he got in. He wasn't normally so nineteen-fifties housewife, so perhaps he was just being kind under trying circumstances. They'd barely had time to exchange a few words that morning, after yesterday evening when he'd got home to find Adam zonked out on the sofa. Maybe they'd get the chance to chat later today. In the meantime he had an interview to conduct, and on his own. Anderson was en route to the Florentine with a list of questions, a guarded expression, and the germ of a theory that he'd said he wasn't ready to share with his boss, in case it made him out to be a prat.

Phillips had been transferred to one of the acute wards, his condition having stabilised, but he was being kept in a side room, where Robin ran him to ground.

Jim Phillips looked like death warmed up. His leg was in a complicated traction that appeared excruciating, an ugly bruise covered the left side of his face, and there were stitches on his left hand.

"Luckily it's not my chopping hand," he joked, once Robin had introduced himself and made some small talk about the accident and the damage done. Despite what the nurse had said, the patient seemed entirely up for answering questions. "I'd happily murder that lorry driver, though, cutting me up. I needed my holiday."

"Not the same resting here, is it?" The casual remark about murder, without the usual horrified follow-up that witnesses made when they realised what they'd said, gave Robin pause for thought. In his experience, guilty people tended to be careful about making such off-the-cuff remarks, but there were always exceptions to that rule. "I wanted to talk about Friday evening. Going into Saturday morning."

Phillips nodded. "Busy night. We managed to get cleared up pretty quick."

"I understand you stayed on afterwards?" No cards yet on the bedside locker, but the Florentine staff might have been in contact and discussed the unexpected police visit.

"Yes. I'm one of these control freaks, or so my colleagues at the restaurant tell me. I wanted to leave them a list of stuff to do and not to do." Whatever he'd been up to, Phillips wasn't denying he'd been there. Perhaps he'd told the rest of the staff he was leaving straight away because he'd wanted to hide the fact he didn't trust them.

"Wouldn't it have been more efficient to tell people what you wanted face-to-face?"

Phillips's scowl showed his contempt at the suggestion. "Nah. It'd go in one ear and out the other. Leave them a checklist and they have to tick it off or explain why something didn't get done when it should have."

"Did a bloke called Thomas Hatton drop in to see you?"

"Tom? Yeah, he did. He handles our accounts and was supposed to be in for a meal earlier, but his girlfriend couldn't make it. He rang me on the off chance, then dropped in for a natter. Always enjoys our red wine." Phillips's expression changed. "Here, before you ask, he was the one on the sauce, not me. That lorry burst a tyre and slammed into my car. Nobody's fault."

"It happened out near the industrial estate, didn't it?" Robin nodded. "I don't believe that's on your way home."

"No, but it's where the nearest box for franked mail is. By the bloody Tesco depot." Phillips frowned. "It's a pain in the arse to have to go out there, but I couldn't ask the girls to do it. Not on the night before the new moon."

"The post couldn't have waited?"

"I wanted it gone on Saturday morning, and I wouldn't have had time to drop it off before my flight." It was a convincing story, although there was a hint of something—relief?—in Phillips's eyes at Robin's nod.

"When did Hatton leave?"

"A bit before I did. About half two." Phillips narrowed his eyes, wary for the first time. "Why?"

"Because he was attacked nearby in the next half an hour."

"What the fuck?" Phillips slumped on his pillows. "Is he all right?" If his surprise was fake, Phillips had reached an Oscar-winning standard of acting.

"He's dead, I'm afraid. Stabbed."

"Stabbed? Tom? No, he can't be." Phillips, ashen faced, clutched at his chest and arm. His breathing, forced and rasping, alarmed Robin, who didn't like that blue-tinged pallor either. "Sorry, this is a hell of a shock."

"I bet it is. You can't think of why anybody would have wanted him dead?"

"No." Phillips gasped. "I'd never have slashed him. Nobody would have. Look, I honestly don't feel well."

"I'll fetch a doctor." The deathly pallor that filled the chef's face couldn't have been put on.

Robin called for help, then grabbed his coat before edging out of the room. Phillips, flapping away the doctor's hand for a moment, called after him, "I'll do all I can to help find who did this."

"You won't be doing anything until you're well," the doctor said, glaring at Robin.

"Of course. It'll have to wait." Robin stood outside the door for a moment while the health professionals treated their patient. That surprise about Hatton's death, and the offer of help, had seemed genuine, and there'd been no attempt to cover the fact the murdered man had been drinking there. So why was he left with the impression that Phillips was hiding something?

He rang Anderson as soon as he got into the car park, but came up against a voicemail response saying that the sergeant would ring back later. When he did, he was as happy as Campbell when he got given the last sausage.

"Nothing about Hatton, sir, except that he did their accounts."

"Tell me what I don't know. He was drinking there with the chef until half two on Saturday." Robin got him up to speed with the rest of his interview with Phillips. "Not sure there's anywhere else to go on this lead at the moment."

"I wouldn't be so sure, sir." Anderson sounded horribly smug. "The staff were remarkably chatty. Nice crowd. I asked them whether Phillips often stayed late and they said it was only an occasional thing, except for the eve of the new moon. He always insists on being around to see the girls back to their cars. He even paid for a taxi home for one of them on Friday because he was worried about her using public transport."

"Seems a decent chap. Where is this going?"

"The Abbotston Slasher. He attacks between three and four in the morning. He didn't attack on Saturday. Maybe something stopped him."

"There's nothing to link Hatton to being the Slasher. Inspector Root checked his DNA." The last time, the Slasher had been careless, catching himself on the sharp point of a bolt attachment. Root had regarded it as a breakthrough, but the profile hadn't matched anyone on file.

"I wasn't thinking of Hatton."

"Phillips?" The man who made the remark about his chopping hand.

"Yes. The people at the Florentine said he gets angry the day after an attack, asking if 'he'd' struck, slagging the Slasher off and saying what he'd do if he got his hands on the bloke. I wondered if it's a case of excessive cover-up."

"Whatever he was saying it for, it's not enough for us to get a warrant to search his house."

Anderson laughed. "It wouldn't be *us* applying for a warrant, sir. Not our case."

"So it's not enough for Root to get one." They'd have to brief him on their suspicions, though.

"Well, I thought we could mosey down to the car pound, which is where Phillip's vehicle is supposed to be. For a little look."

"For black suede gloves or camel-coloured coats?"

"Something like that. And if there happened to be a spot of blood on the upholstery, we'd get a CSI down to give it the once-over."

"Hm." Robin still didn't like it. He could imagine some smart brief applying for the evidence to be disregarded because it had been obtained in irregular circumstances. Something flashed like a green light in his memory. "Phillips used a peculiar phrase. When he was insisting he hadn't harmed Hatton, he told me 'I'd never have slashed him.'"

"That's enough for me, sir."

"Right. Meet you at the car pound. I'll get a CSI to come down." They could justify taking a blood sample, anyway, to eliminate Phillips from the Hatton enquiry. The fact they didn't have anything tangible to match it to was by the by. That weapon might turn up yet.

And Campbell might sprout wings and fly.

The policemen arrived at the car before the CSI did, so their investigation had to be done gingerly, suited and gloved, in case Anderson's hunch was spot on. There seemed to be evidence of blood on the seat, possibly where the windscreen glass had sliced into Phillip's left hand. Not his chopping hand, Robin recalled with a shiver. No sign of clothes on the back seat, but they'd leave the boot to the expert.

They were still circling the vehicle when a bright female voice shouted, "I knew there had to be trouble brewing!"

"Grace!" Robin smiled at the arrival of his favourite CSI. She'd been covering all the Slasher crime scenes so was absolutely the person for the job. "We need this car processed. Blood for DNA matching, fibres—" He stopped as Grace raised her hand.

"Yes, I did do the training, sir. Is this connected with Hatton?"

Robin nodded. "The last person that we know for certain saw him. May be a possible connection to another case."

"Oh yes?"

"Have a shufti first, then we'll let Anderson share his theory." Robin pointed a gloved finger towards the boot; the lock had taken the brunt of an impact. "You'll have to prise it open."

"You don't fancy doing it while I have a shufti for evidence?" Grace flashed Anderson a smile.

"Of course. The insurance assessor has already been down here and taken a million pictures. I'll get someone to give me a jemmy." Anderson, with a cheery grin, went off on the cadge.

Grace got her kit prepared while Robin stood around feeling like a spare part.

"Fibres would be useful," he said, moving across, next to Grace.

"They usually are. We're looking for some in the Slasher case too."

Robin peeled his gaze away from the car. "Really? I'd not heard about that."

"Inspector Root has kept it pretty close to his chest, sir."

"But he let the story about the blood spot get out?" Robin would have played it the other way round. Details about fibres might ring a bell with someone who knew the Slasher, family or friend, whereas everybody had blood.

"He thought it might make the Slasher panic." Grace rolled her eyes.

Robin refrained from commenting. Anderson was on the way back and the boot would soon be opened. When it was, it proved a profound disappointment, nothing made of black suede—gloves, coat, or hat—nor of camel-coloured wool leaping into view, even when they peered beneath the floor panel. So unless such things turned up when Grace started rummaging under the seats or anywhere else that took her fancy, there was no apparent link to Hatton's killing, just as Robin had suspected.

There *were* fibres of all sorts, on the floor of the boot, some only visible to a well-trained eye. Nobody needed skilled eyes to spot the pair of knives there, though, but they would—as Robin had to keep reminding himself—have been the tools of Phillips's trade.

"You look like a cat who's got the cream," Anderson said, watching with evident pleasure as Grace worked.

"I'm a cat who's got some bits of wool," she said over her shoulder.

"Camel coloured?"

"No. Green. And, without getting too excited, they're awfully like the ones we found in connection with the Slasher."

"Yes!" Anderson punched the air.

Grace glanced up at the sergeant, then at Robin. "What's going on here?"

"I had a hunch that Phillips might be the man Inspector Root is after." Anderson sounded fit to burst with pride. "Not least because he was laid up in hospital when the Slasher didn't strike."

"That sounds like the dog that didn't bark in the night-time." Grace grinned.

"There's a pretty good chance of getting some DNA samples from inside the car. You'd be justified in taking them, given what you found in the boot."

"Thank you, sir. They didn't cover that in the training." Grace rolled her eyes. "I'll be taking those knives too!"

Robin and the sergeant left her to it.

"Well done on your theory." Robin clapped Anderson on the shoulder. "It's over to Inspector Root now. I hope he appreciates your efforts."

"*Our* efforts, sir." Anderson's words might have been self-deprecating, but he smiled like a loon.

"Okay. *Our* efforts, but never forget it was *your* hunch. Although perhaps you'd rather disown it. If it turns out we've solved his case for him on the back of your mad idea, I'm not sure he'll be too happy."

"I'd love to be a fly on the wall when he reads the report, assuming the DNA matches." Anderson frowned. "There *is* another downside, not just Root's temper."

"Yeah, at least I'm ahead of you on that one. If they catch the Slasher, they'll have capacity to take back the Hatton case." Robin shrugged. "We won't have long to wait to find out. Grace will rush the samples through processing, and Root will add his clout. In the meantime, we need to concern ourselves with Hatton. He was drinking with Phillips, so we can account for most of the missing time, but if our chef didn't kill the man—and he convinced me on that point—then who the hell did?"

Adam left his classroom, heading for the lower-school classrooms, last pupil safely out of the door and no parents nabbing him about a perceived indiscretion on the school's part with their little Olivia or Calum.

He rarely felt a frisson of discomfort now when passing what had been the door to the children's kitchen, but today the hairs on the back of his neck stood up. Last spring there'd been a dead body slumped over the table in that room, and the corpse's face still sneaked into Adam's thoughts at the most inappropriate times. Chris Waldrom had taken the right action, of course, finding a pot of funding to get a reconfiguration of that part of the school pushed through during the winter. Now the place where Ian Youngs had been strangled lay behind a row of cabinets in the cleaners' storeroom, and the pupils made their fairy cakes where the mops and buckets had once been located.

The children had been pretty stoic back then, soon getting over the murder and the makeover, but the adults had longer—and more vivid—memories. Life had to go on, however, and Adam couldn't make a detour every time he had to go past the storeroom—like today, when he was seeking an after-school-hours talk with Luke. He took a last look at the old kitchen door, trying to find something good out of the evil. Was the fact that the murder had been the means of his meeting Robin enough to be grateful for? He strode on, entering Luke's classroom with a cheery, "Had a good afternoon?"

Luke, who'd been putting some of his children's work on a display, jumped a mile. "Do you always sneak up on people?"

"Sorry. Force of habit. Too used to flushing out the year sixes when they're arsing about in the bushes." Adam laughed, although he noted the unsettled edge in Luke's voice. "It's 'The Jolly Postman' tomorrow?"

"Yep. My planning's on the desk. They're going to be writing their own letters to fairy-tale characters."

"Cool." Adam checked over the lesson plan, with half an eye on Luke, who kept sneaking a look at him. "Are you okay?"

"Yes. Why shouldn't I be?" The forcefulness of the response belied the words.

"No reason. Hang loose." Adam raised his hands as though surrendering. "This planning's spot on, by the way. You have learned well, young Brunning."

Luke's scowl turned to a smile. "Sorry I snapped at you. Had a bit of a weekend."

"Been on the sauce?"

"I wish." Luke came over and perched on the end of the desk. "I can tell you this because you get it, and you won't go shooting your mouth off. I'm worried about Sam."

"Oh yes? What's the matter?"

"He's been edgy the entire weekend." Sam and Luke both lived at home with their parents on a smallholding between Lindenshaw and Stanebridge. "I thought it was worrying about the match. He was out on the lash on Friday, and he was like a bear with a sore head on Saturday night. He's still edgy. I think his girlfriend might have given him the push."

Adam made a sympathetic face.

"She's a police officer, too. Wendy May."

"Wasn't she involved with taking statements at the Desdemona? Robin was pretty impressed with her abilities."

"That sounds like her. Shame if it is all off, because we really liked her, despite . . ."

The fact she's black? Adam let Luke flounder.

"Despite the fact it isn't a good idea to mix work and romance," he managed at last.

"Excellent advice." Adam nodded. "It leads to far too many complications. And you never get any absence to let your heart grow fonder." He wasn't sure that made as much sense as he intended.

Luke didn't appear to notice, blowing out his cheeks and tapping nervously with a pencil on the nearest desk. "Can I pick your brain about phonics?"

"You can try. I'm probably as much use at them as at being an agony aunt."

Luke seemed a lot happier at the prospect of phonemes than talking about his brother. "Thanks. We don't want police business getting in the way of school again, do we?"

"Too true." Adam recalled the unease he'd felt when passing the old kitchen door, the unexpected evocation of memories. Please God Robin's latest case, unlikely as appeared at present, wouldn't end up involving the school a second time.

Chapter Four

The first working morning of the week had dawned bright, with a hint of warmth in the sun; Carol, the queen of the BBC weather forecast, had promised a few lovely days ahead, even though she'd warned that Monday itself would turn a bit iffy in places. Adam should have taken better note of her.

The dazzling morning that had conned him into riding his bike into school faded into a grey afternoon, and by the time the teachers were heading for home, the heavens had opened. Five minutes cycling home were going to feel more like fifty in this weather, although at least he had his waterproof jacket and a cap. Luke only had his umbrella, which didn't look sturdy enough not to blow itself inside out before he even got to his car. Lack of foresight all round.

Adam didn't dawdle, desperate to get home, get dry, and get stuck into the selection of Waitrose Indian meals he'd simply stuff in the microwave for tea once Robin was back. If they had to fight off Campbell, who'd no doubt want a mouthful, that was a small price to pay. There might even be a couple of bottles of Cobra beer to wash it down with.

As he turned into his road, some idiot was standing on the pavement, gazing up and down the street as if lost. Whoever it was resembled a drowned rat, a daft drowned rat that hadn't the sense to wear a coat or bring an umbrella. Adam cycled past with a feeling of self-satisfaction, wondering why the guy's face seemed vaguely familiar and why anyone in their right mind would be dithering about and getting soaked.

His smugness drained away, like torrents down the pipes, two minutes after he'd got in, when the bell went and he opened the door to find the drowned rat standing there. Anybody might have been unsettled by the apparition on the doorstep, not least because it was dripping wet and had no apparent reason for being there.

"Does Inspector Bright live here?" the spectre asked. "I'm Max Worsley. It's about that murder in Abbotston."

Adam flinched. Robin had mentioned a Worsley to do with the case, and how Anderson had made a snap judgement, saying he'd be trouble. Looked like the sergeant was right, if the witness was here on their doorstep.

"He's not here." That didn't give too much away. How the hell had Worsley found out where Robin was currently living? Surely not from the electoral roll or anything legitimate, because they'd not entered Robin's name when the form had come round. It had felt premature. "You should contact him at the station, not chase around catching your death of cold."

"I can't. See him at the station, I mean. There are reasons. I want to speak to *him* and him only." Worsley stuck out his lip like a petulant child.

Damn. Adam had seen that expression before, and he couldn't say where or when. It wasn't at the Desdemona; he'd only gone there the once and had quickly decided the place wasn't his scene, so Worsley wasn't likely to have been some fumbled encounter after a few too many down the hatch.

"I know he lives here. Don't ask *how* I know." Worsley grinned, despite the rain hammering behind him. "I've got contacts."

"You could ring him at the station." Adam's willpower was fading, the need to protect Robin—to keep Worsley, someone he knew nothing about, out of the house—fighting with his inherent instinct to be a Good Samaritan. He was always telling his class they shouldn't miss out on any opportunity of helping somebody in need. Just like he told them to stay away from "stranger danger."

"I don't want to ring him. It could be dangerous. For both of us." If Worsley was lying, he was doing it well.

"Look at the state of you. You're bloody well soaking." The Good Samaritan had won, even if there was another element that had subtly strayed into the mix. Worsley was handsome, in that square-jawed, rugged, lock-forward way Adam had always liked. Sopping wet, he was a distinctly more attractive version of Mr. Darcy, the film version.

"I left my coat in my office—got a bit distracted. Had to talk to Inspector Bright as soon as I could." The rain and the wind seemed to be stealing Worsley's words away, leaving his sentences half-formed. Nevertheless, he smiled through the rivers of water running down his face from his drenched hair.

"You'd better come in. I don't want your illness on my conscience." Adam ushered Worsley into the hall. "I'll see if I can rustle up something dry for you to put on—you'll catch your bloody death of cold. Stay here." He left Worsley dripping in the front hall, with a suspicious-looking Campbell growling softly, clearly making sure the unwanted visitor didn't go and nick the family silver.

"You'll find the loo by the front door, if you want to towel yourself off," Adam shouted over his shoulder as he managed to put his hands on a sweatshirt and track suit bottoms that would have fitted pretty well every size. It wasn't sensible to let a stranger into the house, but his previous encounter with a murderer had at least left him confident in Campbell's ability to deal with whatever problems he had to face. Anyway, Robin would be home soon to straighten everything out; although maybe Adam should sneak his cricket bat downstairs while he was about it, in case things turned nasty.

He came down the stairs, then stuck an armful of clothes round the toilet door, not wanting to barge in on Worsley if he'd stripped off. He stroked Campbell, which always helped to clear his mind, and dithered about offering to put the kettle on, when a car pulled onto the drive. Adam opened the front door, glad that the rain had at last let up, slipped out and caught Robin while he was in the driver's seat.

"You've got a visitor. That Max Worsley bloke." Now the *name* as well as the face had started to ring a bell, away from the Hatton murder.

Robin's eyes narrowed, face taking on a guarded expression. "What the hell's he doing here?"

Adam shrugged. "Says he wants to see you and refused to go to the station to do it. He got hold of our address somehow."

"Somehow?" Robin puffed out his cheeks. "That doesn't surprise me. He's supposed to be a computer whizz-kid."

"Oh, yeah. I remember." Adam recalled Robin talking about what Worsley did, in the context of some potential connection with the secret services. Those guys could find out what your granny had for breakfast. "I think it's important, given that he's soaking bloody wet and in a bit of a state. I've found him dry clothes to change into."

Robin groaned. "You'd better get the kettle on. I'm going to get changed as well."

Adam took Worsley into the kitchen, where Campbell—who still didn't look impressed with the bloke—settled in his basket and kept his eyes on the visitor. Robin, in a hissed aside before he'd gone upstairs, had insisted that they stay together; safety was more pressing than confidentiality in this instance.

"So, what's so important you had to track me down here?" Robin asked as soon as he came through the kitchen door. "The police station is where witnesses usually go."

"I know. But this is tricky. There are reasons I can't have this particular conversation at Abbotston."

"I'd have seen you at Stanebridge." Robin ran his hands through hair that was damp, probably from the short journey from office to car. "You should have rung there and made an appointment. They'd have got hold of me."

"No!" Worsley held up his hand. "Shouldn't have shouted. I just don't want to be at any police station at present. Not until you've heard what I've got to say. It's a bit of a long story."

"Then you'd better get on with telling it." Robin put his hands to his stomach as it rumbled.

Adam rattled a handful of cutlery, to show he was getting dinner ready. "I'm on the case. Any more of a delay and my stomach will think my throat's been cut. Sorry." Adam made an apologetic face, before turning to Worsley. "You'd better have something as well. It's only Indian meals from Waitrose, but they're pretty good, and we've got plenty of poppadoms . . ."

He stopped, not sure why he was wittering on so much, given the circumstances. Robin shrugged and opened his notepad, which he'd put down on the breakfast bar.

"Thanks, I'd appreciate that. I've not eaten properly since breakfast. And this cup of tea's a lifesaver. More than I deserve."

Worsley's teeth no longer chattered; he cradled the hot mug and smiled, an expansive smile that lit up his whole face. Adam, at last—and with a sinking sensation in the pit of his stomach—remembered where he'd seen Worsley before and why the name was nagging at him so much. Why the hell had he come face-to-face, at this settled stage in his life, with the man he'd fantasised about on and off through several of his formative years?

The last time he'd seen Worsley, Adam had been eighteen, had just done his A levels, and—results allowing—would soon be en route to university to read history before taking teacher training. He'd been called for jury service and had accepted the duty cheerfully, believing it would be a good way to kill a couple of weeks and stop him worrying over results. After twiddling his thumbs for the first day, the second morning he'd found himself assigned to a common assault trial.

He dragged himself back into the present day, aware that two pairs of eyes were fixed on him.

"I'll get on with this curry, then." Adam concentrated on fetching the packs from the fridge, but his mind was going like a train—why hadn't he made the connection earlier? Worsley's face had matured and changed; he hadn't been quite as muscular back in those days and had clearly done a lot of work in the gym since. Why the hell had he come round here, now? Robin had a legitimate reason for being involved in murder cases, but why did they keep wanting to weave themselves into Adam's life?

Robin, voice as icy as the unseasonal rain outside, carried on. "Well, Mr. Worsley. You've imposed on our hospitality. You'd better have something good to tell me in return."

"I don't know if it's good, exactly. I saw the person that Hatton got into a fight with."

"I know. You told us."

"Sorry, I'm not making myself clear. I saw him again. Yesterday. I was in the flower shop at Abbotston Basin. The place that specialises in roses."

"I know the shop. Very upmarket." Robin took a drink of his tea.

Upmarket was an understatement. The Basin was an area of canal frontage, possibly the most exclusive shopping area in the town's redevelopment.

"I wanted to order some for my sister, seeing as I won't be able to get home for her birthday. I was eyeing up the flowers when this guy came in. He had a woman with him. What my mother would describe as a flash piece of goods." Worsley started to grin, then quickly straightened his face. "I tried to give myself time to make sure it *was* the one who'd been in the fight. I dithered about, like I couldn't choose. Let them get served first."

Robin tapped the table with his pen "You're certain it was him?"

"Absolutely positive. I *told* you, I've got a fantastic memory for faces. It must be to compensate for my poor memory for names."

"So what happened in the shop?" Robin scribbled some notes.

"They had a bit of a spat over which variety of red would be best. She didn't like being contradicted. High-maintenance woman, too used to having her own way, I'd have said. She walked out in a huff, and he followed her." Worsley shrugged.

"Grub's up." Adam had waited until the last possible moment to put the food on the breakfast bar. As he laid plates and cutlery alongside them, and encouraged people to help themselves, he avoided looking at Worsley, especially those piercing eyes of his. They'd been almost as piercing back in the court, when Worsley had been standing in the witness box, two days into the assault trial. He would most likely have gazed out at the double rank of jurors and not even taken the least bit of notice of Adam. That had been frustrating at the time; now Adam was glad of that probability.

"Did you ever get round to finding out their names? Did they say or do anything that's actually relevant to the case?" Robin asked as he ladled food onto his plate. The way he was slapping the spoon down suggested his temper was becoming frayed and the poppadoms were going to end up like ground almonds.

"I got their names eventually." Worsley kept his eyes on his food. "Not before I'd got a pile of stick from the florist, though."

Adam was amazed that Robin could pick the important stuff from the mass of irrelevant detail coming out. He'd never been privy to one of Robin's interviews, except for the ones he'd been on the other end of.

Worsley carried on. "I said I thought I used to work with the guy who'd just been in the shop, but I couldn't think of his name and trying to remember it would bug me all week."

"And who was it?" Robin's voice was so exasperated, Adam wouldn't have been surprised if he grabbed Worsley and held his head in the curry until he gave a proper answer.

"He's called Sam Brunning."

"Sam Brunning? But that's—that's none of my business." Adam got his head back down over the food, although his appetite was pretty well gone. "How did you get here?"

"On the bus, seeing as there's no train out here in the sticks." Worsley glanced up from his plate; at least *his* appetite wasn't suffering. "I had to walk here from the High Street."

"Why didn't you drive here rather than get soaked?"

"I don't drive. I've had occasional fits ever since I was a teenager, so it's public transport or Shanks's pony most of the time."

Yes. That had come up during the trial, the smart-alec defence brief trying to throw doubt on Worsley's evidence and the witness giving as good as he'd got, insisting that he hadn't suffered a fit at the time. He'd also asked why the barrister was making such a big thing of his disability by implying that being epileptic made people unreliable witnesses. It had earned Worsley a lot of credit with the jury, two of whom had epileptic children.

Best not to think about those days too much now.

They ate in a strained silence until they'd consumed as much as they could. Adam started to clear away with the plates, with a swift, pleading look at Robin not to ask him why he'd interjected. Not until they were alone, anyway. He offered coffee, was refused, thought of suggesting they crack open the beer in the fridge, then decided that was a worse idea. He'd occupy himself with the washing-up.

"Brunning's a policeman, according to the florist," Worsley recommenced, once the table was tidy.

Robin nodded but held his tongue.

"Which is why I didn't want to go to the police station. What if he followed Hatton after their fight and killed him? What if he remembered me from the Desdemona? I don't want him to know I'm onto him."

"He wouldn't necessarily have known why you'd contacted me. Any discussion we'd had at the station would have been confidential."

Worsley snorted. "Word gets round in any organisation. The police aren't immune."

Even though Adam had his back to the room, he sensed Robin seething. Yes, there were failings in any organisation, but Robin wouldn't tolerate them on his watch. Adam manoeuvred at the sink to get a better view of proceedings via the reflection in the window.

"How do you know you've got the Brunning name right if you have such a bad memory for them?"

"I wrote it on a slip of paper, straight away." Worsley went to find his still soggy clothes, fishing in the pocket to produce a sodden slip, which he passed over to Robin.

Robin examined the paper, then laid it carefully to one side. "So let me get this straight. You're saying that Brunning was definitely fighting with Hatton."

"Yes."

"What about the woman with him? Did you get *her* name?"

Worsley shook his head. "The florist didn't know her. Made a big joke about how I'd have to find that one out for myself. She was tall, though. Black hair. Pretty."

Robin nodded as though the description rang a bell. Maybe one of Hatton's girlfriends, which could explain the fight? Face drawn, he pushed his notepad to one side, bringing things to a close. When it became clear there was nothing further to be gleaned, Adam rang for a taxi to take the witness home, pleased when told that one would be round within ten minutes. He and Robin needed to talk, and not only about Brunning.

"Do you possess anything made from black suede? Gloves or something?" Robin carried on the questioning as they waited in the hall, gathering up Worsley's still damp clothes. His voice sounded deliberately airy—Adam recognised the "lull you into a false sense of security" tone from his own interviews, the year previously. Although he'd been more interested in listening for subtle signs of attraction back then.

"Not my colour, dear." Worsley waved his hand, suddenly camp as a row of tents. "Sorry. I'm being an idiot. No, I don't think I have any suede stuff. Why?"

"Routine. The questions we have to ask everybody."

If the black suede was significant, Robin must have been taking a calculated risk mentioning it. If Worsley did have such a pair of gloves now, he might well not have one by the morning.

"You know Sam Brunning?" Robin asked as soon as they'd packed their unexpected visitor into the taxi and got back indoors.

"Hello and it's nice to see you back from work too." Adam couldn't resist the barb.

"We don't have time to arse about." Robin shut his eyes and appeared to count to five. "Sorry. You didn't deserve that. I'm cross at Worsley being here."

"How do you think I feel?" Adam took a deep breath. "Let's get a beer and sit down."

By the time they'd each knocked back half a bottle, the tension had eased.

"I didn't mean to interrogate you." Robin fiddled with his bottle. "It can wait."

"No. If it's important, we need to deal with it." Adam took another swig. "Sam Brunning. I don't know him personally, but you'll remember his brother Luke."

"At the school? The slightly wimpish bloke we met at that do?" Robin nodded. "I'd forgotten he had a connection to the force."

Adam managed a grin. "For a wimp, he's got the potential to be a good teacher."

"He's not mentioned anything the last few days?"

"No-o. Not at first anyway. I mean, we were discussing the murder in the staffroom. What had been on the news about it."

"Not at first?" Typical Robin to pick up on the small, all-important phrase.

Adam shrugged. "Later, Luke came across as preoccupied. I don't know if this helps or makes things worse, but he's worried about Sam. Said his brother was edgy this weekend, although he put it down to girlfriend trouble. Your friend WPC May."

"May?" Robin stuck out his lip. "Davis *said* she was going out with a dog handler. But I didn't get the impression she was upset on Saturday. Apart from having been up most of the night taking statements."

"Could she have been one of Hatton's women? Or possibly he'd been chasing her and Brunning didn't like it?"

"And that's what they fought over?" Robin made a face. "May's certainly not the woman in the florist's, although *she* sounds like one of Hatton's ladies. More likely the spat was over her."

"Good point. Guess that's why you're the cop and I'm the teacher."

"This cop says you mustn't assume it *was* Brunning in the shop or in the fight. People do pretend to be coppers, and people do make mistakes on identification, no matter how good a memory for faces they say they have."

Adam could guess how awkward an identity parade would be if it featured one of their own, but he didn't want to mention yet that he knew how reliable a witness Worsley could be. "Why should he lie?"

"Because people do. Not least to divert our attention. From themselves." Robin reached down to stroke Campbell, who had suddenly appeared, his dogdar—or whatever canine instinct should be called—evidently informing him that one of his masters needed affection. "I've half a mind to take along somebody other than Anderson to the florist. He's not exactly unbiased as far as Worsley's concerned."

Adam almost said, *I'm not exactly unbiased, either*, but held his tongue. He'd developed the worst case of cold feet about blurting everything out now; there had to be time to get his own thoughts straight before sharing them, especially when he and Robin both seemed to be walking on eggshells at present. "Not WPC May, given the circumstances," he said eventually. "Although you without Anderson would be like cheese without chutney."

"I'll take that as a compliment." Robin gave what looked like a forced smile. "And you're right. If this does turn out to involve one of ours, I'd likely need to keep those in the know as few as possible, for the moment."

"Hell of a mess, isn't it?"

"You said it. Bad enough with the possible IRA connection, but internal matters make things even darker and dirtier. I'll ring Cowdrey first thing. He'll have the Independent Police Complaints Commission aspect top of his agenda." Robin pulled back his shoulders, clearly easing some knots of tension. "This can wait until tomorrow. When I can think straight."

"You need a proper night's sleep. Have an early night while I do some marking. Campbell can keep me company."

"I always play second fiddle to that dog." Robin kissed him—more than just a passing kiss, one that spoke of deep needs.

"Quite right. Get to bed."

Adam watched his lover trudge up the stairs, then went to pour another beer. It would oil the marking wheels and help him concentrate.

Eighteen. That's how old he'd been when he did jury duty. Eighteen and a raging mass of hormones. Lust at first sight had been an everyday event. He remembered alternating between hanging on Worsley's every word in the witness box, and getting his head down and making notes, in case anyone spotted how his tongue was almost touching the floor. He'd spent too many nights during the trial, then all that summer and part of his first term at uni, having steamy dreams about the bloke. Even called out Worsley's name once, when he was in the height of passion with some other man. Not Robin, thank goodness. The "juror gets off with the witness" obsession had trailed off years ago, after Adam had started going steady with his first serious boyfriend.

Campbell yelped as Adam stepped back onto him.

"Sorry, boy." Adam bent to give the dog a hug. "Miles away there. Come and help me mark."

They settled down on the settee in the lounge, but Adam could only give half his mind to the books, the other half clearly picturing Worsley—who was barely a year older than he was—getting distressed while giving evidence against a thug with a history of homophobic attacks. Only they hadn't given them that particular title in those days. The case had stung like hell. Adam hadn't been that long out to his parents, and most of his friends had no idea he was gay. Worsley had been in his first year at Imperial College; Adam remembered every detail about him, even though the case itself was little more than a fuzzy memory.

What was the name of the man they'd found guilty? How infuriating not to remember such an important thing.

He roused himself from his thoughts to look at the pile of marking, still untouched, before turning to Campbell, who was eyeing him as though peering into his master's brain, worried about the tangled knot of emotions there.

"I know," Adam said, rubbing the dog's ear. "I'm being stupid."

He should get on with his marking, forget about Max sodding Worsley, think about the man upstairs, who meant more than a dozen teenage fantasies combined. He should, but it was easier said than done.

Chapter Five

Tuesday morning, Anderson wasn't impressed at the prospect of being dragged down to a florist's shop, especially when Robin explained that they had a trail to check out, and whose information they were verifying. He wasn't happy about the Brunning aspect, either. He'd spoken to Cowdrey, who was awaiting further developments.

"We've got to take it seriously, even if you think it's all wrong." Robin didn't like investigating one of their own any more than his sergeant did, but they had to follow every lead. No matter how much he'd taken a dislike to Worsley.

"I didn't say I thought this is all wrong. Just peculiar. Peculiar makes me suspicious." Anderson's eyes narrowed as he got out of his car and locked it. "Especially as he came round to your house. I told you he'd be a troublemaker."

"I know you did. Although if he's given us a good lead, you might have to change your opinion." If anybody else had come with that story, would he and Anderson have been so insistent on double-checking it, or was it because one of their colleagues had been fingered?

"I'll believe it when I see it. I don't trust him as far as I could throw him, which isn't far given how he's built." Anderson sniffed, loudly, as they walked along the waterfront. "Going to visit you was out of order. He could have come to Stanebridge station if he didn't want to go to Abbotston."

"That's what I pointed out. But he was insistent it couldn't be on official ground because of Brunning. I'm relieved Adam was there to witness the conversation."

Adam, for some reason, had been unsettled by that encounter with Worsley. He'd not slept well, tossing and turning, and hadn't been himself this morning. Probably it was the shock of a witness coming to his house—an unwanted, unnecessary corollary to being a rozzer's partner—that had upset him, and they'd need to talk it over. Although there hadn't been time over the cornflakes, and probably wouldn't be for the foreseeable future. He'd given him a big hug and promised they'd go out for dinner as soon as Hatton's killer was caught. The offer had done the trick.

He stopped just outside the shop. Should he get Adam a bouquet to show his appreciation of his lover's patience? The strategy probably wouldn't work, given that Adam had never been much of a flowers bloke, so maybe Robin would have to earn his brownie points elsewhere. "Perhaps I should order a bunch of flowers for Mum's birthday, while we're here."

"You'll have plenty of choice." Anderson jerked his thumb at the shop window.

Robin had never seen so many different sorts of roses; how the hell would he ever make up his mind? His mother liked red, hated pink, and loved a vibrant yellow. That was satisfactory when he was simply grabbing a bunch of the things from the entrance of his local Waitrose, but her sixty-fifth birthday was too special an occasion for taking a gung-ho approach. Not to mention the fact that when the blooms were such a subtle mass of delicate and contrasting colours, the simple preference of red or yellow seemed irrelevant. He took a sideways glance at Anderson, but the sergeant seemed just as bewildered.

"Bloody hell, sir. Do people really come and buy these?"

"Apparently. Or why would they sell them?"

"It's like being at a restaurant when the sweet trolley comes. You can't make a sensible choice when there's too much on offer." Anderson pointed at a large bunch of white blooms. "And look at the bloody prices."

"I've seen them." Shopping might be off the menu; they'd restrict their visit to asking questions about Brunning today, although how he could afford to shop at this place on policeman's pay was anybody's guess.

The florist—a cheerful young man with an air of efficiency and something that pinged Robin's gaydar—laid down the orange variegated roses he'd been arranging, at the sight of their warrant cards. He insisted they call him Charlie and said he'd be thrilled to help the police. Davis, that rooter out of unconsidered gems, had managed to find pretty passable pictures of the key players, so Robin was able to launch straight into identifications.

"I know him." Charlie slipped on a pair of reading glasses. "Yes, that's Max. No memory for names. Bloody hopeless."

"Does he come in here a lot?"

Charlie smiled. "Every couple of weeks. But once seen, never forgotten. And he likes his flowers."

Robin remembered the profusion of blooms in Worsley's flat, and nodded. "He told us that he asked you about one of your other customers."

"Oh yes. A typical case of his forgetfulness." Charlie raised an eyebrow.

"We've some pictures here." Anderson produced the file Davis had compiled. "Is the man Worsley was asking about among them?"

"I'll have a gander. I can confirm his name for you as well."

"Is he another regular?" Anderson asked.

"Not if it's the man I'm thinking of." Charlie smiled again, then glanced through the small dossier of vaguely similar men, into which Robin had slipped the picture of Brunning. The picture the florist immediately pointed at. "That's him. He was here with a woman. They had a bit of a spat."

Robin's heart sank as the first part of the story was verified. "Go on."

"She accused him of being a cheapskate or something. Stormed out. He came back later and ordered some flowers to collect. I've got the original order in the book." Charlie picked up a thick, old-fashioned tome.

Robin, transported back to days before computer terminal and card transactions were the norm, remarked, "I'd have thought it was all done online now."

"You'd be surprised." Charlie made a deprecating face. "Lots of customers like the paper trail. As does my lady who makes the bouquets up. Ah. Here. Brunning. Sam Brunning."

"Thank you." That appeared to confirm Worsley's story. "Was there a name on the message card with them?"

"No. The customer wanted that left blank so he could do it himself. If they were for the woman who stormed out, I can't help with her name, either."

"Maybe *we* can." Robin produced a picture of Zandra Williams, one where she had her hand by her face.

"Yes, I think that's her. I'd remember her nails, anyway, because they were flawless bar a couple that looked like she'd been chewing them."

"That helps, thank you." Robin picked up a business card from the holder on the counter. "May I keep this?

"Of course. You can have a discount any time you return."

For the first time in ages, Robin felt himself flushing in the face of blatant flirtation. He mumbled another thank-you and ushered Anderson out.

"No comments," he said as they walked back to the car.

"Never crossed my mind to comment, sir."

"Just as well. Anyway, Worsley was probably correct about Brunning."

"Only at the florist's. Doesn't have to have been him at the club." Anderson jangled his car keys in his hand.

"Easy enough to check." Robin tapped his sheaf of photos. "I'm talking to Cowdrey first though. Right now." He got out his phone and entered the number.

By the time he'd finished explaining things to his boss, Cowdrey had gone into damage reduction mode. *He* would talk to Brunning. *He* would visit the Desdemona and complete the identification there; Davis would run off more copies of the photos. If they needed to set the wheels of an internal investigation in motion, they had to play by the book, and Robin might already have strayed off the page.

"We've plenty of other angles to cover. I assume it's okay for us to go back and talk to Zandra?" Robin waited for his boss's assent before asking if there was any news on the IRA front.

"Nothing useful, no. We'll talk this afternoon."

"Yes, sir." Robin ended the call, then updated Anderson, who'd become increasingly agitated.

"Rather him than me. Never good when it's one of us involved."

"Innocent until proven guilty." Robin wagged his finger, like Adam might at a naughty child. "Let's see what Zandra has to say."

But Zandra wasn't saying anything. Her mother had taken a turn for the worse, so she was back at the hospital, or so the message on her answerphone told them. They left a message, but with no great hopes of it being returned any time soon.

"Where next?" Anderson jangled his car keys, clearly frustrated.

Robin took a deep breath. He didn't want to let go of the Brunning angle so easily, irrespective of procedure. They could do with finding somebody safe to talk to, safe as in neither Cowdrey nor Root getting wind of it. Safe as in doing no harm to any eventual internal investigation. Somebody with a connection to the force—ex-copper possibly—whose ear he could confidentially bend.

Pike.

"I've had a brilliant idea. Let me get Davis to rustle up a number for us, and with any luck we'll soon be getting into the Batmobile."

For once, luck was on their side.

"So where are we going?" Anderson said as they pulled out of the car park, a couple of phone calls later.

"The industrial estate on the Newbury Road, about half an hour from here. Do you know it?"

"Yep. Did I hear we're going to visit somebody called Pike?"

"That's the boy. Maurice Pike. He's retired from the force now, but he used to work at Stanebridge nick. Spent some time with the dog handlers too."

"Ah. Got it." Anderson nodded. "I've heard his name mentioned. Only good stuff."

"I'd expect nothing less. He's one of the best of the old school." He'd always been a proper pal to Robin, even when Robin was a wet-behind-the-ears, university graduate fast tracker. "He was at Stanebridge when I started, and he took me under his wing. Got out just before you joined us. He must have known you were trouble." Robin grinned.

"I'll have to bend his ears about your misdemeanours."

"Don't you dare." Pike had been a godsend back then, nurturing Robin with valuable advice and a healthy dose of sporting chat, convinced that Detective Constable Bright would end up being the youngest-ever chief constable.

"When I'm retired, I'll tell all my mates down at the allotment that I remember when you were first out of the training college, and no use to anyone. And you can tell all the posh people you meet that Sergeant Pike gave you the best guidance."

"He gave good advice, though. Simple. Keep nicking people, keep your nose clean, and keep your paperwork up to date." There'd been a bit more to Robin's career than that, but it made a solid foundation.

"Sounds as if I'm going to like him."

"You are. We need to stop off and get the bribes in advance."

"The bribes?"

"Oh, yes. Didn't you know the way to a man's heart is through his stomach?" Robin grinned. "And if you dare say, 'Trust you to know that, sir,' I'll have you up on a disciplinary."

The bribes—hot bacon sandwiches from the little station cafe at Abbotston Junction—filled the car with their seductive aroma. It was as well the industrial estate was only five minutes' drive away from there, or Anderson might have expired from unquenched desire. Hot, crispy bacon was the ideal way to get into anyone's good books, even if it was torture to defer the pleasure. They parked outside an impressive new office block, then bore their packages through the door and up to the security desk, where Robin smiled broadly at the sight of his old colleague. Pike might be in his mid-fifties, with greying hair that might have lured any villain into trying to leg it, but that wiry frame suggested he could probably take on most scamps over four hundred yards and still catch them.

"Morning, Mr. Pike."

"Morning, Mr. Bright." The security man grinned. "Got nothing better to do than come and annoy hard-working ex-coppers?"

"Any more cheek and I won't share my bacon butties." Robin laid down a couple of greaseproof-wrapped packs on the security guard's desk. "This is my sergeant, Anderson."

"Pleased to meet you." Pike thrust out his hand. "He needs someone to keep him under control. Although perhaps that nice teacher of his does that?"

"Blimey. How quickly does gossip travel around here?" Robin started to unwrap his own bacon butty. He was going to need it if these two ganged up on him.

"Good news travels fast." Pike smiled. "How's domestic life suiting you?"

"It's good." Robin put the tension of the last few days to the back of his mind. Once this case was over, he and Adam would return to normal, surely?

"Glad to hear it." Pike gave Robin a long, scrutinising look. "I'll get you both a coffee to go with that butty. Then you can tell me what you're on the cadge for. Sugar?"

"Don't call people 'sugar' until you know them better." Anderson seemed delighted at his joke, but Pike shook his head. He settled the pair on his side of the desk, fetched the drinks, and waited.

Robin wiped his mouth. "I'm picking your brains. In your capacity as one-time looker-after of the still-in-nappies members of the dog squad."

Pike glanced up over his butty. "Honest? Seems like it's you and everybody else."

Robin had been about to dig into his sandwich, but that remark quelled his appetite. "Everybody?"

"Well, two people. You and that smarmy inspector with the same name as the cricketer."

"Root?"

"Yeah. You've got it in one. Just put the phone down from talking to him.

Robin frowned at Anderson, who shrugged back. "What was he after?"

"Said he was asking around about some of the lads. Career development. I didn't believe him," Pike added with a knowing grin. "I said if he wanted personal information, he had to go through the proper channels. I'd write a reference, but otherwise it could be seen as idle gossip, detrimental to the force. Asked him if it was a proper internal investigation and all that."

"Are you going to make *us* go through the proper channels?" Robin's heart sank. Had Pike turned jobsworth? Maybe he'd clam up about the dog handler, and all they'd get from today would be a decent brunch. Sod's law.

Sod, however, must have been on holiday, because Pike took another bite of sandwich, wiped his mouth, and said, "Of course not. I trust you two, so if I had a smidge of gossip, it would be safe in your hands. You just have to keep some people in their places."

"Too true." Anderson nodded.

"I'm guessing from the glint in your eye you're going down the same track. Personal information about one of the dog handlers."

"You've got me bang to rights." Robin fortified himself with another swig of coffee. "Sam Brunning. Did he ever blot his copybook?"

"Not that I remember." Pike's brow furrowed. "I mean there was a bit of hijinks now and then, practical jokes and the like, but nothing I had to jump on from a great height."

"Never been on the take or anything like that?" Robin held up his hand on seeing Pike's horrified expression. "I've got to ask, Maurice. I know you kept your nose clean—and if you didn't, nobody found out, so don't shatter my illusions now—but it happens."

"As far as I know, Sam never did anything like that. I mean, he's not the brightest spark plug on the engine, but he's not bent. Oh!" Pike made a face. "Didn't mean it like that."

"I know you didn't." Robin grinned. He and Pike went back a long way; they knew where the boundaries sat. He and Adam should invite Pike and his wife round for dinner one day, once things were back to normal.

"What's this about? Or can't you tell me?"

"I can't, but I will. However, if you snitch, there'll be no more bacon butties." Robin waggled the last part of his sandwich to emphasise the point. "Brunning might have got into a fight with someone. Someone who was later found dead, stabbed."

"That bloke in Abbotston? Stabbing doesn't sound like Sam. As for the fight—" Pike shrugged, "—could be, if he'd had a few and a woman was involved."

Anderson and Robin shared a glance, but Pike was ploughing on.

"Anyway, I'm glad you got in contact. Saved me the bother of a phone call. It was the stabbing I wanted to talk about. Hatton. The name rang a bell."

Robin, who'd laid his notepad down on the counter, picked it up again. "Go on."

"If it's the same bloke I'm thinking of, Hatton gave us valuable information about an assault, hmm . . . ten years ago?" Pike's brow wrinkled. "Might be even longer than that, but not much."

"There's nothing about it in the official records," Anderson remarked. "I've trawled them."

"There wouldn't be. Some things only get stored here." Pike tapped his forehead. "And it's not only a case of sloppy record-keeping. We were told to keep his name out of things."

"Why?"

"He was working for GCHQ at the time, and *that* mob wanted to keep things under wraps. There was something else as well, to do with the victim. Had friends in high places. Anyway, it was very odd."

"Sounds it." Robin didn't have much time for people who tried to buck the system and unduly influence due process. Even if that was what *he* was doing.

"Anyway, once we ran the perpetrator down, we had enough witnesses and forensics not to need Hatton's eyewitness evidence."

"Was there some IRA connection in that case?" Robin didn't want the answer to be a positive one, not least because it would be another feather in Anderson's smug cap.

"Not that I'm aware of. A common or garden thug. Can't remember his name, but if you go back through the records, you should be able to pin him down. Assault took place up on the Rings."

The Rings were an Iron Age hill fort, not far outside Abbotston, popular with dog walkers, ramblers, and—after dark—courting couples of every combination of gender. "How serious an assault was it?"

"Beating up, rather than indecent." Pike stopped, clearly weighing his words. "I remember talk that the victim had been under suspicion for kiddie fiddling, which might have been the motive for him getting done over. But those friends in high places made phone calls, so a lot of the background didn't come out in court. Most of it will be in the files. Except anything about Hatton's tip-off. You *do* know who the arresting officer was?"

"You?"

"No." Pike rolled his eyes. "Root. Sergeant Root, as he was in those days. His first case at Abbotston."

Anderson whistled. "Would he have known about Hatton's involvement?"

"I doubt it. They weren't that sure of Root back then. Early days."

"I'm not sure what to make of him now." Anderson snorted, contemptuously.

Robin ignored the jibe. "What was the matter with him? He's a successful enough copper now."

Pike, making a mouth like he had a mouthful of lemon, shrugged. "Yeah, he's okay. Back in those days he was regarded as a soft touch. Bleeding heart. Felt sorry for the little scrotes he had to nick."

"He's not like that now, or so Anderson's spies say." Robin swigged the last of his coffee. "That's our work for the rest of the day sorted, then. Thanks. Thanks for everything."

"That sounds like a line from the kind of romance film the missus likes." Pike put the back of his hand to his forehead. "Must you go so soon?"

Robin groaned. "Since when have I become your straight man? No, don't answer that. Too much scope for another of your stupid one-liners. Let's leave it at me owing you a pint for this."

"That's more like it." Pike stood to shake their hands. "Catch whoever did this, right? Hatton struck me as being a fundamentally good guy."

"We'll try our very best," Robin promised, meaning every word.

They'd hardly been back at the station an hour when Cowdrey appeared in their office. The superintendent hadn't been idle and wanted to tell them all about his Brunning-related activities. He'd been to the flat over the Desdemona, getting two of the staff grumpily out of their shared bed to look at the picture of Brunning.

"One thought it was definitely him in the punch-up; the other wasn't sure. I left at the point where a major domestic was brewing over the matter." Cowdrey blew out his cheeks. "Then I spoke to Brunning, with his union representative present as well. Informally, at the moment, to see what his account was of that evening. We're close to setting official wheels in motion."

Robin nodded. The boss clearly liked this as little as he did. "And?"

"And he denies that he was in any fight. He said he was at the Desdemona for a drink, with a mate of his who's gay but in the closet, which is why—he says—he was reluctant to mention the fact when this blew up. Didn't want to get stick from the rest of the lads, and didn't want to shop his mate." Cowdrey made a face, although whether it showed distaste at the laddish attitudes prevailing at the station, or disbelief at Brunning's story—or both—Robin couldn't tell.

"And after he got thrown out of the club?"

"He says he wasn't thrown out. Just left of his own accord, then went to bed, so he was ready for duty at the Cup game, although he's got no alibi for that part. He stays at a pal's flat sometimes, when he's on duty in Abbotston, but this pal was away for the weekend on a stag do. He says the people at the Desdemona must have mixed him up with somebody else." Cowdrey ran his hands through what little hair he had left. "The other officers said he didn't look like he'd had an altercation when he reported for duty. No bruising or anything."

"I told you Worsley was trouble. So much for his photographic memory." Anderson snorted.

"Unless they're closing ranks." Robin didn't feel like defending Worsley, but they had to get behind the "he said, she said" and find the truth. "It happens. Root must have his suspicions too."

"Root? I'd keep your head down where he's concerned. He's not happy about you treading on his case." Cowdrey, on the other hand, appeared delighted.

"Technically, sir, his case has trodden on mine."

Grace had already reported that the fibres from the boot matched those left by the Slasher, although they still awaited the DNA results.

"I agree, but don't tell him that. He's given his boss grief too, about the Hatton case." Cowdrey sighed. "We'll have to wait and see on that one. Returning to Hatton. I'm listening."

"Remember Maurice Pike? We talked to him today."

"About Brunning?" Cowdrey frowned. Thank God they had something more to offer than that, but the rest could wait until Brunning was sorted.

"He was for starters." Robin brought his boss up to date with what Pike had said, such as it was. "He reckons Brunning's exactly the sort to get into a fight, especially over a woman."

"Circumstantial evidence." Cowdrey shrugged. "Useful but anecdotal."

Robin gazed through the window at the brilliant blue sky, the type of sky he wished he was out under, with Adam and Campbell at his side. Why couldn't this have been a simple domestic murder, all done and dusted within forty-eight hours?

"I've got *my* boss following the IRA thing," Cowdrey continued. "He can make phone calls behind closed doors to people who won't want to tell us anything. If there is a connection to some aspect of national security, then the rules will change."

"Could be interesting." Anderson was clearly pleased that his favourite investigation strand was getting an airing. "Back to Brunning for a moment. We understand Root was picking Pike's brains on the same subject before we got there."

"Ah." Cowdrey grinned sheepishly. "I believe I know why that was. He's pretty sure you were right about Phillips—not happy about the fact, but he'll claim it as a success for his team—and he's expecting a quick wind-up to the case. He's got the Hatton murder in his sights now."

"He would." Robin shared a despairing look with his sergeant. Although. . . "How did he know that we were investigating Brunning's activities?"

"That would be me, I'm afraid. Because Brunning was working out of Abbotston last weekend, I had to go via the proper channels, which included Root's boss—I bet *he* let word slip. They want to get one back on the Stanebridge yokels." Cowdrey rubbed his hands together. "I don't think they've ever forgiven us for solving the Lindenshaw killings. Anyway, Brunning's on gardening leave until it's sorted out. Best for all concerned."

Robin nodded. "Pike had another lead for us. An old case that Hatton—strictly on the quiet—provided a tip-off for. Davis is on the trail of it now."

As though the phrase gave birth to the action, there was a sharp rap on the door, then Davis's cheery face appeared round it.

"Got it, sir. The assault." She placed a file on Robin's desk. "It's detailed in there, but basically a chap called Edwards was sent down for it. Very little chance of it being a miscarriage of justice. He was released last year."

The other three officers nodded. Ex-offenders; usually re-offenders.

"There's another thing, though. I went down the list of people involved, in case any of the names rang a bell. And they do." She grinned, wide as the Cheshire cat.

Robin, delighted at her moment of glory, said, "Go on."

"Max Worsley was one of the witnesses."

Anderson, who'd been leaning back in his chair, shot forward, almost propelling himself out of his seat. "Bloody hell."

Bloody hell indeed.

Adam, glad to be home after a tiring day that had seemed to consist more of settling disputes between children than actually teaching them anything, opened his front door and got a chest full of Campbell.

"Hello, boy. Yes, I love you too." He eased the dog off him. Robin must be home, or else the door from kitchen to hallway would be shut. "Hello? Any fit policemen around here?"

There were no policemen of any sort in the house, so either Campbell had worked out how to use part of his paws as an opposable thumb on the handle, or Adam hadn't secured the door as he thought he had. Or . . .

Or somebody had been in the house. Adam took a quick look in the lounge, but the television and the Bose music system hadn't gone, and he wasn't sure there'd be a lot else for burglars to target. And, given the fact that Campbell didn't have his chops smeared with burglar flesh, it seemed unlikely a stranger had got in and got away again. With a sickening feeling in the pit of his stomach, he remembered Worsley. Was there any chance the bloke had been back? Although why the hell he'd have wanted to come in and poke about . . .

A whine from Campbell reminded Adam that the dog would need to visit the garden as soon as possible. En route to the back door, he found a note on the fridge, from their cleaning lady, saying she'd had a phone call that her daughter had been sick at school, so she'd had to leave in a hurry and would text them to let them know when she'd be back to finish the ironing.

What a bleeding idiot you are for missing the obvious. That would explain the door, and anything else that had subconsciously triggered Adam's fears. He knew he was being stupid, imagining such things, but he'd been on edge since Monday, a jumble of old emotions coming to the surface. They should be moving forward now, on the back of Robin having relocated here. Adam hadn't wanted to press him about why his flat hadn't been rented out yet. Maybe that wasn't the root of the problem, only a symptom. Didn't everything return to Robin's bloody job and the way it gnawed into their lives?

Campbell came back into the kitchen, scowling at Adam, as though the dog knew his master was having treacherous thoughts about policemen.

"All right. I *do* love him. And I *will* clear the air on this, I promise. Now, priorities. Your tea." He went to get a tin of dog food while Campbell wagged his tail contentedly. If only everybody was as easy to please.

Adam had a box full of odds and sods he kept meaning to sort out but had never quite got round to. Now seemed an ideal time to make a start, while his own tea was cooking; it might help to both calm and clear his mind. He got it from the bottom of the wardrobe, then rummaged through pictures, matchbooks, shells, the oddments collected through time. He put some of them in the bin, although he couldn't be as ruthless as he wanted. Memories were hard to discard.

He found the newspaper cuttings he'd clipped about the trial and kept at the end of his jury service, the keepsake that helped to mark his move from boy to man—the experience had felt like an important rite of passage.

Re-reading the clipping brought it all back. The case had looked to be going tits up, a wily defence barrister bamboozling witnesses into saying they might have misremembered everything. At the hands of the old fox, they'd probably have admitted to getting their mothers' names wrong.

Max had been the only one to hold his ground, under severe cross-examination and not a small amount of personal attack about what he'd been doing up on the Rings. At the time, Adam had added moral fibre and a hint of the embattled warrior to the list of qualities in Worsley to admire, not least of which was him being drop-dead gorgeous. He'd had to keep his rampant hormones in check when the jury had entered its deliberations.

Worsley remained handsome, but whether he still possessed moral fibre was up for debate; Anderson had clearly taken an instant dislike to him, and the sergeant was nobody's fool.

The sound of Robin's car pulling up on the drive, coinciding with a beeping noise from the oven to say that the shepherd's pie was cooked, made Adam hurriedly scoop the bits and pieces back into the box. Like Campbell, Robin would need feeding and some TLC before he was up to dealing with important things.

Robin gave him a résumé over dinner of what he and Anderson had done during the day: a rose shop, bacon butties, an old colleague—the glamorous life of the jobbing detective.

"Can I ask if Worsley was right about Luke's brother?" Adam asked at a convenient break in the narrative.

"You can, because I'll trust you not to say anything to Luke." Robin eased shoulder muscles that were clearly knotted with stress.

"Here, let me rub that back of yours while you tell me." Adam got to work on the tension in his partner's neck.

"That feels better." Robin leaned into the massage. "If I were a betting man, I'd have a tenner on Brunning being involved in the fight, even though he insists he wasn't."

"Sounds like the kids after there's been a scuffle in the playground. Two or three different versions of the same story, every one of which the teller swears is true." Adam's fingers pummelled at the hard knots of tissue along Robin's spine.

"Perhaps I should employ your expert eye to work out which is which in this case."

"Nah. I've only got the knack with ten-year-olds." Adam flexed his fingers and started to rub again. "Bad pennies in every profession, though. Teachers can be the same. Put people in a position of authority and you'll always have those who abuse it."

"And there was me thinking that everyone in teaching was as squeaky clean as you are."

"You'd be amazed. Or perhaps you wouldn't, given what you must have seen down the years."

Robin reached up to stroke Adam's arm. "I'm sure I haven't lost the capacity to be surprised."

Adam squeezed his hand. "Well, there's not a week goes by that two or three teachers somewhere round the country don't get barred from teaching. 'Prohibition Order,' they call it."

"Sounds like they've been bootlegging." Robin returned the squeeze. "Go on. Horrify me."

"Well, it's usually something horribly prosaic and stupid. Dipping their fingers in the school accounts, falsifying pupils' work, incidents that bring the whole profession into disrepute." Adam wrinkled his nose. "Then there are the ones who've overstepped the safeguarding line. Clipping a pupil's ear. Touching up. I don't need to spell that bit out, do I?"

"No. I get it."

"I find it quite sickening." Too many cases across the media, some going back years and some horribly recent, of teachers who'd done the most disgusting things to the pupils in their care. Adam began a soothing manipulation of muscles that were at last starting to relax. Robin's school days had hardly been happy ones, although the worst he'd suffered at the hands of teachers was their turning a blind eye. "Do you think Brunning killed Hatton?"

Robin shrugged. "I suspect that might have a connection to an old case."

"Really?"

"Yeah. An assault, up at the Rings. Hey, don't stop. I was enjoying that."

"Sorry." Adam resumed the massage, mind racing. He knew what was coming next.

"Young man got beaten up. Suggestion it might have been either homophobic or revenge at a supposed paedophile. The guy who did it was called—"

"Mike Edwards," Adam cut in. "And Worsley was one of the witnesses."

Robin's head spun round. "How the hell did you know that?"

"I was on the jury. I'd forgotten all about it until he came round here on Monday. I kept wondering where I'd seen him before." That was close enough to the truth for the moment. "It was only today I remembered the rest of it. I used to fancy him, back then."

"I'm not surprised. He's pretty hot."

Well, that was simple.

He and Robin had often sat in a bar, eyeing up the guys passing— eyeing up the cakes in the Waitrose bakery section, they'd called it—and it hadn't been a problem. Why had he expected a jealous reaction this time? Robin couldn't see into his head and know what mucky thoughts had lain there.

"What do you remember about Edwards?"

"He didn't look like a thug, despite what people said, but you can't judge on appearances." Adam left off the massage. "I kept some news cuttings about the case and went through them earlier."

"Eyeing up Worsley?" Robin smirked, evidently finding the connection amusing rather than annoying.

"Leave it out. There aren't any pictures of him anyway. Come on." He took Robin into the lounge and opened the box he'd left there.

"What were the jury like?" Robin asked, as he settled onto the sofa.

"Mixed bag. A couple who said you only had to look at the defendant to know he was guilty. A bit like Oliver Narraway used to be." Adam smiled ruefully at memories of a man who'd been a continual thorn in the flesh but whom, in a strange way, he now missed. "Another couple who'd only have convicted the defendant if they'd seen a video of the attack, with the defendant clearly committing it. And possibly not even then."

"Sounds like the usual mixture." Robin snorted. "How did you break the deadlock?"

"We applied to the judge to allow a majority verdict, and that's what we brought in. Guilty as charged and sentenced to a stretch behind bars."

"He's out now. Has been for a couple of years, apparently, but he's supposed to have kept his nose clean. Running his own business up on the industrial estate by the motorway."

"Maybe he was just led astray, although if so, he let it happen time and again. He had a criminal record, or so we found after we'd reached a verdict. Here." Adam passed Robin the clippings. "Have you talked to him?"

"Only over the phone. He's in Glasgow, but he's flying back tomorrow. He was quite happy to meet us then."

"Here, lend me that one from the *Abbotston Chronicle*." The picture showed the convicted man when younger, with his parents and siblings; Adam held the fuzzy likeness next to Robin's face. "It's never struck me before, but he looks a bit like you. Possibly."

"You think so? How do the press always manage to root out this sort of thing?" Robin peered at the picture, then moved it into a better light. "Maybe if you saw him in a dark alley, he'd look like me."

Adam shuddered. "That's one place I wouldn't want to meet him, reformed or not."

Robin put his arm round Adam's shoulder. "You could always take Campbell the wonder dog with you."

"Don't let him hear that name. He's big-headed enough."

Robin laughed and rifled through the clippings once more. "Nobody else from those days ringing a bell?"

"No." Adam ran his finger along the picture. The parents, Alec and Rosemary, his sister Katie, brother James. Some of them must have been in court, but he'd not noticed at the time and certainly hadn't encountered them since. "I've been racking my brains, but these are total strangers to me."

"Forget about it. You'll end up straining to make connections where there are none."

"Yeah. Like that brother having the same dodgy haircut as Luke Brunning." He studied the picture once more. "James may have died young. The defence lawyer had lots of irons in the fire, in case he couldn't persuade us it was a case of mistaken identity. Edwards had a bit of a record, but the lawyer kept saying how he'd only gone off the rails because he'd never got over his brother's death. Close-knit family."

"Hm." Robin's eyes narrowed. "Anything suspicious about how James died?"

"I don't think so. Leukaemia?"

"Okay. It's probably not relevant. Is there anybody who's lurking on the periphery of this case who might have been around back then?"

Adam shut his eyes, trying to picture those days spent in the court, the jury, the judge, the police officers. "I'm pretty sure Brunning wasn't involved."

"He'd have hardly been out of nappies! Well, still in school, anyway." Robin grinned. "No point flogging the proverbial dead horse. You know how it goes. If you remember anything else, tell me. Can I keep these?" At Adam's assent, Robin put the slips of paper into a tidy pile on the table. "I wish I'd had the opportunity for jury service. It would have been good preparation for this job, understanding a bit more about the processes affecting people's perceptions and judgements. Not least because it could help me to be a convincing witness."

"I bet you charm the birds out of the trees when you're in the box," Adam said, a bit too soppily, although if Robin noticed the feeling of guilt he was covering up, the man wasn't letting on. "Useful development for me too, because it taught me to keep proper notes. I couldn't get over how some of my fellow jurors had 'remembered' things being said in court that never *had* been said."

"I wish you were on the jury for my cases." Robin leaned in for a long, soft kiss.

"That's nice. Seems like ages since you kissed me like that."

"It *is* ages. Only, this is a case of 'not tonight, Josephine.'"

Adam tried to hide his disappointment. Bed didn't solve everything, but it would have reminded them both how much they meant to each other.

Robin planted another kiss, then stifled a yawn. "Sorry to be a killjoy, but all I want to do is put my feet up and watch the football. Any chance of a beer for a tired copper?"

"Chance of beer for both of us." Adam ruffled his lover's hair. "We'll watch the Arsenal together. Then I won't feel guilty about the planning I need to do while we're at it."

"If I snore, don't poke me too hard."

"Only if you promise the same."

Adam went to fetch the beers from the fridge.

"Yes," he told Campbell as he encountered him en route. "I've opened up the box of stuff to your favourite person. No, he didn't mind. Anything else is going to have to wait."

He glanced at the kitchen door, remembering his panic when he'd come home. If Edwards was involved with Hatton's death, maybe they'd have bigger and nastier fish than Worsley knocking on their door to worry about.

Chapter Six

Edwards might have come home on Wednesday, but Robin didn't get to interview him. By the time his flight was in, they were no longer on the case.

The men's toilet facility at Abbotston police station wasn't the most salubrious place for a team meeting, but it was somewhere Robin and his sergeant could talk in private before facing Root for the handover. He'd just about calmed down after hearing the bad news, although the sergeant had kept up a constant stream of moaning all the way over from Stanebridge, even when they stopped at Costa. Anderson had bought them each a large coffee. Proper coffee. Three shots, by the taste of it, which was about the amount of caffeine they were going to need to get through the imminent briefing.

Of course they were delighted the DNA had shown that Phillips was the Slasher, but were both livid at losing a case at the point when it was starting to take some sort of form.

"Kick the porcelain if it makes you feel any better." Anderson leaned against the wall.

"The way things are going today, I'll probably break my toe. I know it's logical for us not to be involved anymore. I simply wish *they* weren't so smug about it." Smug and patronising over the phone as they'd arranged the handover, thanking the small-town rozzers for the way they'd held the fort. The meeting would be perfectly amiable, Robin was sure: Inspector Root and his local guys and gals taking the files, waving the yokels goodbye.

"We should finish off here and get back to business as usual." Anderson swigged the last of his coffee. "Blimey, we'll float all the way to Stanebridge on this."

"They make it strong." Robin eyed his paper cup, then took a sip, wincing at the strength. Anything to help him stay polite and smiling for the next hour. "Helen won't be unhappy. She's got a set of shelves she wants me to hang on the wall. And at least your Adam will get to see a bit more of you."

"True. I've promised him a meal out. He's spent too much time putting up with me falling asleep on the settee and snoring through whatever he's trying to watch." He'd not been himself the last few days, either. Distracted, or something.

"You look like you've lost fifty quid."

"There's this strange feeling I can't shake off." Robin shrugged. "The sensation you get when you let some hard-arsed villain get away, rather than handing over an investigation. I've got an itch about this case and I'd have appreciated the chance to scratch it."

Anderson moved over to the entrance door, leaning against it. "Just so we'll know when we're about to be interrupted. When you've got a feeling like that, it's usually got a basis in fact. I can't decide if you're extremely insightful or simply a lucky bastard."

"They say the harder you work, the luckier you get. If there's something wrong, I'm sure Root will run it to ground." He smiled, but wasn't confident on that point.

"If there's a terrorism connection, he's welcome to do the running." Anderson wouldn't let that IRA aspect drop. Always a chance he'd prove to be correct, like he'd been about the chef. "I wouldn't have minded the experience, though. Maybe if we'd had a few more days, made a bit more headway . . ."

"They couldn't have taken the case off us? Don't you believe it." Robin took a deep breath, immediately regretted it, given the location, before setting his shoulders for the skirmish. "Let's get this out of the way, *then* we can get back to the sanity of Stanebridge. I wouldn't mind getting home on time for once."

"Helen would appreciate me getting home on time too." Anderson grinned. "Perhaps somebody will be obliging enough to commit an armed robbery right in the middle of *our* patch, so we won't get bored. In which case we could get some of the limelight as well."

Robin shivered, that sudden, unpleasant sensation his mother called "somebody walking over your grave." "My granny always used to tell me to be careful what I wished for."

"Your granny sounds too superstitious." Which was a bit rich, coming from *him*. "We'll probably have nothing more exciting than shoplifting to deal with."

"I wouldn't wish for that. It wouldn't be good for either of our careers."

Anderson rocked back, then moved to let the door to the toilets swing open. A tall, muscular man in a smartly cut suit came in, stopping at the sight of Robin and his sergeant. "Mothers' meeting, gents?"

"Morning, Root." Robin made a face. "Can't a man go to the loo in peace?" He made a point of washing his hands.

"Do what you like. I haven't got time to hang around gossiping. Got a killer to catch." Root entered one of the stalls, Anderson raising a couple of fingers at him once the door had shut.

"Come on. We've got stuff to do." Robin muttered. "This place gives me a bad taste in the mouth."

"You're never satisfied, sir."

"Too right." Robin smiled, but those careless words had suddenly dug deep. He had the prospect of promotion on the horizon, and Adam back in Lindenshaw to snuggle on the sofa with—so why didn't he feel contented?

Wednesday had been a long day for Adam as well. Monday night's lack of sleep, tossing and turning and trying to get Worsley out of his mind, the kitchen door business on Tuesday, and the frustration at hardly having any downtime with Robin had at last caught up with Adam. He'd had an appointment with a parent straight after lessons ended, which had taxed his patience to the limit, although she'd been sent away happy—or as happy as anyone can be who has had to be gently dissuaded of the notion that her little Sophie was a genius who should be doing GCSEs at ten years old.

He needed a big mug of tea, two custard creams, and ten minutes to clear his head before doing anything productive. By the time he got to the staffroom, it seemed like everyone on site was crammed into the place, and a buzz of gossip filled the air.

"What's up?" he asked before he even started to fight his way to the kettle.

"You've not heard?"

"Heard what?"

"They've caught the Abbotston Slasher!" Jennifer Shepherd, who should by rights have been in the front office presiding over her administrative kingdom, was instead in the staffroom, holding forth while other staff members fiddled around on the internet, probably getting the latest news. "Matched his DNA to somebody."

"The chef from the Florentine," Luke said over his shoulder as, surrounded by women desperate for news, he scrolled down an internet page.

"Oh!" Jennifer put her hands to her face. "Not that chap off the telly. Miles Benneton."

"He's only nominally in charge. I suspect he doesn't cook there very often," Luke reassured her.

"Oh yes." Sally, whose face was less haggard than it had been the last few weeks, spoke with the authority of someone who followed the every move of celebrity chefs. "He's got three restaurants and his television career to worry about. I'm not sure whether he'll think a murder is good publicity or bad."

Adam filled his mug with hot water, drowning the tea bag. "They say no publicity can be bad publicity."

"Honestly?" Sally's eyes widened. "It might put everyone off going."

Adam snorted. "More likely to bring out the ghouls."

"True," Luke said. "I hope they've got the right bloke. It wouldn't be the first time the rozzers have got it wrong." He glanced up, met Adam's eyes, then hastily looked away again, cheeks burning.

Does he know that I know about his brother?

Luke ploughed on hastily. "My brother has got stories that would beggar belief."

"I bet he has." Adam smiled and tried sounding non-committal. "We'll soon know, hopefully. Let's think of it as good news, anyway."

It might be good news for Robin too, if he got some help with the Hatton case as a result. Surely there wouldn't be too much else to occupy the minds and hands of the Abbotston police if the Slasher really had been run to ground. Robin was going to need all the help he could get if Sam Brunning was mixed up in things, let alone ex-cons and terrorists and who knew what. Why did murder cases have to resemble those over-complicated plots you saw on the telly, the ones that Robin always made fun of?

"Perhaps he killed the other man as well." Sally nodded. "Right night. Same kind of weapon."

"Wrong sex of victim, different style of attack," Adam said, carelessly. That was too close to discussions he'd had with Robin. "It isn't only chefs who have knives."

The arrival of the headteacher, with news about the impending visit of their new contact at the county education department—replacing the one who'd hardly covered himself in glory during the previous murders—turned the conversation away from stabbing. Apart from the suggestion that a knife might be useful when the Ofsted inspectors came round.

The conversation in the staffroom was, unbeknownst to anyone concerned, being mirrored in Stanebridge police station, Anderson having heard the latest gossip from his fount of inside knowledge at Abbotston.

"Apparently Phillips confessed to the stabbings," he told Robin. "As soon as they confronted him with the forensics, he started to talk and everything came out. Perhaps that car crash affected him."

"Intimations of mortality? Semi-deathbed confession?" Robin snorted.

"Could be, sir. Maybe he thought it was a sign from above. Got to his conscience or whatever."

"More likely he saw he was up the creek and took the easiest course. We'll see if he sticks to it, though." Robin didn't believe in *those* sorts of divine signs, and he knew it wasn't unusual for people to confess, then retract everything and plead not guilty in the dock. "Or rather, Root will."

"Phillips swears he didn't kill Hatton. Says he was genuinely shocked when you told him. Root believes the bloke."

"I believed him too." Robin shrugged. "I've been through it a dozen times in my head." MO. Forensics. Victim. Motive. It didn't add up.

"What does your gut tell you?"

Robin took a deep breath. Despite objective thinking being key to good police work, the sifting of evidence to construct a coherent case that would stand up in court, sometimes instinct had something significant—if subjective—to add to the process. A sudden, slightly different way of looking at things.

"My gut tells me we—all of us, not just Root—are nowhere near the truth. It'll turn out to be more complicated and more simple than we've guessed so far. And it's not our case anymore, remember?" He shut the file on his desk. The afternoon had been surprisingly productive, lots of catching up done, but he felt washed out and ill at ease.

"That sounds good to me. If this were one of those TV programmes they keep rerunning, it'd be the point where the poor old weary sergeant gets to relax at last with his best mate over a pint or two. Before he goes home to the old woman to have his pie and chips." Anderson pushed his chair back from the table, looking every bit the old married copper.

"You turn into Dixon of Dock Green and I'm arranging a transfer for you."

Anderson grinned. "You know, I was thinking, sir. There aren't that many TV detectives who have happy home lives. Morse goes from woman to woman, never finding the right one." He counted them off on his fingers. "Lewis, Gently, both widowed, both wives killed."

"Barnaby's happy enough."

"Even he's got his troubles. His wife's lovely, but she can't cook."

"Thank God it's not real life, then." Robin got up from his desk. "None of them seem to have blokes waiting for them at home, for one thing."

"I don't believe your Adam would want to be compared to Mrs. Barnaby, or any of the others."

"His cooking's better, anyway. Right, see you tomorrow." Robin exited the office before the conversation could continue. He was certainly better off than most TV sleuths, with somebody at home who wasn't simply waiting, nineteen-fifties style, to welcome home the master of the house and indulge his every whim. Adam was his equal, his partner, the man who shared their home.

Their home.

Funny how he sometimes thought of Adam's place like that and sometimes even now thought of it as Adam's alone. Robin felt a pang of guilt over his own property, still having the mortgage paid on it and still mothballed despite the fact it could be generating a pile of money in rental. Why didn't he take the even better option, selling up and making a proper new start?

All Robin needed to do was get back to the letting agent and give him the green light, so why did he never seem to get round to it? Trouble was, he hadn't had the time for anything important recently. He needed to buck up his ideas, go home, and make the evening a special one, or even Adam's apparently endless store of patience might run dry.

Campbell must have heard the car approach long before Adam did, or perhaps his canine sixth sense had cut in again; he was waiting at the door well in advance of Robin opening it.

"Hiya!" Adam called from the lounge. "You're home early."

Robin's face appeared round the door, grinning. "Sorry, shall I come back when you've sent your bit of rough away?"

Adam ignored the joke, vaguely worried for a moment that it might be referring to Worsley. "I'll rephrase that. Nice to see you home early for once, my dear. Caught Hatton's killer?"

"I wish. We're off the case." Robin launched into an explanation about the consequences of Anderson having run down the Slasher. "Back to Stanebridge and less glamorous stuff."

"Death's not at all glamorous." Sudden memories of Ian Youngs's dead body, of the double murder that nearly ripped his school community apart, played over in his mind's eye.

"No, you're right. Sorry." Robin, yawning, ran his hand over his brow. "I was getting into TV cop speak. Been listening to Anderson too long."

"You need a proper meal, some footie on the telly, and an early night. You'll be back to your usual self in the morning." Adam pulled his partner into an embrace, rubbing his head against the side of Robin's neck. "Go and have a proper soak in the bath while I get the rest of that casserole out of the freezer. Beef. You need it to build you up."

"Sounds like heaven." Robin gave him a smacking kiss. "Talking of which, when you say 'early night', do you have any plans for it apart from sleeping?"

"Wait and see. Maybe if you smelled less like a wrestler's jockstrap, you'd be in with a chance."

"Bloody hell, I'd better get in that bath, then." Robin stifled a yawn. "You should come and bang on the door every five minutes. I could sleep for a week."

"Take Campbell in the bathroom with you. Newfoundlands are supposed to be ideal for water rescues." The dog, evidently hearing his name, went to wait at the bottom of the stairs.

"No way, boy. You'll be in there with me." Robin patted the dog's head on the way past. "We'll go out Friday night. Make up for missing lunch at the weekend."

"It's a deal." Adam headed for the freezer . . . and the wine rack.

An hour later they were snuggled up on the sofa, like they had in courting days—days when they'd had to exercise a load of self-restraint because of the potential complications. Now it didn't matter if they shared a sofa, or a kiss, or a bed.

"You've been incredibly understanding about the hours I've had to put in." The red wine was beginning to speak loud and clear. The apparent difficulty in enunciating those simple words was an unmistakable sign that Robin had overindulged. He was *likely* to have a hell of a headache in the morning, which wouldn't help on top of the lack of sleep that would probably result from this evening. He had *that* gleam in his eye. "I always knew you were wonderful. Add that to the fact you're gorgeous and I want to snog you more than I've wanted anything all day. All week."

"Big smoothie." Adam leaned into the kiss. "Do they teach you this stuff at police college?"

"Plonker."

Adam enjoyed the rippling, tingling sensation working its way up the back of his neck. Robin's kiss was stimulating enough; their legs touching, thigh on thigh, was almost unbearable. Or would have been if he didn't know what was going to happen upstairs very soon.

"Flatfoot." Adam rubbed his hand along Robin's six o'clock (or in this case eight o'clock) shadow. "Fancy a naughty time with a school governor?"

"Only if the governor in question looks like you, rather than any of the others I've met."

True. It wasn't vain of Adam to admit he was hardly representative of the type.

Robin tickled his ear. "Are you propositioning me, Mr. Teacher?"

"Of course I am. Only don't talk like a daft teenage schoolgirl with a crush. It's a passion killer." Adam rubbed Robin's cheeks again. "Interested?"

"As you said, of course I am."

As they pulled each other up the stairs, progress hampered by the number of times they had to stop for a snog, Adam's thoughts went back to the first occasion he and Robin had made it to bed together. Or, to be accurate, onto an extremely comfortable sofa. While they'd been entirely forthright through their courtship proper—he didn't count as courtship the cagey period when they'd been a rozzer and witness who fancied the pants off each other—they'd not discussed the thing that could make or break the fledgling relationship. Politics, religion, sport— everything that mattered, they'd managed without a cross word.

But the finer details of romantic arrangements, who preferred what and where—which tab and which slot—hadn't been aired until that evening on that sofa.

Robin, who appeared to have picked up Campbell's ability to read minds, stopped as they reached the bed. "Do you remember what a mess we almost made when we first did it?"

"How could I ever forget?"

Robin had got completely and utterly flustered in his effort to make things as good as possible, launching into a big, complicated speech as they both sat half-dressed downstairs. *I suppose that we should really consider our preferences and all that. I mean to say, it's just possible that we might not, you know, and then it would be rather awkward to . . . because I wouldn't want . . ."* The incomprehensible nature of his words and the subsequent set of giggles they'd got had nearly wiped out all chances of a romantic encounter. Especially when Adam had pointed out that if that was the sum of what Robin had to say, then there was very little chance of any tab going anywhere until it ended up too old and wrinkly to be of use to any slot.

"You've simply got to give it a try and hope for the best," Adam said, quoting his words from back then. "We can play around, find out what we like. We'll make it work."

"Sounds like an admirable way to live your life." Robin pushed him onto the bed. "And to spend the next hour."

And it was.

Chapter Seven

Thursday morning had hardly got itself into gear before Robin's granny's prophetic words had come true.

The proprietor of the open-all-hours petrol station on the main road north out of Stanebridge rang in to say they'd been robbed by a pair of blokes—he assumed they were blokes, although with balaclavas and big bomber jackets he couldn't be sure—wielding knives. They'd appeared at the point the lad on the night shift had gone into day mode, opening the door rather than doing all the business through a small security window. They'd made him clear the till, then left him trussed up with plastic cable, the sort you used to keep computer wires tidy, until the first proper customer of the day had found him.

"It only happened about an hour ago, so we can hotfoot it on the trail." Anderson, who'd barely got through the door when the call had been put through to their office, slipped his coat back on.

"Your turn to drive, then." Robin, aching and tired, and only in part from the excesses of the night before, would have to put up with his sergeant's eccentric driving style. "You say they used knives? Any chance of a connection to Hatton's stabbing?"

Anderson grinned. "Probably only in your imagination, knowing the way our luck's going at present. The best way to find out is to catch the scumbags. It would be nice to solve Inspector Root's case for him. Again," he added smugly.

Robin couldn't help returning the grin. "He'd go mental if we did that. He fancies himself as being on the fast track, and that business with Phillips has applied the brakes a bit. Right. Down to the petrol station."

The cashier was shaken, but able to give a good description of the knives, though he had little to offer about the people carrying them. "They were covered up, with only their eyes showing. Could have been my mum and I wouldn't have known."

"You got a better look at the knives?" Robin asked.

"Yeah. Big things, like they use on the cooking shows on the telly, for slicing up steak or something. Sharp as anything." The cashier blanched. "Didn't fancy seeing if they'd slice up me."

"I don't blame you." Anderson tapped his pen on his notebook.

"There are knives everywhere these days," the garage manager chipped in. "I don't know what Abbotston's coming to." She took a drag on an electric cigarette. "My nerves are shot to pieces."

"At least you can go out without worrying about the moon, now." The cashier made a face behind his boss's back.

Oblivious, she shuddered. "Yes, but there's that other bloke who got stabbed. What if it's the same people who did this?"

Robin exchanged glances with his sergeant. It was a reasonable connection to make, given the previous rarity of knife crime in the area, although what connection there could be to Hatton escaped them for the moment. And it wasn't their case, as Robin kept reminding himself, even though Root's business seemed determined to get under their noses.

"That's our job to find out," he reassured them. "So anything that you can remember about the incident, no matter how small, would be of help."

Anderson pointed at a camera up in the corner. "Any CCTV?"

The manager smiled sheepishly. "It's out of order. Bloke's supposed to be coming today to mend it."

"Isn't that always the way?" Anderson nodded. Maybe he wouldn't have been quite so sympathetic if the manager had been male.

"They were an odd couple." The cashier, who'd wrinkled his forehead, clearly racking his brains, piped up at last. "Like one of them knew what he was doing and the other was learning the ropes."

This was more like it. "What gave you that impression?"

"Something about the way they were talking to each other. The way the bigger of the pair took the lead on everything. And I'm sure that one was a bloke. Unless it was a big woman with a deep voice." The cashier shrugged sadly. "Sorry, it's not much to go on."

"Not much to go on" was the story of their lives at the moment.

As they walked back to the road, Anderson remarked, "Does this sound like an old lag with a young apprentice?"

"No evidence it's an old lag. They don't all get caught, for a start."

"Okay, let's be pedantic. Experienced villain with a young apprentice. Not a familiar pattern of crime for round here though. Possibly he's recently moved into our area."

"Could be." Davis, of course, was on the case, looking at anyone with a history of committing similar crimes, in their county or out of it. Seeing if any of them had not long been released from prison. "Any idea if Edwards ever turned his hand to armed robbery?"

They'd reached the car. "Not in his record. What brings him to mind?"

"Not sure. Wishful thinking? Your remark about old lags?"

"Wishful thinking that this case might connect back to Hatton?" Anderson grinned.

"You've got me bang to rights, guv'nor." Robin had put on his best TV villain accent. "Come on, talk me out of it. You can make a lot of enemies in the force by queering other people's pitches."

"Okay. This is your semi-official warning." Anderson wagged his finger. "Only, despite what the manager said, in the greater scheme of things there hasn't been a lot of knife crime round here, so we'd be stupid to ignore the fact that the weapons are similar. Maybe the knife used to kill Hatton didn't get chucked away because it was needed today."

"There are plenty of similar knives, though." Much as Robin wanted to support a possible connection, they had to be realistic. "Go down to any big department store or specialist cook shop and there'll be a whole wall of them. Adam's got a collection big enough to murder half the county. Not that it has to be a cook's knife, anyway. Just pretty big, straight, and bloody sharp. Could be a fisherman's or something for DIY or camping or—"

"Yes, I get the picture." Anderson held up his hands. "Keep an open mind."

"You've got it." Robin gazed up and down the road at a cluster of industrial units, then across at a small terrace of houses, none of which looked that promising. "Time to do some legwork round the locals, in case anybody saw or heard anything."

"You take the east side and I'll take the west?" Anderson reached in his pocket. "Or will we toss for it?"

"Take what you like. I'm not feeling optimistic."

Robin's intuition turned out to be accurate; an hour later the sum total of useful information was two items. The first was a description, from an old man who lived in the middle of the terrace, of a black saloon car that had left the garage forecourt in a hurry, tyres squealing. It could have been a Toyota, he'd told Anderson. Although, as he'd pointed out, "All cars look alike these days." He hadn't rung the police at the time as he'd assumed the driver had been simply getting petrol.

The second snippet was more promising. As Robin waited for his sergeant, he prowled the garage forecourt, spotting a small concrete ridge where it appeared somebody had recently taken a tumble, leaving behind a few little shreds of black denim, possibly where the knee of a pair of jeans had split open. Robin had taken photos and a sample, the forensics person having long gone from the scene, so the likelihood of the sample being driven over increasing with every moment now the police had given the go-ahead for business to resume. He'd drop that in for the lab when they got back to the station; maybe Davis would have been more successful at winkling out some gems of information.

As luck would have it, she was waiting at the door to Robin's office as they returned. "Saw you pull in, sir. Thought you'd like a briefing."

"If it's useful, I'd love it. Come in and grab a pew."

"It's entirely useful, I think." She pulled up a chair to the desk and placed her file of notes on it. "Even if it's for elimination purposes. The MO of the attacks isn't that helpful. Those sorts of armed robberies may be rare round here, but elsewhere they're ten a penny. None of our local villains usually go in for them, though."

"Haven't you got any good news for me?" Was it becoming hackneyed to expect Davis would always produce one of her little nuggets?

"Might have." She smiled like Campbell with an unexpected bone. "There was a bloke called Selby put away for a string of armed robberies over in Surrey and up in Shropshire. Yeah, I know, 'have blade, will travel.'"

"And . . .?"

"And he got out about a month ago. Lives over Essex way."

"That doesn't sound promising." Robin leaned forward, trying to catch a glimpse of Davis's notes. "Come on. I know you're dying to tell us whatever it is."

"Less 'what' than 'who.' He did time with Edwards. Same nick, same wing, chances are they'd have met. May be nothing in it, certainly not enough to get either of them in to question, but coincidences always make me wonder."

Robin glanced at Anderson—who'd put on an innocent expression, as if to say, "I wasn't thinking anything in particular"—then back at Davis. "Carry on the good work. Whatever you can turn up that'll give us an excuse to talk to either of those gentlemen would be very useful."

"I'm on it like the proverbial car bonnet, sir. Toyota or not." She bundled together her papers and left.

"Back there again, sir." Anderson's blameless expression had been replaced by the expected smug grin the minute Davis was out of the door. "All the threads weaving together."

"Really? Are you sure they're not unravelling?" Robin shook his head. "Or like we're seeing them connecting up but somehow missing the vital link."

"We'll find it." Anderson flexed his hands. "I'll start by seeing if this Selby has a black Toyota."

"Or a car that resembles a Toyota. Or a black car of any sort." Robin forced a grin, one that soon faded and didn't reappear all afternoon. Anderson rooted out the fact that Selby didn't own a car, possibly because he always used other people's. He had a record for taking and driving without permission, and—true to form—a black Toyota Avensis had been reported stolen that morning, and it turned up abandoned by teatime. Somebody was adept at covering their tracks. The rest of the day brought nothing of interest, except for the rumour that Root had got the name of the ex-IRA man who'd made the threat, and was heading out to Belfast to interview him.

At least Robin could get home to Adam, where the tense atmosphere of the last few days had been blown away by the previous night's romantic interlude. And maybe by no longer having the aura of the murder case hanging over them. Their plan for Thursday evening consisted of nothing more exciting than walking Campbell and sharing gossip about the neighbours, and would be none the worse for that.

By the time Friday morning dragged itself into existence, everything had changed. There'd been another armed robbery—at a betting shop—little more than twenty-four hours after the one at the garage, and with an identical MO. The chief constable had been on the lunchtime news to calm fears about the crime wave that appeared to be infesting their previously peaceful community. He assured people that the police—by which he meant Robin and Anderson— were busting a gut trying to make progress, although he didn't give their names or use so common an expression, at least in public.

But lunchtime brought the first sniff of a lead, with a handy little local nark of Anderson's ringing him up and mentioning a name that might be of interest to him, a young lad called Porterfield who was suddenly flush with cash and cagey about where he'd got it. The nark was happy to dob in the lad because the bookie's shop was the one *he* used, and he wanted whoever had robbed it found. What was the world coming to if a man couldn't have a flutter in peace?

They'd set off straight away to lay hands on Porterfield, but as Robin rang the front door bell, the man in question had attempted to do a runner out of the back, only to find Anderson waiting for him and ready to give chase. Trying to scramble out of the garden and into an alleyway, Porterfield had tumbled off the top of a fence, landing awkwardly and winding up in hospital with a suspected fractured wrist and a concussion. The doctors had insisted he couldn't be questioned until he'd fully regained his wits. Robin had begun to suspect that both fate and the entire medical profession were conspiring against him—how many more people were going to end up in hospital just when he wanted to talk to them?

Robin knew that Cowdrey himself was under intense pressure to get the robberies dealt with, but they were having to kick their heels. With the witness floating in and out of consciousness—and not being terribly coherent when he *was* awake—they could do little more at present. To be honest, Robin and Anderson both needed a break or they'd be sod-all use to anyone in an interview room. There was a team already searching Porterfield's house, a rota of constables had been placed at his bedside to tell them when he awoke (and if he had any significant visitors), and the best thing they could do, Cowdrey reluctantly agreed, was to go home, have a beer, and get a decent night's kip.

Robin was looking forward to a decent evening out; he'd been on autopilot for too long. And he could get a proper early night afterwards, unlike the very pleasant but extremely tiring early night he'd had two evenings before.

Having a beer with Adam (only the one, in case he got called in) and a meal in the best Chinese restaurant in Abbotston would fit in with his boss's suggestion. When his hurried message, "Fancy a plate of spare ribs with a flatfoot tonight?" got the enthusiastic reply "Do I ever!" he rang to book a table, only to get an automated message telling him the Water Margin was closed, although simply for refurbishment, rather than for serving dog or horse meat. That buggered things up.

"Where should I take Adam tonight?" he asked his sergeant as he ended the call.

"Go upmarket. The Florentine."

"The Florentine? Isn't that pushing the boat out for an ordinary Friday night?"

Anderson wagged his head. "Not at the moment. I had half a mind to take Helen there tonight, but I won't cramp your style. They've got a special deal on, so it won't cost the usual arm and a leg."

"Special deal? That's never been their modus operandi. I thought they had to fight customers off . . . oh." Of course. "Phillips."

"So it appears. How the mighty have fallen." Anderson rolled his eyes. "Helen says there's a rumour going round that Benneton wants to get shot of the place. They've apparently lost business hand over fist and are trying anything to win customers back."

"I thought there was no such thing as bad publicity?"

"Not in this case. There's a Facebook campaign by the families of Phillips's victims, wanting the place shut. And another one supporting the present staff, saying they shouldn't have to pay for what the chef did. Usual bloody nonsense. I'd get in while you can."

Robin reached for his phone, then stopped. "There's no thought in your head of me returning to the scene of the crime, is there? You know, in case I hear something totally by chance?"

"Wouldn't dream of it, sir. That would never have been why I wanted to take Helen there either." Anderson's guilty grin belied his words. "Anyway, my mole at Abbotston nick says Root's convinced it's to do with the IRA, so he's not going to know if we happen across any local connections."

"*You* were sure it was the IRA," Robin reminded him.

"That was before I knew about Edwards. I didn't have all the information."

"And what does Root think about Edwards?"

"That's he's definitely turned over a new leaf. He's got a proper business—facilities management—that he ran with his old man, then took over when he died. It's supposed to be doing well." Anderson sniffed. "Too well to need to supplement it by armed robberies."

"Did Root say that?"

"Apparently. Although I didn't get it first-hand, so who knows?"

The "who knows?" bit could be a summation of everything to do with the case. Robin needed to clear his head, let his subconscious work on things—perhaps going back to the vicinity of the crime could act as a trigger. He rang the Florentine, then messaged Adam, who'd be having his lunch break. It would have been easier to ring, but Lindenshaw St. Crispin's school remained a mobile signal black spot, clearly reluctant to embrace the twenty-first century. Sometimes you could receive a text by hanging your phone out the window, but calls usually involved a walk down the lane or gatecrashing the ladies' loo.

Why not the Water Margin? Adam replied. *I've been dreaming about crispy duck.*

Robin explained about the renovations and the meal deal he'd got at the Florentine.

Sounds good. Mixing business with pleasure?

Would I do that? Don't answer.

LOL. It's a deal. My turn to drive, so I can pick up your mother's birthday present on the way. Get the train to Abbotston then you can have a pint.

Good thinking all round. Thanks.

And thank goodness for the boon to modern living that was the John Lewis "click and collect" service. An elegant green glass vase—hardly the most glamorous of presents, compared to the roses, but exactly what she'd asked for and about the same price—was sitting at the Waitrose branch in Abbotston, and Adam collecting it that evening would save a trip on Saturday and maybe ensure the chance of a lie-in before Robin picked his motor up from the police station car park.

Six o'clock. Adam, parcel stowed carefully under his arm, navigated the Waitrose car park, taking suitable care given the average age of the drivers; crossing these yards of tarmac was almost as dangerous as going over the top, large pieces of metal liable to come at you from every direction. He was so busy keeping an eye on an old bloke negotiating his Mercedes out of a slot too narrow for it that he walked right into a muscular mass. A mass that turned out to be Max Worsley.

"Sorry," he said automatically. "Oh. Hello."

Worsley smiled. "Hello again. I should have realised I might run across you here. Only Waitrose branch for miles."

"It's a honeypot for the foodies. And the pensioners," Adam added, as they had to leap out of the way of a pensioner with a lethal trolley-pushing style.

"I'm glad I saw you. Got something I wanted to tell your inspector."

"You need to see him at the station, then. He won't be happy if you come round. Although he may not want to meet you at the station, either."

Worsley made a slightly theatrical bemused face. "Sorry?"

"It's not his case anymore. You'd need to talk to somebody at Abbotston if it's about Hatton."

"Oh. Right." Worsley frowned, clearly not relishing that prospect. "Anyway, the other thing. That time I came round to your house, I was sure we'd met before. Good memory for faces, you know."

Adam didn't reply.

"I'm pretty sure I've remembered where it was. I was witness in a court case, years ago. You were there, although I can't recollect why. You weren't the judge or the defendant, I know that."

Adam hadn't realised he'd been holding his breath until the rush of air surprised him as he opened his mouth to reply. "Yes. That's it. I was on the jury. I thought we'd run across each other. I have a good memory for faces too." Especially *his*, but he wasn't going to admit that.

Worsley slapped his hands together. "Yeah, that's it. Your hair was a different colour then though, I believe."

Adam grinned. "That was my 'dyeing it' phase. Titian or some poncey name like that. I thought I was cool. I suspect I wasn't." He stopped, aware that nerves were making him prattle on.

"It's a better colour now."

"Oh." Before Adam could get any further words out, and make a prat of himself in the process, Worsley carried on.

"That was one of the scariest experiences of my life. Like all your exams and driving tests wrapped up together. I must have spent hours in that courtroom, one way or another. I remember looking the jury over, wondering if you'd give a fair verdict. That's when your face must have registered. It's a nice face."

If this conversation had happened pre-Robin, Adam would have baited his hook with "I'm surprised you noticed me," but the time for that had passed, surely?

"I think we gave as fair a verdict as we could, given the makeup of the jury. No," he raised his hand to forestall any questions. "Please don't ask. You know I can't discuss what we said. Even now."

Worsley nodded. "Yeah, I get that. And yeah, I thought the verdict was spot on."

"Did you know Edwards is out of prison?"

"Is he?" Worsley seemed surprised. "Hm, yes, I suppose he would be now. Time flies."

"It does."

"Or goes down the plughole, along with my love life."

An uncomfortable crawling sensation wormed its way up Adam's neck. "Sorry?"

Worsley grinned. "I should be the one apologising, badgering comparative strangers about my non-existent love life."

"That's all right." How very British he was being—but then Adam was used to old ladies regaling him with the details of their latest operations. He'd been blessed—or cursed—with too sympathetic a manner. He didn't have any "previous" with the old ladies, though. "Things will turn round."

"Will they? My ex keeps telling me to get a life. Real blokes, not the ones on Dieux du Stade. But you can't buy a bloke off the internet like you can a calendar."

"You'd be surprised. I know somebody who fell in that trap—a ripped Russian guy promising everything if his nice, kind English sugar daddy would send him the money for airfare." Adam stopped. Why the hell was he even getting into this conversation? Was Worsley hinting that *he'd* be a suitably real bloke? Time to change the subject. "Have the police been in touch with you about the Hatton case?"

"No." Worsley winced at the sudden change of direction. "Not heard from anyone since I talked to you."

Adam frowned. Surely Inspector Root or one of his minions should have followed up this angle already, even if he'd only had the case a few days. "Don't be surprised if they do. There's some suggestion—" Adam stopped. "Well, they'll tell you all about it when you see them."

"I don't want to go to the station. You know why. Can't I find somewhere to only talk to *your* bloke?"

Adam exhaled, slowly. Should he say something about how the police station coast was clear of Brunning, at least for the moment, or was that breaking confidences?

"I'll get him to give you a ring. You can work it out between you."

"Thanks, I appreciate that." Worsley held out his hand.

Adam wasn't sure that Robin would be quite so appreciative, but he shook Worsley's hand anyway.

"I'm glad we've met again. Shame that you're already hitched up with somebody, though. Missed my chance."

Adam cringed as a flush raced across his cheeks. "Yeah, shame," he managed to blurt out.

"If your circumstances ever change . . ." Worsley shrugged.

"Yeah." Now he just felt stupid, lost for the right words to say. He backed off, gesturing towards his car. "Got to go. See ya."

And precisely how much of this encounter was he going to relate to Robin?

Robin was already settled at the table with menus, a pint of beer, and a bottle of sparkling water—Adam's preferred brand, to boot— by the time his favourite teacher arrived. At first they chatted about nothing in particular, ordered, relaxed, did the little things they hadn't done in too long. It was halfway through the main course when Adam said, a touch too casually, "I saw your favourite person earlier."

"Who's that?"

"Worsley, naturally."

"Worsley?" Robin looked up, piece of steak poised on his fork. Adam, who kept his eyes on his food, had a distinctly sheepish expression.

"Yeah. I bumped into him, literally, in Waitrose car park, after I picked up your mother's present. He said he'd recognised my face that evening he came round, and he'd worked out where."

"How romantic." How predictable. Worsley was probably exactly the type of bloke to flirt with anything in trousers, and Adam was a particular handsome thing in trousers.

"Don't be daft. He wanted to talk to *you* again—he reckons he's got something to tell you—and I said I'd ask you to ring. He refuses to go to the police station. And yes," Adam waved his knife, "I told him you were off the Hatton case, but he wasn't keen to talk to anybody else."

"I'll call him tomorrow." Robin scowled. Why did work have to pursue them everywhere they went? "And did you simply happen to bump into him? Seems a bit too deliberate."

"What do you mean?" Adam looked up this time, frowning.

"It could be he's stalking us."

"I didn't think of it like that. Could be." Adam didn't sound convinced. "Perhaps it's that weird coincidence thing, like where you hear a name you haven't heard in ages and then it crops up three times in a row."

"Shame I can't pass on a third time with Worsley. He caused enough work the first two. Are you sure it wasn't *him* who did the assault at the Rings, rather than Edwards?"

"I'm not that stupid, to miss such a gross miscarriage of justice, and neither were the rest of the jury." Adam jabbed with his fork, emphasising the point.

"Okay, it was just a joke. What's eating you?"

"I could ask the same thing. You're more on edge about this case—these cases—than usual."

"Can you blame me? It's like being in a hall of mirrors; nothing making sense. One minute I'm chasing a murderer, and then I'm not, only I find somebody else's murderer in the meantime." Robin took another bite of steak, chewing it fine before continuing. "And all these elements connect, returning to that court case of yours."

"*I* don't want to return there, thank you very much. Water under the bridge."

"So you keep saying." Robin wasn't sure he believed it. Adam was rarely cagey about anything. What you saw was almost always what you got, but this time he was holding something back. "What's bugging you?"

"Bugging *me*? Nothing."

"Not got Worsley on the brain? The man who made your trousers twitch?"

"Oh, for goodness sake." Adam scowled. "So what if I did fancy him once? That was a long time ago. And if he fancies me, that's his lookout."

"He fancies *you*?" Robin felt like his CD had skipped some bars, and he'd lost the thread of the music.

"Yeah." The scowl faded. "That was a turn-up for the books."

"I bet. Did he say that, right in the middle of Waitrose car park?"

"No. But he gave me the sob story about his 'non-existent love life,' as he put it."

"I bet that was edifying."

"I felt sorry for him, to be frank." Adam fingered his napkin. "He must be desperate. Said if I ever found myself in other circumstances, I knew where I could find him."

Robin wondered what noise his fist would make if it impacted with Worsley's nose. "Let me get this straight. Back then, was it only in your mind or did you actually hook up with him? Is that why he knew where you lived? Old flame?"

"Don't be a pillock." Adam jabbed at a potato with his fork. "It was one-way, as far as I knew. More like . . . like the obsession girls get about whoever the latest teenage pin-up is when their hormones start raging. Somebody I'd never get the chance to meet, like a film star. It was safe thinking about him. He wasn't real to me."

"He looked real enough to *me*." So did Worsley's fists: real enough to cause trouble, as if he weren't causing plenty of trouble already.

"Oh, for heaven's sake, you weren't bothered about him last time we discussed this."

"Last time I thought he was out of our hair." Robin eyed the remaining piece of steak, speared it as though it were Worsley himself on the end of the fork, then ate it. The meat was tender, full of taste, but he wasn't doing the flavour justice. "So, Waitrose car park. You two just happened to be in the same place at the same time."

"What the . . . Are you saying I meant to meet up with him?"

"No. But perhaps he meant to run across you." Robin pushed his plate from him. "He could be stalking you. Have you thought of that? All that crap about him going out of his way to get your home address and turning up on the doorstep without realising it was yours, wringing wet and like a waif you couldn't turn away."

"He came to see *you*. It's *your* address as well. Or maybe it isn't." Adam, face flushed, stared down at the remnants of his food.

"What's that supposed to mean?"

"Exactly what it says." Adam's eyes welled up. "You keep the other flat on, but there's no sign of a tenant moving in. Is it really that you don't have time to deal with it, or have you left things so you can run back there when you're fed up with me?"

Robin winced. That was below the belt, on both counts. He lowered his voice, aware of the horrified glances of the couple at the next-door table. "What the fuck are you going on about?"

"I'm not sure where I stand with you. I expected the long hours, but I didn't expect witnesses turning up at the door for a cosy chat.

And I didn't expect to continue arsing around with your flat when you've lived at mine so long."

Guilt flooded Robin's brain. "If you'd rather I went back to my place, that's what I'll do."

"I didn't say that. You're twisting my words." Adam pushed his own plate away. "But don't let me stop you if that's what you'd prefer. I hope you'll be happy whatever you choose to do."

"You hope? I suppose you hope Max Worsley will come knocking on the door again." Robin shoved back his chair, got out his wallet, and put a handful of notes on the table. "He can come here and help you with dessert. I'm sure he has plenty of spare time."

"What the—"

Robin didn't wait to hear the rest. He was out of the door and storming along the road, heading for the rank to get a cab to Stanebridge. Thank God he *hadn't* rented the flat out or else he'd have had to go and cadge a bed from his mother for the night, and end up getting a lecture with it. She was bound to take Adam's side. Perhaps he should go there anyway and get the telling-off over and done with, because if it wasn't delivered tonight, it would be served with dinner on Sunday.

Fifty yards past where Hatton had been stabbed, a narrow alleyway led down towards the station and the taxi rank. It would knock a good five minutes off Robin's journey, although it wasn't as well lit as the main road. As he reached the entrance to it, the first spots of rain arrived and he dived in. A group of young people were coming along, chatting among themselves, and letting him pass when their paths collided at the point another passage cut in from the left. Nice to know that good manners hadn't been lost entirely.

Robin heard their steps fade, then registered a set of footsteps behind him—probably somebody else taking the shortcut. He slowed down to negotiate his way around a large wheelie bin, as the person following caught him up.

"You go first." Robin pulled in to the side to let him or her go past, so the unexpected fist to his stomach caught him sideways on. "What the—"

Another punch, this time to the side of his head, sent him spinning, shoulder hitting the wall. He launched himself at his attacker, pushing away from the brickwork and landing a punch in their ribs before getting another in return. This time he lost his balance, tumbling to the ground before a foot impacted with the small of his back. A strange buzzing sensation filled his head, reminding him of being put under anaesthetic when he'd had his tonsils out as a twelve-year-old. Time expanded, events going into slow motion as he thought of everything he'd miss if this was the end. Then somebody put out the lights.

Chapter Eight

Robin came to in a vaguely familiar white-and-grey room, with unsettling noises all around. He'd had to interview people in the new casualty department at Abbotston Hospital, so it didn't take him long to recognise his whereabouts. It did take him another minute or two—and a reminder from the pounding sensation in his head—to figure out why he was there. Somebody had *thump*ed him, but who? And how had he ended up here rather than still lying in an alley? That seemed too much to mull over in his befuddled brain, so he succumbed to sleep once more.

He surfaced again to find that the morning sun was now peeking through the windows and he didn't feel *quite* so groggy. Ironic that he'd been cursing fate for putting their witnesses in a hospital bed when it had never occurred to him he'd end up there himself. It hadn't exactly been the way he'd intended getting away from Adam's house

A head came round the door. A cheery young doctor, from the white coat and stethoscope that soon appeared, probably no more experienced than house-officer level. "You're awake. Good."

"I am." That was stating the bleeding obvious. "What's the diagnosis?"

"Nothing worse than bruising and a bit of a bump on the head." Doctor Easter, which was what her name badge said, came over and started the usual medical-type tasks, checking eyes and tongue and pulse and the rest of the signs. "We'd like to keep an eye on you until lunchtime, but if everything's okay, we can discharge you. Hopefully you won't need anything other than painkillers."

"How did I get here?"

"In an ambulance. Somebody rang for it. Your Good Samaritan." She took Robin's arm: blood pressure time. "You walked in here of your own accord. Kept asking if Adam was here. Is he a mate of yours?"

"My partner." Memories were starting to trickle back. The meal, the argument, some bloke—he assumed it was a bloke, but he shouldn't assume—who had landed a few hefty punches. A vague memory of the scent of aftershave. He even had an equally vague recollection of the ambulance, and a nice West Indian paramedic who'd said, "You'll live. Just take it easy."

"Do you want us to ring him? Don't want him worrying."

"No, I'll do that, when you're done prodding me." That would save a heap of explanations and possible misunderstandings. Would Adam be worrying yet? Or would he have assumed Robin had gone to his mother's for the night and be waiting for the apologetic message? Would he even care, given what a tit Robin had made of himself last night? "Where's my phone?"

"In the locker with your other valuables, I'd guess." The doctor collected her things, evidently done with him. "Fancy some breakfast?"

"I could kill a cup of tea and a slice of toast."

"I'll see what I can do." She left him to rummage in the locker.

His phone was there, as was everything else he'd had on him, including his small gold signet ring. He'd not been the victim of a mugging, apparently, unless the attacker had been stopped in the act, perhaps by whoever then called for an ambulance. And they hadn't finished him off, either—unless that was another case of being interrupted—so it seemed like more of a warning than a vendetta. Although what was the use of a warning if the victim didn't know what it was about? He stared at the phone as though it might tell him how to tackle the call. He could ring his mother, of course, or Anderson, but that would involve explaining why he hadn't contacted Adam. And at some point he and Adam would have to talk, not least because he wanted a second chance.

Adam was the best thing that had happened to him in years, the only person who'd been able to help Robin even start to get over his unhappy schooldays. Now Robin had done a pretty good job of cocking everything up.

He took a deep breath—or as deep as he could manage, given the bruising—and dialled Adam's number.

"Hello, Robin." Adam's voice was cool, although Campbell's excited yelps in the background suggested at least somebody was pleased to hear from him. "Having a nice time at your place? Or are you at your mother's?"

"Neither. I'm at Abbotston Hospital."

"Working again?" Adam sounded neither impressed nor concerned. "Your suspect's come round, has he?"

"No. *I* have. I'm on the casualty ward."

"Bloody hell." He certainly seemed alarmed now. "What happened?"

"Somebody gave me a thumping. Been out for the count, but they reckon I'm okay. Bit bruised."

"I'm getting in the car and coming round there this minute. See for myself how bad the damage is."

"I'm fine, honestly. And I'm not ready for discharge yet." He wasn't sure he was ready to face his partner so soon either; he needed time to get his thoughts in line.

"I don't care. I'll sit and wait for you. Or with you." Adam sighed. "You're such a bloody idiot."

"I know. I'm sorry. Is there any chance you'd fancy picking up said bloody idiot and taking him back with you?"

"I suppose so. Nobody else would want to put up with your antics." Campbell's happy whimpers in the background suggested he might get a proper welcome from one member of the household.

"Thank you." The tone remained icy, but thank God Adam's words had held some hope of reconciliation. "Chances are I'll get my marching orders in an hour or so."

"See you as soon as I can get there. Behave yourself for once." Adam ended the call. None of the usual "I love you" before the phone was put down, but what could Robin expect after he'd been such a wazzock?

Nothing to do now but wait and work out what he was going to say. That being too painful, he let rozzer mode, rather than victim mode, kick in. Whoever had given him a thumping could land a useful punch, and had enough wit not to let himself—Robin struggled to believe it had been a "herself," not least because of that aftershave—be easily identified. Worsley had enough muscle to be pretty useful in a fight, but what motive would he have, other than trying to stop Robin in his investigational tracks? Unless this was something to do with his fancying Adam, although that trail seemed to be more a figment of Robin's fevered imagination than fact. And why would Worsley have made a point of saying he wanted to talk to Robin if he was intending duffing him over?

He stifled another wave of guilt at what an all-round prat he'd been the evening before and what a prat he was being now, then got his mind back on the attack.

Thinking of Worsley made him think of Adam's box of clippings, the chance remark about how Edwards had looked a bit like *him*. Was it possible that somebody had mistaken him for somebody else in that dimly lit alleyway, and Robin had simply been in the wrong place at the wrong time? Surely that was stretching credulity, it being more likely *he'd* been the intended victim, done over by someone who wanted to make sure he stopped investigating the robberies. Or maybe even wanted him off the Hatton case, not realising that Root had already managed that?

The tea and toast arrived, the smell of warmed bread reminding Robin of how hungry he was. Perhaps if he could satisfy the body, then the brain might make some sense of what had gone on. At least he'd have a good excuse for not ringing Worsley today.

Adam wasn't the greatest fan of hospitals. The smells and the scraped paint and the slightly disconsolate air were liable to bring down even the cheeriest of spirits, although the hunky junior doctor who greeted him at the casualty ward door made up for them this time. Handsome bloke, well spoken, bit of class about him. You could admire the crumpets in the baker's window even if you were on a diet, couldn't you?

With a shudder, he remembered the crumpet in the witness box, Max Worsley, and the reason Robin had gone off alone last evening. Okay, Adam couldn't have guessed that his partner was going to take that shortcut and end up being done over, but that didn't stop him feeling guilty. If he hadn't been so defensive about Worsley and so hot under the collar about the pressure-of-work issue, they'd not have argued. They'd have gone home together. *Together*, without anybody's job impinging on them—the very outcome he'd wanted.

Adam had spent a hell of a night as well, consoling Campbell, who'd been bereft at Robin not being there, and consoling himself with half a bottle of white wine. Lucky he'd not had the lot or he mightn't have been able to drive safely yet.

"I'm here to see Robin Bright." He gave the doctor a smile.

"You'll find him in that side room, number nine. No, it's not so bad he's had to be isolated," the doctor added, clearly noting Adam's worried face. "It was just as a precaution in case this was anything to do with one of his cases. We found his warrant card, so knew he was in the force."

"Thanks for the reassurance." Although somehow very little of that had been encouraging. Robin had sounded chipper enough, but he'd had a good grounding in hiding his injuries, physical and emotional.

"He's ready to be discharged, according to my colleague. What he needs is rest, painkillers, and to follow the advice we've given him. He got away lightly."

Adam swallowed hard. He knew that, and it didn't make him feel any better.

"I'll be in there in a while to do the formalities. Tell him he's out on bail." The doctor laughed at his pathetic joke; Adam forced a grin and made his way to the side room, to frown round the door.

"Look at the state of you," he said before entering properly.

"Don't overwhelm me with sympathy." Robin, who didn't appear to be quite so close to death's door as Adam had anticipated, grinned sheepishly.

"Oh, you . . ." Adam sat on the edge of the bed and gingerly put his arms round him. "You gave me a hell of a fright."

Robin nestled his head on Adam's shoulder. "I gave myself a hell of a fright."

They sat a while in silence. There was a lot to be said, a lot of air to clear, but it would have to wait. This wasn't the time or the place.

"Any idea who did this to you?" he asked eventually.

"Plenty of ideas and none of them worth a spent match." Robin slipped out of the hug and settled on his propped-up pillows.

"You're not top of anyone's hit list?"

"Hit list? I hope I'm not even on one, let alone top." Robin shrugged, then winced as something or other must have hurt. "We all make enemies; it's almost inevitable for anyone who works in our business. Family members don't like seeing their nearest and dearest put away."

"Family members don't like seeing their boyfriend beaten up." Adam shivered at the thought of anyone wreaking revenge on his lover. "But have *you* made anybody want to beat the crap out of you?"

"Bound to have." Robin snorted. "But I learned early on that there's no point worrying about it. Look over your shoulder too much and you'll fall into a hole."

Adam bit his lip. Robin might have learned that early on, but *he* was still finding his way. "You need to fall onto the settee and stay there for a while. I'll put Campbell on guard."

"I'd rather go and soak in a steaming hot bath full of Radox for an hour."

Adam didn't offer to join him, no matter how appealing the idea was. There was some healing to be done, but they didn't get a chance to embark on it, the doctor entering the room to finish off the paperwork.

As they left, Robin stopped at the desk to exchange parting words and smiles with the nurses—a simple, typical, bit of courtesy that made Adam's chest swell with pride.

My bloke. See what a star he is? A total and utter tit at times, but nonetheless a star.

Perhaps there was still hope.

As Adam and Robin reached the front entrance to the hospital, Anderson came through the big double doors towards them.

"If you've come to visit, you're too late," Robin said, with a cheerfulness he didn't feel.

"That was only half of my plan, sir. Glad you're walking wounded, though." Anderson's voice lacked its usual breeziness; he was clearly more concerned than he wanted to let on.

Robin, not wanting a scene, asked him what the other half was.

"Seeing Porterfield," Anderson said sheepishly. "His doctors have given the go-ahead for him to be interviewed, so I thought I'd do that en route to seeing you."

"I'm coming with you."

"You are not!" Robin's partners—professional and personal— spoke in unison.

"You're coming home to take it easy," Adam added, glancing at Anderson.

Robin thought about arguing, but opted for suggesting a compromise. "What if I simply go along to observe? Twenty minutes at most. Then you can strap me to the sofa for the whole of what's left of Saturday."

"Twenty minutes." Adam tapped his watch. "Not a second more. I'll be waiting outside."

"I'm not a child. I can take care of myself."

"Like you did in that alley?" Adam scowled. "You need constant supervision."

Anderson stepped in. "I'll boot him out, don't worry." Before Adam could respond, the sergeant turned, consulted a scrap of paper, then said, "Ward E5. Let's use the lifts."

Robin, grateful for being rescued from the inevitable ear-bashing, made the trip up to the ward in silence.

Porterfield had been put into a side room. He was supposed to be twenty-one but looked about fifteen, lying in stripy pyjamas in the hospital bed, sheet tucked up around his armpits. Apart from his wrist being in plaster, he seemed to have escaped his fall lightly.

"I can't tell you anything about those robberies," he said in response to Robin's scene-setting question.

"So where did you get this money you've been flashing about?" Anderson asked.

"Had a good win on the horses last week." Porterfield flashed a cheeky grin.

Anderson made a note, but his snort showed he didn't believe the explanation. "Then you can tell us which bookmaker you used, and we can verify it."

"It was on the course. Up at . . . Ascot. Can't remember which bloke I visited. He wore a big hat," he added, less credible with every word.

"There wasn't a meeting at Ascot last week. Hasn't been in ages." Anderson's face wore its smuggest smile. "Why not do yourself a favour and tell us what actually happened? Nobody's going to know that you snitched on them."

Porterfield didn't appear to be convinced. He glanced at the door, then back at the policemen. "I didn't want anyone to get hurt. The knives were only there for show, to put the frighteners on. What with the Slasher and that, everybody's wary of a blade, although the geezer who talked me into it said these attacks had spoiled things. That knives should only be used for putting the wind up, rather than hurting people."

Robin's eyes narrowed. He'd been ready to be sympathetic to a young lad who'd been drawn into something bigger than he'd wanted to get into, but he felt less understanding now it was clear Porterfield had gone with both eyes open. He let Anderson carry on with the questioning.

"What was the name of this other bloke?"

"Selby. Ryan Selby."

That was easy. Maybe too easy, unless Porterfield was trying to make things straightforward for himself as quickly as possible, having realised he wasn't fooling anyone. For all his promises about observing, Robin had to chip in. "Did Selby pick up the cars too?"

"The car?"

"Yes. Like that big black metal thing with four wheels you used to get to the garage. The car that belonged to someone else." Robin, whose adventure in the alley hadn't left him full of the milk of human kindness towards any villains, enjoyed watching Porterfield squirm. "Did you nick it or did Selby?"

"It was Selby. He has family around here, so he knows the area. He was visiting his sister Julie when I met him in the pub. He made me an offer—"

"One you couldn't refuse?" Anderson asked waspishly.

"Eh? Nah, I was a plonker. I know that now." He sounded genuinely contrite, although that could always be at getting caught. "Can I cut a deal?"

Anderson rolled his eyes. "You've been viewing too many American cop shows."

"We *could* talk to the CPS, see what they think. So long as you give us the help we need," Robin cut in. "Like telling us about Edwards's involvement."

"Edwards?"

"I thought you'd stopped arsing about. Selby knew Edwards when they were in prison together. He's local as well."

"Oh, right." Porterfield nodded, having obviously twigged who they meant. "Is he the one who did time for an assault up on the Rings? Selby thinks he's a diamond geezer. Edwards protected him when a fight broke out inside. Selby reckons he saved his life. Sort of bloke who always looks after his own."

"Really?" Davis hadn't rooted that out.

"Yeah. He was there at the pub that night I got tapped up to help with the robberies. Earlier, though. Selby says his old mate's on the straight and narrow now, so he didn't want to talk about anything dodgy in front of him."

"Glad to hear it. About Edwards. Assuming it's true." Robin felt himself drooping. "Sergeant Anderson will take your statement. Be as helpful to him as you can, remember?"

"I will."

Anderson accompanied Robin to the door. "I'll get Selby brought in, sir, and his house searched. This will be pretty straightforward, so you go and get a rest. I'll keep you updated."

"Thanks."

Robin found Adam sitting, waiting, on a chair. Adam glanced up from the magazine he'd been idly flicking through, face as pale as if he'd been the one incarcerated overnight. He got up, patted Robin's shoulder—none too tenderly—and said, "We should get you back home."

"Sounds good." Funny, given the conversation of the previous evening, how it did feel like going home and not just to his lover's house.

"Maybe a glass of wine would help your painkillers." Adam steered him towards the lifts at a pace, possibly afraid that Anderson might re-emerge and catch them.

"I won't argue." Robin reached up to rub his sore head, then winced, drawing his hand away sharpish. "I must learn not to do that for a while."

Once they'd reached the ground floor, they walked back to Adam's car at a slower pace than they usually employed.

Robin halted for a moment, flexing his muscles, before heading off again. "I feel like an old man."

"You *look* like an old man, the way you're walking. Take your time. Enough harm done."

"I should have come back with you last night." Robin sighed. "I'm an idiot."

"You should. You are." Adam stopped, catching Robin's arm and making him turn round. "I'm sorry you got thumped. I have to say it wasn't me who did it, getting my own back after the argument, I promise."

"Surprisingly enough, you're almost the last on my list of suspects."

"Only almost?"

"Yeah. Campbell's rock-bottom."

Adam linked Robin's arm and steered him towards the car park. "At least you've not lost your sense of humour. And you'll need to apologise to Campbell when we get home. Once he was satisfied you weren't lying in the morgue, he decided he's not happy with you at all."

Campbell was certainly unhappy with Robin, as he proved by ignoring him, making a beeline for Adam instead, letting himself be fussed over while giving Robin only a cursory glance.

"I must be in the doghouse." Robin went to pat the Newfoundland's back, then withdrew his hand in case Campbell's bad humour ran to a nip on the fingers. "With both of you. I'd say I was sorry once more, but I'd sound like a cracked record." He waited, trying by sheer willpower to force Adam to look at him.

"I don't want to get into bed with Max Worsley." Adam kept his attention on the dog.

"I know that. It was the stress talking. Or my own special brand of stupidity." Robin rested his hand on Adam's. "I'm a twit, I know, but I can't quite believe my luck at times. Our relationship has already lasted longer than any other I've had, and there's a voice in my head telling me that the good fortune can't carry on indefinitely. That you'll get fed up with me or the job or whatever and give me the boot."

"Is that why you keep your flat? Because you think I'll chuck you out?"

"Something like that."

"I take back what I said about you being an idiot. That word's totally inadequate to describe your level of stupidity." Adam squeezed Robin's fingers. "I can't imagine me living without you, not at present. And neither can Campbell, despite the huff he's in at the moment. But it's bloody hard for us. We can get our heads round hardly seeing you when there's a big case on, but when something like this happens, it breaks our hearts."

The dog turned his head, gave Robin a sympathetic look, then rubbed himself against his leg.

"I don't deserve either of you." Robin choked back a tear.

"Oh, for goodness sake, don't say that, or you'll start to actually believe it. There's nothing about deserving things in love, is there?"

"No." Adam was right. Adam was always right. "I'll ring the agent on Monday and get the flat rented out. I promise."

"Don't promise, just do it."

"I will. And you can string me up from the yardarm if I forget."

"You've forgotten we don't have a yardarm." Adam grinned, eased himself out of his seat, then leaned in to kiss Robin's cheek. "Or a grating to flog you at, which might be more useful for keeping you in line. Instead, I'll have to rely on *himself* to keep you in line."

"Where are you going?"

"I need to get milk and things. All the stuff I meant to do this morning, but . . ." Adam spread his hands. "I'm pleased the doors have got Chubb locks. Make sure they're secured while you're here alone. Even if you're here with Campbell. If Worsley managed to get your address, other people could too, and if you were beaten up by somebody who wanted to halt your investigation . . ."

It was a valid point, one that Robin had been forcing himself not to think about. "I'll be fine. Don't fuss."

"Don't fuss? This is deadly serious." Adam's stern expression matched his words. "I know the dog saved you last time, but there's a limit to anybody's luck, even yours."

"I'm sorry. You're right. As usual." Robin pulled him into a hug. "I promise not to make a target of myself. I won't act like some stupid tart in a bad American thriller, putting on high heels and an evening dress so that if I have to make a getaway, I'll be in as impractical an outfit as possible."

"You should do that. The sight of you in that outfit would scare anybody off." Adam nuzzled against his neck, voice unsteady. "I won't be long. Don't let me come back to find that my favourite rozzer's been thumped again."

"I have every intention of making sure that doesn't happen. My mother would kill me anyway if we don't turn up for lunch tomorrow."

"You should get her round here, then. She'd scare off any muggers."

That was too accurate to be funny. "I'd better ring her. Or else she might die of fright when she sees the state of me." Robin was developing quite a shiner of a black eye; by Sunday he'd look like he'd had a kick from a mule.

"After you've had a bath and a rest. Doctor Matthews's orders." Adam got his bunch of keys from his pocket. "And I'm locking you in. I mean it."

Robin was left with little choice but to have that bath, after which he sprawled out on the sofa, flicked through a bit of sport on the telly, and dozed, all under Campbell's watchful eye. The dog had taken his guardianship duties so seriously he'd even insisted on wedging himself in the bathroom doorway so it couldn't be closed.

By the time Adam came back, Robin didn't feel quite so much like he'd been under a steamroller, and Cowdrey had rung to wish him well, ordering him to get a couple of days' rest in the process. He'd told Root and his merry men at Abbotston that they'd have to delay taking any statement until the evening, unless there was anything urgent to pass on, but that had been ignored. One of their team turned up on the doorstep hard on Adam's heels, as soon as they'd got settled on the sofa with a cup of tea and thirty French rugby players. The match was into the second half by the time he'd escaped.

It wasn't pleasant, getting grilled and being made to feel like you were the guilty party rather than the victim. Did Robin's interviewees undergo the same thing? He resolved not to be too harsh on them in future. There was no pleasure in the boot being on the other foot.

When he got back to the sofa, Adam budged up to make room for him.

"Good game?" The scoreline suggested a bit of a try fest.

"Cracking. Good legs, too. Rougerie's got them up to his armpits. Or shouldn't I mention them in case you think I'm going to run off with Sergio Parisse?"

Robin put his hands up. "Okay, point taken. How many times are you going to make me suffer over this one? If I go and pay my penance by licking out Campbell's bowl, can I be forgiven?"

The dog, stirring in his sleep at the mention of his name, nestled against Robin's foot.

"You don't need to go that far. Just ring the agent. And take care of yourself."

"I promise. On both counts." He turned his attention to the rugby; even the stern French referee sounded like he had it in for troublemakers like him, although the sultry continental tones made the on-field instructions come across as faintly seductive. "*Flexion. Plie. Jeu.* Sexier than 'Crouch. Set. Bind,' isn't it?"

"I was thinking that accent improves everything. I mean, when they ask, 'Is there any reason I cannot award the try?' it smacks of 'Would you like to come to bed?'"

Robin grinned; it seemed he was on the way to being forgiven at last. "I have to admit that when it used to be 'Crouch, touch, pause, engage,' I always used to have dirty thoughts. Can I ask if it's okay to admire a peachy backside, or a particularly muscular thigh?"

"You can admire as much as you want, so long as I can too."

Back there again. Luckily the referee used a small fracas to make as much of an ass of himself as Robin had the evening before, sending the wrong man to the sin bin.

"Is that what happened to you?" Adam voiced Robin's own thoughts. "Got the wrong man?"

"Could be. Are you thinking of Edwards? You reckoned he looked a bit like me."

"Yeah. I guess it feels more comforting, too, if they weren't actually out to get *you*."

"Seems like we've got doubles cropping up everywhere." Robin blew out his cheeks. "Anderson says that Sam Brunning is adamant that he'd been mistaken for somebody. Still maintains he was never in a fight."

"Want me to bend Luke's ear on Monday? We've got a training day, so I can buttonhole him." Adam's expression suggested the offer was genuine but sacrificial, this case impinging yet again on their lives.

"I don't know how wise that is." *On any count.*

"Don't you trust me? I can be subtle."

"I know. Calm down." Robin squeezed Adam's hand. "It's just that I don't want you ending up being thumped as well."

"I echo the sentiment." Adam ran his foot along Campbell's back. "God, what a bloody mess."

"I didn't make the Brunnings be involved."

Campbell growled, giving them both the disapproving look he saved for when they argued.

"Sorry." It wasn't clear who Adam had intended the apology for. "Okay. If you *were* mistaken for Edwards, who would want him thumped? The victim in the assault case didn't strike me as somebody who'd take revenge. Too scrawny, for one thing."

"That in itself wouldn't clear him." Robin pulled a face. "It's like straws in a haystack. Perhaps somebody Edwards upset in prison, somebody who doesn't like his business dealings, somebody who thinks he did in Hatton and is getting their own back. There are far too many threads in this case—these cases—and none of them tying up anywhere. Who knows which will be the one that gets pulled and unravels the whole tapestry?"

Adam smiled at last, rubbing Robin's shoulder with something like affection. "You're waxing very poetical. Perhaps that knock on the head's done some good."

"I'd be willing to endure another hammering, if only it would help me make bloody sense of things."

Because nothing else was helping.

Chapter Nine

Robin had prepared his mother for the worst, but it didn't stop her—or his aunt Clare—fussing and fretting over him, before telling him off for going down dark alleys on his own. Even when he reminded them that he was a grown man, they weren't placated, so he let them vent to their heart's content, to Adam's evident satisfaction. Once that was done with, Robin gave her the handsome green glass vase they'd bought, even though the roses to fill it would have to be delivered, recent events having meant he hadn't been able to get back to the shop to collect some.

Mrs. Bright's birthday lunch had the air of a seven-year-old's, considering the number of gifts on display from her family and friends. Only the *presence* of bottles of wine as opposed to brightly coloured juice, and dishes of olives instead of dishes of jelly, gave the game away. Although the talk during preprandial drinks soon drifted from the quantity of presents and back to the amount of bruising that had come up on Robin's face and right hand.

There'd been a mention of the attack on the Saturday evening news, which had sent his mother into a tizzy and a steam of panicked phone calls the night before her party, convinced that everyone was trying to keep the awful truth from her of how bad the assault had been. Both Robin and Adam had tried to reassure her several times, but nothing short of a face-to-face examination of the evidence for herself had been going to help. "Any more of this and you'll put me in an early grave," she said now that she had them sitting safely at her dining table, although everyone present knew that nothing short of attack by a Sherman tank would put her in the ground before her time. Any formidable genes Robin might have inherited came straight from the distaff side. Thank goodness the full extent of the danger Robin had faced in his last murder case had never been completely explained to her, or she'd have been up to the prison, dealing with the now-convicted double murderer who'd dared to be mean to her boy.

"The police are always getting themselves beaten up." Aunt Clare added her two penn'orth.

"Oh, be fair. This is the first time I've been duffed over. I've got away with things pretty lightly." Robin fingered one of his bruises, immediately regretting it. He should have learned his lesson on that score but, like a little boy, couldn't help continually prodding the sore spots. "And we don't even know that this was related to work. Might simply be wrong place, wrong time."

Mrs. Bright's reply, a simple sniff, was laden with more meaning than a dozen words. Robin deftly changed the subject. "You like watching old comedy shows, don't you?"

"Yes. They're better than what passes for humour these days. Why?"

"What's the one with a character called Radar?"

"*M*A*S*H*," Adam chipped in, eyebrows raised. "I thought everyone knew that."

"Haven't you realised yet that Robin is oblivious to most of what goes on around him?" Mrs. Bright grinned. "Radar was a clerical assistant to the colonel. Always knew what was about to happen, hence the nickname. And you still haven't told us why you want to know."

"It's not particularly important. The murder case we had and now don't. One of the people we were trying to trace got called the name, and I wondered if there was a connection."

"Perhaps you're hunting a clairvoyant." Mrs. Bright rose from the table to gather up the plates. "Or a member of the army."

"Or a man who works in air traffic control." Aunt Clare evidently wanted to get her oar in.

"You should let us do that." Adam got up and made a grab for the plates. "It's your special day, Mrs. B."

Robin grinned. "It spoils Mum's day if you don't let her fuss over us. It's more blessed to serve than be served, isn't that right?"

"You're mixing your verses. Probably deliberately." Mrs. Bright, whose father had been a vicar, eyed her son sceptically. "Adam's no doubt run himself ragged looking after you this last twenty-four hours. *You* can come and help with pudding."

Robin made a face at his partner, who raised his eyebrows, then started to chat to Aunt Clare about other old television programmes they liked.

"Are you sure you're all right?" Mrs. Bright asked once they were in the kitchen.

"Yeah. I'm not taking that shortcut again any time soon, but I'm not avoiding Abbotston entirely."

"That wasn't exactly what I was asking about." She put the plates down, leaned against the sink, and fixed him with the kind of expression she'd employed when he was little and hiding some misdemeanour. "You seem not quite yourself. Or maybe not quite *yourselves*. Is everything tickety-boo with you and Adam?"

"Mother!" Robin flicked her with the edge of the tea towel he'd started to use to wipe a spoon. Concentrating on cutlery would let him avoid that basilisk glare. "Not like you to be so inquisitive."

"By inquisitive, do you mean downright nosy?"

Robin looked up at that, but his mother was smiling now. "You don't normally pry."

"I know, but this time I'm concerned. Something's up."

"Where do I start?" Robin concentrated on the spoon again, although there couldn't have been even a molecule of water left on it. "One of the witnesses in the Hatton murder case—the case we had to hand over. He turned up on the doorstep. Never had that happen before, and neither of us liked it."

Mrs. Bright put her hand under her son's chin and tilted his face towards hers. "That's better. I don't like addressing your left ear. There are a lot of things happening at present that apparently haven't happened before."

"No 'apparently' about it." Robin laid down the spoon. Should he mention the unprecedented concerns about Adam, too? Clearly his mother had spotted something. He let out a sigh; time to admit defeat. "Okay. This witness. Adam met him years ago—well, didn't quite meet him, ran across him. He was a witness when Adam did jury duty."

"Quite a coincidence."

"My professional life is full of coincidences at the moment. It makes you wonder how much of it really is chance." Robin laid down the spoon at last. "Especially when Worsley just 'bumped into' Adam on Friday, in Waitrose car park of all places. I'm worried he might be stalking us, but I've no proof." That was as far as he would go for now.

"Nasty. Do you believe he might be the man who attacked you?" Mrs. Bright slipped her arm around her son's waist.

"I have no idea. Could have been."

She rubbed his side soothingly. "I know I'm being a nosy old bag, but what on earth were you doing in that alleyway on your own?"

Robin groaned. "We'd been out for dinner and had an argument. I stormed off."

"I'm not a betting woman, but I told your aunt Clare that's what I'd have put my money on. Did you argue about Worsley?"

"Do you read minds?" Robin flicked her with the tea towel again. "Only partly. I was stressed and stupid and picking on anything. I've been working every hour God sends, and I've failed to rent out the flat."

"Ah. I see." She nodded, gave him a final squeeze, and went to the oven to inspect the pudding. "That needs another couple of minutes. During which I won't pry any further. You do know, I hope, that I've only asked because I care for you. Both of you."

"I know that. *We* know that."

"You always were a hard worker. Adam's the same. Dedicated, the pair of you. You'll have to work that one out going forward, because there's more to life than marking books and nicking villains."

"Yes, oh wise one."

Mrs. Bright flicked him back with her tea towel. "I can remember you as a teenage boy, on the front at Great Yarmouth, unable to make your mind up about what flavour of ice cream you wanted."

"Sorry?"

"Thinking aloud." Mrs. Bright opened the oven, nodded, then brought out of it a bowl of steaming, golden-coloured apple crumble, which she laid on a trivet to cool. "I remember you always chose vanilla. I checked that you didn't want strawberry or chocolate or anything else, but you insisted."

"I never felt happy choosing one of the others. Like I didn't deserve them."

"Oh!" She stopped what she was doing, faced him again. "Did *we* make you feel like that?"

"No. Honestly, no." He went across, then put his arm round her shoulder. "Not you. School. Bullying. You know."

"*That* place." She scowled. "If Adam didn't work there, I'd go and burn it down."

Perhaps it was as well she hadn't comprehended the extent of the bullying when it was happening, or he might have let loose an arsonist.

"Is that part of the issue with Adam? You don't think you deserve to have such a nice bloke?"

"Something like that. I get mixed up in my head at times. Don't mention it, though. We're working through it together."

"I understand. Mum's the word." She patted his cheek. "I simply want you to be as happy as your father and I were. Or is that being too . . . what's the word? I learned it from a television programme about equalities."

"I have no idea." Robin pressed her hand against his face; he bet she'd watched that programme so as to better understand him.

"Heteronormative! That was it. I shouldn't impose heteronormative values on you."

"You might as well be talking Urdu, but I appreciate the sentiment." He appreciated the deeper significance too. When his mother couldn't remember words or names—or pretended she couldn't—then she usually felt deeply and strongly about something. He wound his arms round her, leaning his head on her back. "You're possibly the oddest mother in the entire universe, but I wouldn't have you any different."

"I'll take that as a compliment," she said, kissing him. "Now, this crumble won't eat itself. Let's take it through."

As they re-entered the dining room, Adam was beaming like a boy who'd found the sixpence in a Christmas pudding. "Your aunt Clare is a genius."

"I know she is," Robin laid down the jug of custard he'd been inveigled into carrying. "What's the latest evidence of it?"

"Radar. She's got a connection we've all missed."

Aunt Clare cleared her throat, evidently embarrassed at the compliment. "Back in the seventies, there was a police show. It was quite cutting edge, I suppose you'd call it, at the time, although your generation would probably find the whole thing very tame."

"You're probably right." Robin's ears had pricked up at the words "police show," though.

"There was a police dog, which got shot. I cried my eyes out. He was called Inky."

"Inky? That's—" Robin clammed up as Adam shot him a warning glance.

"That's who?" Aunt Clare asked as she helped herself to crumble.

"Nothing. I shouldn't have interrupted. Go on."

"The replacement dog was called Radar."

Robin resisted the urge to punch the air and shout "Result!" There was no guarantee that the dog-handler aspect was any more than a coincidence, even if it was a pretty impressive accident of chance if accident it was. Although it wasn't his case anymore, was it?

Aunt Clare was carrying on regardless. "I preferred the first dog, though. I don't know how they got him to act dead so convincingly. I thought he *had* been shot. Poor Inky."

"I've never got over them shooting Archie Kennedy in *Hornblower*," Adam said, deftly changing the tack of the conversation onto characters they'd loved and lost.

Robin consumed his crumble, deep in thought, wondering when he should share the latest bit of information with Cowdrey, and why Hatton kept poking his nose into *his* business.

The weekend passed too soon, as weekends always did, wherever spent and under whatever degree of duress. They'd kept Sunday lunch pretty sober, which promised a lack of Monday morning hangover headaches, and Adam even made it to the Sunday evening service, leaving Robin to kip on the sofa, Campbell still keeping guard.

They liked to attend together when they could, the ladies of a certain age who made up the bulk of the evensong congregation apparently delighted at having their very own gay couple in the village, but those ladies would have to go without their fun tonight.

At church, Neil the vicar was on sparkling form, and Adam felt pretty optimistic again, especially as he had an in-school training day on Monday. The last three days had been a bit of a roller-coaster ride, and while he loved his charges dearly, not having to teach them tomorrow would be a bonus, as he didn't feel up to dealing with the helter-skelter of their burgeoning emotions. Even a session on assessing the new curriculum sounded appealing for once, as it would allow him to concentrate on things other than murders or relationships.

As he turned to leave the pew, he spotted someone he didn't usually associate with the St. Crispin's evening service; the congregation was small enough to spot any unfamiliar faces. Only this face was entirely familiar.

"Hi, Luke." Adam smiled and waved as he reached the pew where Luke had just opened his eyes from what presumably was a spot of post-blessing prayer.

"Hi. I thought I saw you sat up there." Luke wore a sheepish expression that suggested he hadn't anticipated getting into conversation.

"Had a good weekend?" Adam asked, not sure whether it was politic to chat, but feeling guilty about simply saying goodbye and moving on. Luke looked like he'd had as ragged a few days as Adam and Robin had been through.

Rescue came in the form of Victor Reed, chair of the school governing body and an ever-present at the six thirty service, who came up grimacing theatrically and holding his face. "I bet you've not had as bad a weekend as I have. Barely slept a wink. Dental abscess, under three teeth. Needs endodontic surgery."

As a small crowd of female parishioners assembled to hear the gruesome details and fuss over Victor, Adam realised he was more stuck in the church than ever. So much for being rescued. An especially grisly description of dental symptoms gave Adam the chance to feign queasiness and make an escape, only to find Luke hard on his heels, having grabbed the same opportunity. He'd just have to be civil.

"I do like Victor, but there's nothing worse than somebody else's symptoms, is there?" Adam breathed deeply of the cool air.

"Yeah. I can't bear anything to do with teeth, unless they're my own." Luke walked in step with him down to the lychgate.

"You've chosen the wrong career, then. You're bound to have to deal with a couple of milk teeth coming out every term." Adam unhitched the big gate and let Luke through. The security lamp from the property across the road flicked on, illuminating them in its stark white light.

"I'll have to hope I have a classroom assistant to help me, in that case." Luke's smile couldn't mask his nervous, fidgety air.

Should Adam ask what was wrong? He was Luke's official mentor, for goodness' sake, but probably discretion would be better for the moment. Robin had rung Cowdrey straight after they'd left Mrs. Bright's house, in case they'd stumbled on the truth of the Radar nickname; it was entirely possible that events had moved on apace since then and Sam Brunning had been hauled in off his gardening leave to account for why he'd lied.

In the event, Adam didn't have to ask anything. Luke kicked at the gatepost and spat out, "You shouldn't have dobbed my brother in."

"I'm sorry?" Could news have travelled so quickly?

Luke kept his eyes firmly fixed on his boots. "You shouldn't have dobbed my brother in when I told you about his woman trouble."

Adam blew out his cheeks in relief. Luke had to be referring to their conversation in the classroom the previous Monday, rather than events since, although why had he taken so long to mention it? "I wasn't aware *I'd* snitched on anybody. The information went through the proper channels. There's a witness who reckons they saw your brother in a fight with Hatton."

"And he says he wasn't there."

Had the news from Robin's call not filtered down yet, or had Cowdrey simply dismissed the "Radar" connection as ridiculous?

"This isn't the time or the place to be discussing this. In fact," Adam lowered his voice, "we shouldn't be discussing it full stop. Police business, not church."

"Yeah, well, this is personal. For both of us." Luke kicked the gatepost again.

"I know it is, and it isn't going to be easy for you to deal with it, but you're going to have to find a way to carry on working with me, whatever the outcome. Unless you want to ask Chris to appoint you another mentor." Perhaps that would be best for all parties.

"Maybe I'll do that very thing." Luke slammed his right hand against the gate itself. "Shit!" He gingerly cradled it in his left.

"Are you okay? That looks nasty." Adam reached out to help, but Luke turned away from him.

"I'm fine. Just caught it awkwardly. I'll go home and put another batch of ice on it." Luke backed off. "Don't worry about me. I can take care of myself."

Adam watched him go, suddenly sure that *he* had to get in first to tell the headteacher why two of his staff weren't likely to be talking to each other for a while. If Sam Brunning was economical with the truth, would his brother be any more factual?

Chapter Ten

Monday morning, Robin was back at work, despite the protests of Adam, who reckoned he needed more rest; Cowdrey, who threatened to send him home at the slightest sign of concussion; and Anderson, who said Robin looked like death and *he* didn't want to have to spend his day nursing him.

Robin, now sitting at his desk and on his second coffee of the day, stared at the piece of paper in front of him and tried to concentrate. With Porterfield's statement safe in hand, they should be sorting out these armed robberies, but his brain couldn't focus on the job.

Anderson's voice cut into his thoughts. "You okay, sir?"

Robin scowled. "That's not the most sensible question you've ever asked."

"Sorry. You just don't seem yourself. Even for a man who's been coshed."

A great shiver went through Robin's body, like wind through a cornfield, as Anderson might have said when waxing lyrical. "No, you're fine. I should be the one to apologise. I shouldn't have snapped. I can't get into gear today."

"You either need to go home and have a rest or get out and get detecting."

"Thank you, Dr. Anderson." Robin grinned. The bloke was spot on. It was no use sitting here feeling like crap.

"Davis is trying to pin down Selby's whereabouts. He's not home, and we haven't got enough information to locate his sister, except Porterfield reckons she's called some name like Judy or Julie."

"Leave him for a moment. I want to return to where I was thumped."

"Is that wise? It's Abbotston's jurisdiction—area and case. They think it's linked to Hatton."

Robin knew about that. One of the reasons for his foul mood was having to give that witness statement when he'd got settled at home on Saturday. Word was that Root had got his lads and lasses checking the alibis from Friday night of anyone involved with Hatton. "What if it's linked to the robberies, though? That's *our* baby."

"Can't be Porterfield. Might be the mysterious Selby."

"Come on. Back to the scene of the crime. You can drive." Robin wasn't the happiest passenger, especially when his sergeant was at the wheel, but today was an exception.

"You mustn't be feeling well if you'd rather I drove." Anderson's eyes narrowed. "Are you sure you're ready to return there?"

"Of course I am. Best get it over and done with, or you work yourself into a complex about things. I'm fine now. Soon be my normal self." Robin smiled, then winced.

"Hm. I'll take your word for it. Say if you need to have a rest."

"I'm not an invalid," Robin reminded him. "Nor am I eighty-three. And don't you dare say that's how old I look."

"Wouldn't dream of it, sir." Anderson grinned, but before he could fish out his car keys, Cowdrey appeared at the office door.

"Got a minute?" he asked in a low voice.

"Always got time for you, sir." Robin straightened himself in his seat while Anderson pulled up a chair for the chief superintendent, who had carefully closed the door behind him.

"Brunning insists it wasn't him in that fight. And he's got an alibi for Friday evening, too."

"Right. Thanks for keeping us in the loop."

"There's a bit more to it than that." Cowdrey ran his hand over his bald pate. "Root keeps going down the terrorism line. They've found Hatton's friend from GCHQ, a bloke called Harry Lewis, and he confirmed that they were threatened when they were out drinking, though it was a few years back. More than once, to boot. The Ulsterman's called O'Driscoll, and Lewis reckons he could be a vengeful relative of somebody *he* helped to put away. He's given Root some clues to help track him down. Lewis has kept his ears open—he clearly wasn't as casual about the threats as he tried to sound—and he's heard a rumour the guy might be back in England again, which means he could have been in Abbotston the Friday before last. And the Friday just gone, too."

Robin, who was itching to find out where the conversation was going, rubbed his chin. "You've a nose for a case, sir. Do *you* think there's a connection between this Harry Lewis and Hatton's death?"

"I'm not convinced. I blame the television—it's always MI5 or the CIA or the KGB at the bottom of things. It rarely is in real life." Cowdrey spread his large, muscular hands on the desk. "Which is why I'm here. The business stinks of red herring."

Anderson, who'd clearly been biting his tongue, leaped in. "The sort you go sniffing after while the real culprit legs it."

Cowdrey tapped quietly on the arm of his chair. Robin had seen that movement before; it meant his boss was considering his options, and possibly a few of those options stretched good practice a bit. "Root is convinced this is about an old enemy getting revenge. I suspect that's narrowing the field too much."

Anderson seemed about to say something, but Robin silenced him with a wave.

"I've seen him do the same thing in another division," Cowdrey continued. "He got a fixed idea about a case, and it turned out he'd got things totally wrong."

"And do you think history is repeating itself?"

"Quite possibly, although—much as it irks me to say it—we shouldn't be pursuing a case that's not ours anymore." Cowdrey leaned back in his chair, evidently trying, and just as evidently failing, to appear innocent. "Of course, if somehow there was a connection between certain elements in the Hatton case and your armed robberies . . ."

"Ones which we didn't realise returned to Hatton until we were too far through the investigation to call a halt?" Robin raised an enquiring eyebrow.

"Something like that. There is an obvious connection, given the similar description of the knife." Cowdrey nodded. "In an ideal world, you'd be able to find a reason to go back and talk to that woman. The one who went out with Hatton and knows Brunning."

"Zandra?"

"That's the one. She'd be able to settle once and for all the business of whether Brunning was in a fight at the club, or whether anybody calls him Radar. In an ideal world."

"Okay, so what reason might we find?" Robin had seen the twinkle in his boss's eye; Cowdrey was up for anything that wasn't strictly out of order. "Worsley says he wants to talk to us. That could be a start."

"Make it so." Cowdrey nodded. "I'll have your back if Root makes a fuss. And you getting nobbled could be to do with those robberies. Abbotston nick may be investigating the assault itself, but if it isn't linked to Hatton . . ."

"What exactly *are* you thinking, sir?"

"That Abbotston are trying to scoop up the entire pot of investigations for some reason. I don't like it." Cowdrey curled his lip in disgust.

Anderson chipped in. "Maybe they simply want to black our eyes a bit. Because we fingered Phillips."

"I hope it's nothing more than that." Cowdrey's expression of distaste turned to one of cunning. "I heard that Zandra girl knows Selby's sister."

"Blimey." Anderson, who'd been rocking back in his chair, shot forward again. "We don't even have her name yet."

"Neither do I, for that matter." Cowdrey grinned.

"I think Mr. Cowdrey is trying to subtly supply us with a good enough reason to go and interview Zandra again." Robin and his boss shared a knowing look.

"Although don't forget, what's said in this room stays in this room. I might deny it all to Root." Cowdrey rose from his chair, heading for the door. "Of course, it would be a public duty for us to use our eyes and ears if certain of our colleagues are too blind to see what's under their noses. We wouldn't want a miscarriage of justice, would we?"

"Indeed we wouldn't, sir." And putting Root's nose out of joint would make Robin's sore head worthwhile.

The crime scene investigator had given the alleyway a good once-over, but if there had ever been anything to find, it was long gone by then. Robin could, however, retrace his steps from the main road and follow the sequence of events as best he could.

"This was where I ran into the group of youngsters."

"We've put out an alert for them to contact the police if they saw something suspicious." Anderson looked up and down the cut way. "You were lucky they were there, or things might have been worse."

"Don't I know it?" Robin shivered. "What if it had been a quiet Tuesday and nobody around?"

"Yeah. Makes you think that whoever it was who lumped you must have been desperate to chance their arm. I mean, plenty of people use this shortcut."

"Of course they do. Otherwise I'd have not been stupid enough to come down here." Robin gingerly rubbed the back of his head.

"Definitely not a mugging gone wrong?"

"I don't think so. He might have been after my wallet or my phone, but he didn't ask for them, or make any attempt to get them out of my pockets." Robin shrugged; it still didn't make sense. "Unless he thought I was a Millwall supporter and got his own back."

"Everybody's saying that it's not convincing as a real attempt to kill you. Not like that last murder. Our friend with the revolver."

Robin shuddered at the memory of the other case they'd been involved in and how close it had come to either him, Anderson, or Adam breathing their last. "I'd rather face a football supporter in a dark alley than a fifty-something woman."

"Why you this time? I mean, last time we were arresting a killer. Was this wrong place, wrong time, or was somebody out to get you in particular?"

"Thanks for stating the bleeding obvious, Sergeant. Otherwise I'd never have thought of that."

Anderson grinned, unabashed. "Could be whoever it was thinks you remain in charge of the Hatton case?"

"Already considered that option. And if it was a friend of Phillips avenging him for us having found that blood. Or the possibility whoever it was mistook me for somebody else."

"Yeah. That does happen." Anderson nodded. "I'd still think it's more likely that they wanted to scare you off."

"In that case, not only did they scare off the wrong bloke, they also failed at letting me know what I was supposed to be frightened off of." Robin winced at the awful grammar.

"I'm convinced something happened to change the outcome."

"Change the outcome? Are you trying to find a subtle way of saying the attacker panicked and didn't finish me off?"

"Not necessarily. Perhaps they had a sudden pang of conscience. It happens."

"Perhaps." It was rare, but not unknown, for a desperate hard case, who'd have had no problem with beating some poor sod to a pulp, to have an attack of scruples about doing the same to the "wrong" person.

"I don't quite get why you were here on your own," Anderson said airily. Too deliberately airily to be anything but serious.

No point in trying to lie. "Adam and I argued when we were out for dinner. I got a huff on and stormed off."

"What the hell did you argue about? I mean, you two always get along so easily. No grief on either side."

Robin thought about saying "Nothing" or "Mind your own business," but decided that the truth had to be best this time. "Max sodding Worsley. Our favourite witness."

"Yeah, I remember. The one who came round to your house. The one who strikes me as a bit creepy."

"The one I'm supposed to ring today." Robin gave Anderson a précis of the conversation Adam had engaged in with Worsley in Waitrose car park. "I flew off the handle because I thought Worsley was stalking us and, you know, typical argument, one thing led to another. No logic to it."

"Hm." Anderson's brow wrinkled. "Want me to ring him? Not that I relish the prospect."

"That would be useful. Although I guess we should see him face-to-face." He couldn't entirely trust Worsley to tell him the truth, nor himself not to punch the guy's nose or give him a mouthful for hanging about Adam.

"I'll arrange a meeting and come with you. I'd like to know what he's got to say that's supposed to be 'so important.'"

"Say we'll come over to his work." Robin fished the phone number out of his pocket. "Make it as soon as we can. If what he's got to say *is* significant, I want to hear it now. If it isn't significant, I don't want us to waste any more time on it."

Anderson made the call, keeping it short and forceful, arranging to meet Worsley as soon as they could get to his office. They headed for the car, Robin happier now he was out of the alley.

"Maybe you *have* got a double," Anderson said once they were in the car and on the road again. "I remember being in a taxi a while back, heading for Abbotston train station, when I thought I saw you walking along the pavement. We'd stopped for lights, so I rolled the window down and was about to say hello—well, actually it would have been something slightly more interesting—when I realised I'd made a mistake. Like but not identical."

"When was this?"

"About a year ago. Do you think it was Edwards I saw?"

"Perhaps. I'd only seen that old picture Adam had kept, until this morning. Davis rustled up a more recent one. There's a passing resemblance to me, but he also looks a bit like Cowdrey or Brunning or you. Mister Average. You should see if it's the same bloke."

"I will do. Mind you, none of that proves you were attacked instead of him."

"I know. It would make me feel better, though." Robin stared out of the window at the people passing by. How many variations on the human face could there be, and how could two unrelated people end up being similar enough to be mistaken for each other? "Any news about who has or hasn't got an alibi?"

"Not officially, but my mole tells me that Sam Brunning says he was with his brother, and we know where Porterfield and Phillips were."

And if the attacker was somebody looking for Edwards, then they probably had no bloody idea whose alibis they should be checking.

Worsley seemed happy enough to talk to the police, no hint—as he met them in reception—that he was disappointed at Anderson being there too. As he ushered them into a convenient meeting room, Robin sneaked a glance at the witness's knuckles, but they didn't show any evidence of cuts or bruising.

They took their chairs, Anderson making a show of getting himself comfortable, fishing out his notepad and pen.

"Most people would arrange to come to the station." Robin fixed Worsley with a stony glare. "You have a habit of doing things *your* way."

"Wouldn't you, if you were worried? I know what the police can be like, closing ranks. I was hoping you'd give me a fairer hearing than they would at Abbotston."

"If it's about Hatton, we're not on the case." How many times would he have to say that? Although Worsley's concerns certainly reflected his and Cowdrey's; how fair a hearing would anybody get with Root's team?

"It's concerning Brunning. You can make sure the proper people get informed about it."

"Go on."

"I saw him again, last Friday lunchtime. He was walking down the street out there." Worsley pointed in the direction of the main road, not fifty yards from where they were sitting. "He came over and said he recognised me from the Desdemona. Acted all surprised at having run into me, but I wonder if he'd been hanging around."

Ironic, given that was what Robin had thought happened at Waitrose. Brunning might have been doing the same; Anderson wouldn't be the only one who had a spy inside the Abbotston camp, delivering information. "What did he say?"

"He said I'd been making trouble for him and his family. That I was to tell the police it wasn't him in the fight. That I'd made a mistake."

Here was an echo of Luke's conversation with Adam, as he'd reported it to Robin the previous evening. The Brunnings taking the same approach?

"Did he threaten you?" Anderson asked, mirroring Robin's thoughts.

Worsley shrugged. "Not physically. I could take him on in a fight any day. Not overtly, either. You might say he was clever with his use of words, because there was no direct threat, but an implication of one. I was going to get in touch with you over the weekend, then I saw your bloke. Lucky, that. "

Robin didn't comment. "Lucky" wasn't the word he'd have chosen.

"And you're entirely positive he was the person you saw in the fight? Stand up in the witness box and say it under oath positive?" Anderson clarified.

"Absolutely."

Cowdrey was going to love this. Nobody took pleasure in ruining another officer's career, but he was more determined than most in shuffling rogue coppers out of the pack.

"Thank you. One of our colleagues—one we promise you can trust absolutely—will be in touch." Robin rose to leave.

"That's not everything, though. Well, it was when I asked your bloke to get you to ring."

"More about Brunning?" Robin plonked himself back in his chair.

"No. It's from yesterday evening. I'm not sure how it fits in with anything, but I'm sure it's important."

Anderson rolled his eyes behind Worsley's back, then reopened his prematurely closed notebook.

"Let's hear it, then."

Worsley leaned forward in his chair, hands on knees. "I'd gone out for dinner, because I didn't fancy shoving something into the microwave."

Robin sighed. "You can spare us the domestic details, unless they're germane to the story."

Worsley, who evidently appreciated an audience, frowned. "Okay then. I was in the Wig. Do you know it?"

"Yes." Robin knew the Wig well; the pub was on the outskirts of Stanebridge, an old place all nooks and crannies, now the sort of shabby-chic joint that would have been heaving with customers if it had been in a fashionable area. He and Adam had been there for lunch in their courting days.

"I'd tucked myself in a corner, head down over the iPad, pretending to check my emails while really playing games. Society's new way of being a recluse." Worsley's thumbs jiggled, acting out the movements, before the man realised he was trapped between two stony gazes. "Right. I'd zoned out, until the guy sitting behind me mentioned he'd attacked some bloke, and how it had been the wrong bloke. They couldn't have known I was there, so I couldn't resist listening in. Doing my duty as a citizen rather than being nosy."

"How can someone beat up the wrong bloke?" Anderson, scowling, sounded incredulous, which was good acting for a bloke who'd been discussing the same thing with Robin not a few hours before.

Worsley ignored the frown. "Fairly easily, I'd have thought, if you didn't know the victim personally. The way these guys were talking, it seemed like a case of mistaken identity."

"That makes sense. I think." Robin rubbed his head instinctively, even though it didn't ache quite so much now. Was it possible Worsley was referring to what had happened in that alley? "The men who were talking—what can you tell us about them?"

"One of them had a. . ." Worsley shrugged. "I don't know, Essex accent? Like you'd hear on *Birds of a Feather*. He was the one who'd made the cock-up. Other one was a lot posher. Softly spoken. Home Counties. I didn't recognise either voice, though."

Essex. Selby came from up that way. "The posh one couldn't have been Edwards?"

"The Edwards I helped send down?" Worsley thought for a moment, then shook his head. "Not unless he's had plastic surgery, no. I managed to get a look at them."

Robin nodded. "What else did they say?"

"That the job still needed doing. He had to make sure he got the right bloke next time, but it was going to be difficult." Worsley opened the file he'd brought with him, producing a handful of scribbled notes, which he gave to Robin. "I jotted down what I heard before I made myself scarce. I didn't want to risk them seeing me, but there's a corridor to the toilets and a back door into the yard, so I nipped along and out."

"Good you knew all that in advance." Anderson clearly didn't believe a word of it.

"I was once in the Wig when the fire alarm went off. We had to go out that way." Worsley leaned forward, arms on the desk. "I wanted to get a butcher's, as I said, but I felt a right idiot, sneaking about. Like I was the one doing something illegal, not them."

Anderson snorted; Robin shot him a scowl, then nodded at Worsley encouragingly. "Nothing looks more suspicious than people trying not to look suspicious. Go on."

"I doubled round to the front of the building and had a sneaky peek through that big window the Wig had put in when they did the refurbishments. I saw two ordinary blokes; I've never seen anyone look less like villains."

"They don't all wear striped jumpers and masks and carry a bag marked 'swag.'" Anderson snorted once more.

Robin ignored him. "You keep saying you've got a good memory for faces. Would you recognise them again?"

"Probably. I went up the road, bought a paper at the Co-op, then went back for a second gander. One of them turned his head and caught me in full gawp, so I tried to appear gormless and walked on as if nothing had happened. I got to the end of the road. Then I legged it like a sprinter to the bus stop. When I eventually got there, I couldn't stop shaking. Luckily the bus came along almost straight away." Worsley certainly appeared shaken in the telling of it. "I remembered to check I hadn't been followed."

Anderson rolled his eyes. "So you have no idea who the people were or who they were discussing?"

"No. If I had, I'd have said. And yes, I know it might be a red herring, but you might be able to make sense of it." Worsley smiled pleadingly at Robin.

Assembling such small jigsaw pieces, images that made no sense out of context, could make a pretty decent picture of a case.

"Did they give any indication of when or where this erroneous thumping took place? Or who the victim was?" Robin asked.

"Not really. The bar started to fill while I was listening, so they got cagey. It was in Abbotston, though. And sometime during the last few weeks."

Robin and his sergeant shared a glance.

"Is that significant?" Worsley asked.

"It might be." Robin, determined to remain non-committal, let Anderson carry on with the questioning; the antagonism between this pair might help flush out something.

"The thing is, Mr. Worsley," the sergeant said, "I always get nervous when people try to be too helpful. Inspector Bright here reckons it's me being naturally suspicious. He says I'd be checking my own mother out if she kept 'stumbling across' information entirely by chance, then telling me about it."

"Credit me with some sense." Worsley shook his head, frowning and drumming his fingers. "If I were up to my arse in this, I'd have got myself a proper alibi for the time of Hatton's death, rather than being at home alone. And for whatever happened on Friday night," he added. "Your mates from Abbotston rang up and asked me what I was doing then, too. Somebody else get stabbed?"

"Not quite. A policeman was attacked." Robin kept his voice unemotional.

"Ah. That explains how zealous the questioning was. I've got no alibi for it, unless my Sky box can verify all the flicking between channels I did."

"Shame we can't ask it." Anderson raised his eyebrows. "But wouldn't you agree that this procession of accidental meetings seems worryingly coincidental?"

Worsley's temper finally flared. "Worryingly coincidental? What do you think I'm playing at?"

Robin raised his hand. "There's no need to shout."

"There's every bloody need. I nearly caught my death of cold trudging to Lindenshaw to give you information last week. If I'd stabbed Hatton, wouldn't I be trying to distance myself from the case?"

"Not if you were trying to deflect our attention elsewhere," Anderson replied bullishly.

"Oh, for goodness' sake." Worsley slammed his hands on his knees. "I can't win with you. Next time I come across anything, I'll keep it to myself."

"No, don't do that." Robin shot his sergeant a warning glance. "We appreciate your help, but you have to understand our point of view. People don't always tell us the truth."

Worsley exhaled loudly. "Okay, I get that. And I also get that you believe I might have imagined the whole conversation, or something, but I swear to God I'm not yanking your chain. When I came round to your house, all I was trying to do was help. That's all I'm doing now."

Robin took a deep breath. There was a chance they were misreading Worsley. Perhaps he was being candid with them. Perhaps he was dealing them a load of tripe. Robin would play a straight bat and see what happened. "If that's the case, then I'll thank you properly." He got out of his chair, proffering his hand for Worsley to shake. "You see, it's a bit personal. The policeman who was attacked on Friday night—that was me."

"Bloody hell." Worsley pulled his hand away post-shake as though scalded. "You think they were talking about you? Who did they mean to do over?"

"I have no idea." And if he had, he wouldn't share it with Worsley.

Davis hadn't managed to run Selby to ground, so next stop was the Wig, to find out anything about the men whom Worsley said he'd overheard. For once the police struck as lucky as *he* seemed to—the bar staff from the night before identified one of them from the pictures Anderson showed. Selby, just as they'd expected, although who the other man was remained as much a mystery as who was supposed to be beaten up. Could being a bit of a ringer for Edwards be the key? Selby certainly might have a reason to bear a grudge against Edwards, given that they knew each other. It would also explain why the attacker hadn't finished him off, having realised his mistake.

"Seems like it's true, then." Anderson kicked angrily at a stone on the pavement as they walked back to his car. "Although doesn't it beggar belief that of all the seats in all the pubs Worsley might have chosen, he ended up next to them when they're having that particular conversation? And why would anyone with an ounce of sense have such a conversation in such a public place?"

"They might not have realised they were being overheard. You saw the place. It's a right rabbit warren."

"Hm." Anderson clearly couldn't shake off his distrust. "Worsley always has a spot of information to give that deflects the attention from him. Or means that he gets to see you again."

"I'm sure I'm not his cup of tea." He hadn't considered that possibility, and he didn't want to. "Anyway, in the case of Selby, he was spot on. Chances are he was about Brunning, too. Maybe it's like that snout of yours who fingered Porterfield. Big ears and a bagful of luck."

Robin's phone vibrated; there was a text from Davis, saying that Zandra's mother was home from hospital and being cared for by her daughter. Zandra would be happy to talk to them if they went round to her house now. He'd have preferred to see the woman at the station; the unfamiliar, unsettling location often worked wonders at getting into a witness's mind, even if they were innocent and trying to protect a third party. But the station was officially off limits at the moment for obvious reasons—if Anderson had spies at Abbotston, Robin bet the reverse applied.

When Zandra opened the door to them, her appearance was distinctly less groomed than before, although her nails were now manicured, growing back, and painted a subtle pearl colour. Perhaps she'd found time to do that while she'd waited at her mother's bedside.

"You seem to find my hands fascinating," she said to Robin as she ushered them into her lounge, where a woman—clearly her mother, given the facial resemblance—sat reading a book.

The remark caught him off guard, but he rallied. "I couldn't help noticing last time that they weren't as well turned out as the rest of you."

"Blame that hospital. I snagged two of them on the edge of Mother's trolley when we were hanging around in casualty, waiting for them to do something sensible with her appendix."

Mrs. Williams said, without looking up from her book, "They couldn't rush me into theatre because it was too soon after I'd had a meal."

Zandra smiled indulgently. "I suppose so. Anyway, I didn't even have an emery board to hand, so had to nibble the dangling bits off. It was awfully embarrassing."

Was she over-elaborating? Why give elaborate details about a snagged nail, for goodness' sake, unless it was to cover up that she'd bitten them away worrying about what Brunning had done? Then again, *they'd* been the ones so obsessed with the bitten nails that they'd taken the first opportunity to inspect them. Better to get back to business.

"Could you take a look at some of these pictures? We're wondering if you—or Hatton—had come across any of them before." It was a long shot, and more an excuse to interview her than any firm expectation she'd know the armed robbers.

"Certainly." Zandra studied each in turn, shaking her head at Porterfield, Selby, Edwards, two random blokes they'd put in to make up the numbers, and Worsley. The last, and crucial, picture was that of Sam Brunning.

"That's Sam." Zandra smiled. "Do you remember Sam Brunning, Mum?"

Mrs. Williams glanced up from her book. "Oh, yes. Nice lad. Always been spotty."

"He's pretty well lost the acne now." Zandra handed the photo to Anderson. "We've known Sam for years. Dad used to coach the local youngsters' cricket team, and I'd join in, keeping wicket. I went on and played it at uni, before you ask. I was pretty good."

Robin, who struggled to imagine anybody with such a manicure donning the gloves, nodded, then brought the conversation back to the matter in hand. Just in case Anderson was tempted to talk about the woes of the England cricket team. "Are you and Brunning romantically involved?"

"Oh, you have to be joking." Zandra flapped her hands like a bird struggling to take flight. "He's not my type at all. More like a little brother."

"But you were with him in the rose shop, on the waterfront in Abbotston, buying flowers?"

"Of course I was, but they weren't for me." Zandra, laughing, shook her head. "He can't be trusted to do something like that on his own, so I offered to advise him. They reckon you should say it with flowers; he needed help about what sort would best say, 'Sorry for being a jerk.'"

Anderson asked. "What had he been a jerk about?"

"His tangled love life, as usual," Zandra said, in the condescending tone she adopted every time she spoke to the sergeant. "He's not a bad-looking lad, now the spots have gone, and the girls like him. Only he can't keep things as neat as Tom managed to."

"Two women?" Robin clarified.

"Only the two, yes. And one at least had her nose put out of joint. He can be such an idiot at times."

"But you argued, in the shop?"

"We did. There were some lovely peach-coloured roses on display, but he wouldn't buy a proper bunch of them, because he's not simply an idiot, he's a cheapskate. I know he can't earn that much in the force, so I offered to put something towards them, and he went all nineteen-fifties on me."

Robin was warming to Zandra. Inside that icy exterior, there was a genuinely nice person. "Who was the woman he had to mollify?"

"Not that policewoman, for a start." Zandra's mouth formed a little pout of disapproval. "She's given him the heave-ho, although he wasn't too bothered. Nothing injured but his pride. He's never been lucky in love."

Anderson's impatience had at last overcome his reticence. "So who *was* he bothered about?"

"Don't you know?" Zandra's snort of disapproval was cut short as Mrs. Williams pointed out that it was highly unlikely that the police were psychic.

"Sorry. Mother's right. It was Beryl. Tom's Beryl. They were at school together, and he's always carried a torch for her."

"Bloody hell!" Anderson immediately raised his hands apologetically. "Sorry. Bit surprised. Is that who he fought Hatton over, at the Desdemona?"

"Absolutely." Zandra stopped. "You already knew he was there, didn't you? I haven't dobbed him in?"

"No, you're fine." Robin tried to be reassuring, but he guessed this might put the end to Sam and Zandra's friendship, just when it could be useful. "We'd already heard he was in the fight, although he's denying it. Perhaps you could persuade him to come clean—it would be better all round."

"I'll try, but once he gets a particular idea in his head, you can't shift it."

"He didn't lose that when he lost his spots, did he?" Mrs. Williams muttered, eyes on her book.

"Anyway," Zandra continued blithely, "I guess Tom had a glass or two too many inside him and started sounding off about his love life. Sam overheard and went ballistic."

"Ballistic enough to follow the guy and kill him?" Robin asked the question, then waited, studying Zandra's face, trying to analyse the emotions playing out there.

"I suppose you'd expected me to say 'He couldn't have!' straight away," she replied eventually, "but I can't swear to that. I know it's not in his nature, and he certainly didn't give any indication when we went shopping that he'd been involved in anything worse than a punch-up. And he was distraught at having been stupid enough to get into *that*."

"Does he often get into fights?"

"He did when he was younger. He's got a chip on his shoulder because his dad didn't have as good a job as the other dads or some sob story like that. But a bit of handbags was usually the limit."

Robin nodded. This felt like a measured, thoughtful estimation of character. "So why would he continue to lie about being in the fight? It reeks of guilt."

"Because he's an idiot." Zandra wrinkled her nose. "People often are. They believe that if they keep denying something, they'll somehow change history and it won't have happened. But I don't think he'd have killed Tom just to get rid of a love rival. He'd not have had the ba—guts to face me afterwards if he had. And it would have defeated the object. If Beryl ever got wind of it, she'd never have talked to him again."

That was a shame. The love-rival theory had the advantage of being nearer Robin's "killed by somebody you knew" than the Ulster link did. Although, as he reminded himself for the umpteenth time, it wasn't their case, and coming here hadn't moved them forward in the one that *was*.

Mrs. Williams found her voice once more. "Are you sure it wasn't the Slasher who killed Tom?"

"It's not my case," Robin said, ignoring Anderson's grin, "but we're pretty sure he didn't."

"Jim Phillips was Tom's friend, Mother. He'd never have done anything to hurt him."

"He hurt those women, though." Mrs. Williams folded her book shut; it was one of the more lurid examples of the true crime genre. "Dreadful thing. Mary Carpenter, Katie Russell—she's the one who died—Julie . . ."

"The police aren't interested in your obsession with serial killers." Zandra rolled her eyes. "And anyway, Phillips never actually killed anybody, not during an attack."

Robin shot Anderson a glance—he looked as uncomfortable as Robin at the outbreak of domestic bickering. They left their chairs, thanked Zandra and her mother for their time, then eased themselves out of the door.

"Phew," Anderson said once they couldn't be overheard. "I thought Mrs. W was going to grill us about the most gruesome murders we'd seen."

"I felt the same." Robin rubbed his knuckles together. "We'd better let Cowdrey know about Brunning. I don't envy him sorting out the mess."

"Do you believe Brunning killed Hatton?"

"No. I think Zandra got it spot on. There's something, though." He turned and stared at the house. "One of those two made a remark that rang a bell. My mind's too fuddled to work out what, though."

"I must have missed that. She scares me."

"Zandra or her mother?"

"Both." Anderson grinned. "Take more medicine for that head of yours and maybe the answer will come."

That sounded like a good idea, although Robin didn't have any great hopes it would work. Some things were beyond the power of even paracetamol and codeine.

Chapter Eleven

Dinner on Monday evening was easy. Mrs. Bright had sent them home with a tub of frozen chili con carne, ostensibly because she'd made too much for her to use, but probably because she didn't believe either of them were looking after themselves properly. Adam's own mother was exactly the same. He put it on to cook while Robin went upstairs and got changed.

He didn't want to ask, "Did you ring the estate agent?" as soon as Robin returned to the kitchen, even though he'd been wondering about it all day. What if another major case came along and buggered up everything again?

"Before you ask," Robin said, coming through the door and making a beeline for Campbell, with whom normal relations had been resumed.

"Before I ask what? Or are you talking to Campbell?"

"To you, of course." Robin rubbed the dog behind his ear, which made the answer to the question still uncertain. "I did ring the estate agent. Mum's going to go round there, show him the flat, seeing as I'm a bit tied up."

"Thank you." Adam came over, wound his arm round his partner's waist, then gave him a well-deserved kiss.

"It's funny. Now it's done, it's such a relief. Like a weight off my shoulders." Robin nestled his head against Adam's shoulder, letting himself be held close. "Didn't realise I was so wound up about it inside."

"All better now." Adam hoped Robin would continue feeling better after they'd eaten, because Adam had something else that had been bothering him.

"And even better when we've filled our faces. That smells delicious."

The chili con carne tasted as good as it smelled. After they'd had their fill, Adam suggested they leave the washing-up and take advantage of the fine evening. They could stretch Campbell's legs as well as their own. "If you're not too tired," he added.

"I am, but I reckon half an hour of fresh air would be what the doctor ordered. I could do with clearing my mind."

"Sounds good." Adam got out Campbell's lead, fitting it on to the excited animal—who was evidently elated at such an unexpected treat—while pondering how much he'd be refilling Robin's mind with other stuff.

They wandered along past the church, doing a circuit of the village that would keep them on footpaths rather than blundering down bridleways in the dark. Campbell, who clearly had a fixed notion of where he wanted them to go, tugged Adam round a corner and into the lane leading down to Lindenshaw St. Crispin's school.

"It's not time for me to go back to work, boy." Adam pulled on the lead, but Campbell wasn't to be deflected from his chosen course.

"He's probably doing it to punish me," Robin said, although he didn't have the usual catch in his voice when he referred to schooldays.

"No, he's just reading minds as normal. I had an interesting conversation here today that I need to tell you about."

"Who with?"

"Luke Brunning, of course." Adam lowered his voice, even though they were the only people out and about. "I saw him last evening at church. Struck me as odd at the time. He's not one of the regulars."

"Perhaps he was sending up a prayer for his brother, who's been lying about his involvement in the fight with Hatton."

"That doesn't surprise me. Luke's like a bear with a sore head over it. Blamed me for dobbing Sam in, playing the 'get off, this is personal' card. I pointed out it was personal for me too." Adam shuddered in remembrance of another awkward conversation he'd been forced to have that morning. "Today I asked Chris, headteacher Chris I mean, to appoint Luke a different mentor. I thought I'd better get in and state my side of the case before Luke sounded off. Turns out Luke changed his mind and wanted to stick with me anyway, so I could have saved myself a pile of angst and not made a prat of myself in front of Chris with what Luke called making a mountain out of a molehill."

"I bet you were peeved."

"Bloody livid. There's more to it than making a tit of myself, though."

"Oh yes?" Suddenly Robin's voice took on an official tone.

"He was extremely apologetic afterwards. Asked me to forget what he'd said last evening. How he'd been too upset to think straight. *That* struck me as overegging the pudding, so I wondered if he'd said something he shouldn't." Adam had replayed the conversation in his head until something obvious struck him. "Then I remembered. And when I remembered, I had a quick shufti at his hands."

"His hands?" Robin stopped, clearly bewildered.

"Yes." Adam slipped his arm through Robin's and got him on the move again, following Campbell, who, thank goodness, had at last set his radar for home. "He'd banged one of them on the lychgate last night, and he said he'd have to put another batch of ice on it. Not just put ice on. *Another* batch. Like it was already hurt, which makes sense given his reaction. He didn't hit the gate hard enough to do any real damage, but evidently it was smarting like hell."

"As though his hand was already injured?"

"Precisely. And that's how it appeared. The knuckles had taken a right hammering, and not in the last twenty-four hours." They waited as a car came along, temporarily blinding them, before crossing the road. "I was too nervous to ask him what had happened, but luckily Sally did when we were getting coffee. Luke said he'd been playing football and ran into the goalpost."

"And you didn't believe him?"

"Too right. Not least when he started going into great detail about how the accident had happened. Protesting too much." Time to get his thoughts entirely in the open. "I wondered whether he had an alibi for Friday evening."

"He and Sam were supposed to be together. *I'd* been wondering whether Luke was covering for his brother, but it could be a case of vice versa." Robin kicked at a small stone that lay on the path. "I'd better ring and let Cowdrey know when I get home. Might be coincidence."

"Might be. Although my gut tells me it isn't."

"Hm. What is it with your school?"

"My school? It was yours as well."

Robin snorted. "If I had kids, I wouldn't send any of them there, not with the way it keeps connecting itself to murders."

He was clearly making a joke, but Adam's hackles rose. For all that Lindenshaw St. Crispin's would soon be his *ex*-school, when he left to take up his deputy headship, he still felt protective over the place. *He* was allowed to make snide remarks about it, but others—even ex-pupils—had to watch their manners.

No. Unfair. Robin's got every reason to hate the place. Can you really blame him?

Adam softened his voice. "Maybe . . . it wants to call you back there or something." He'd been about to say, "Maybe it's taking its revenge on you," but that would have been below the belt. "Anyway, it won't be my school for much longer. I can soon shake the dust of it off my feet forever, thank God. I thought I'd feel bad when the moment came to leave, but now it can't come soon enough."

"We'll have to take Campbell up there and let him pee against the railings."

"We'd never persuade him to. He has standards." Adam pulled Robin closer as they stopped at the kerb to let another car pass.

"If it was Luke who thumped me, that would make a lot of sense."

"In what way?"

"It would explain why he left it as a whacking. A hard-nosed villain would have finished me off. We'd been assuming—yes, I know, you should never assume—that the most likely scenario was that somebody had mistaken me for somebody else and only realised mid-thumping."

"Then thank God he's a teacher and retains some sense of morality." Adam shrugged. "He's a nice lad, you know. He could be a very good teacher if he got some of the fire from his belly."

"They say the same of his brother." Robin exhaled loudly, sending a cloud of vapour into a night that was turning chilly.

"I've never told you this, but the Brunnings boys are adopted. They were taken away from their parents before Luke even started school. Violent father, so I'm told. Possibly it's showing in the sons."

"It happens." Robin shrugged. "How did he know where to find me? Find *us*? I'm paranoid enough about Worsley stalking us. Please don't tell me the Brunnings are at it as well."

"I think there's an innocent explanation for that. One which might be another mark against him, though."

"I'm all ears." That professional tone was back in Robin's voice.

"Last Friday I was checking my messages in the staffroom. I asked Sally what she thought of the Florentine, as she'd had her birthday do there last year. Luke was close by; he'd have heard."

"We'll have to get him in for questioning. I can leave it until after the end of the school day tomorrow, if that would help."

"I'd be grateful, thank you. And so would Chris. We've only recently recovered from the last lot of bad press. I don't think Luke will do a runner." Adam laid his hand on Robin's shoulder. "I'm sorry if it turns out to be him who thumped you. Especially if I acted as a catalyst."

"You can repay me by keeping an eye on him tomorrow. I'm sorry if this business ends up causing any trouble for you." It was a dark night, so they risked a kiss before crossing the road and getting into the last stretch of their journey home.

"All worth it if I get paid in kisses."

"It's a mystery, though," Robin said as they broke the embrace.

"What is?"

"Who the people Worsley overheard were discussing, because it doesn't sound like it was me."

"I have no idea what you're talking about."

Robin slipped his arm round Adam's shoulders. "It's work talk. Do you honestly want to hear it?"

"So long as it doesn't involve either of us getting thumped, yes."

"Then I'll tell you about it as we walk home."

Tuesday morning, Robin was straight into Cowdrey's office. He'd thought about ringing in the previous evening but had decided to sleep on it, wanting to reassure himself he wasn't just jumping to conclusions. After Robin laid out what Adam had told him, Cowdrey agreed that Luke had questions to answer, and decided that he and Robin would conduct the interview together at the end of the school day. Robin had begun to plan how best to use the time till then, because they didn't appear to be making any headway on the robberies front, when there was a knock on the door and Anderson appeared, wearing a smug grin.

"They've tracked down Selby. The chap we spoke to at the Wig, the one who identified him, saw Selby in there again last night, with a woman this time, so he did a bit of asking around once they'd gone."

"If only everybody were as helpful." The ironic note in Cowdrey's voice struck a chord with Robin. It certainly would make their investigations simpler.

"He managed to get the girl's name and address, because she'd once lost something at the Wig and had left contact details in case it turned up. He phoned them in this morning. You'll be pleased to hear it's not Beryl or Zandra this time."

"It never crossed my mind." The sergeant would be happy not to be going back to Zandra's again, though.

"We've sent a car to see if he's still lurking there."

"Good work." And very good news. Even if Selby hadn't stayed the night, the woman should be able to give them the heads-up on where he was. Robin got his head down, catching up with paperwork and crossing his metaphorical fingers that they'd soon be in interviewing action.

An hour later, Selby was brought into Stanebridge station by two burly constables who Anderson reckoned had been recruited for the sole purpose of apprehending absconding villains. This particular villain was taken straight to an interview room, where Anderson got the recording equipment set up and Robin went through the proper procedures, among them offering the services of the duty solicitor.

"Got my own, if I need him." Selby shrugged.

Robin, surprised at an old lag not playing the "I want everything I'm entitled to" card, made a note of the refusal for the purposes of the tape, then asked Selby where he was at the time the garage was robbed.

"At home, in bed."

"Honestly? Because we've got a witness who puts you at the scene of the crime, brandishing a knife."

"What witness?" Selby looked affronted. Perhaps he didn't know that Porterfield had been arrested, or he was simply good at acting the innocent. He'd probably had plenty of practice.

"Your friend Porterfield, for a start. He's given us a great account of your mini crime spree." Anderson tapped the manila folder he'd laid on the table, a folder which might contain Porterfield's statement or might be a useful prop.

Selby blanched but managed to keep up the show. "Oh, that wan—idiot. You don't want to believe everything he says. Whoever he was working with, it wasn't me."

"Well, we'll soon verify that. We've got a warrant to search your home, and your girlfriend's. We'll be particularly interested in any knives we find. And any sudden, unaccounted-for influx of funds." Anderson tapped the file again. "No honour among thieves, eh?"

"Anyway, we're in no hurry," Robin said, leaning back in his chair. "We can wait for the search results; they'll be worth it. Meanwhile, we can talk about Mike Edwards."

"Edwards?" Selby started, apparently genuinely surprised this time.

"Yes. You were in prison with him." Robin spoke slowly and facetiously. "Remember?"

"So what if I was? I was in prison with a lot of people." The affronted attitude had returned.

"I bet. But it's Edwards we're interested in. No grudges against him?" Even though it appeared increasingly likely that Luke had been Robin's assailant, they had to keep exploring all the avenues. No assumptions until they had proof.

"Grudges?" Selby's eyebrows shot up. "No way. He's a great bloke."

"Great bloke when he's not duffing people over?" Anderson gave one of his habitual snorts.

"He couldn't help going astray. His brother died and it broke Mike's heart." Selby gave the sergeant a dirty look. "Even the copper who picked him up felt sorry for him."

"You're breaking *our* hearts." Robin mimed playing a violin. "You became friends when serving time."

"Yeah. Mike took me under his wing while I was inside, used to say you had to take care of your family and your mates. I'd have come a cropper if it weren't for him. Did you know he saved my life when some idiot had got hold of a knife and went ballistic with it?"

"Shame he didn't keep taking care of you." Anderson sneered. "We've been told he's gone straight since he came out, although we're not sure we believe it."

"Maybe you've been told right. They reckon he . . . what would you call it . . . saw the light, back when we were in prison. There was a padre used to come in—big bloke, built like a brick shithouse—and Edwards thought the world of him. Said the padre had made him want to change his ways." Selby screwed up his face. "I'm not a great fan of the milk of human kindness, even if it's being peddled by someone who looks like Henry Cooper and who might beat the crap out of you if you don't play ball."

"Is that why Edwards has given up crime? Because he thinks this priest will belt him one if he strays?" Anderson curled his lip.

"Ask him, not me." Selby's mocking laugh showed what he thought of the idea.

Robin drummed his fingers on the table. "You don't approve of leopards changing their spots?"

Selby shook his head. "We'll see how long he gets away with it. I tried to persuade him to consider his position, but he wasn't having any. I might have been better off if he had."

"So you admit you did the robberies? And you tried to get Edwards to join in?"

"I'm admitting nothing. We just had a full and frank conversation about our options." Selby grinned slyly.

"Seems like Edwards is more willing to turn the other cheek than wave a knife in somebody's face. Thank God there's one person with a bit of sense." Robin was being deliberately provocative. Okay, Selby hadn't put his hand up for the robberies, but that was surely a matter of holding their nerve until he realised he had no option but to admit his involvement—that and getting the evidence from his house. Whether Selby cracked now or later didn't matter that much, but Robin had become certain there was something else going on in the man's brain. Some aspect of his demeanour rang bells from previous interviews where villains had tried to hide multiple things.

Anderson sniffed. "Perhaps we should get that padre down here. That would cut the crime rate."

"Put you out of a job," Selby countered with another laugh. "Edwards gave me a bit of a sermon about this turning the other cheek malarkey. No more 'eye for an eye.' I don't agree. Punishment should fit the crime, isn't that what they say?"

"Is it what *you* say?" Robin felt like he was being given a sermon and not a very sincere one at that. "What punishment fits your current crimes?"

"Okay, that's enough." Selby slapped his hands down on the table. "I've told you I had nothing to do with the robberies. If you want anything else from me, I want my brief with me."

"Feel free to contact him as soon as you want, but I'm afraid that's *not* it." Robin was determined to keep control of the interview. Surely they could squeeze a little bit more out. "We've got other things to ask you about. Like where you were on Friday."

"Friday? Which Friday?"

"The Friday just gone," Anderson said, in the sort of voice you'd use for a four-year-old.

"I was out with my girlfriend. The one whose domestic bliss you so rudely interrupted this morning." Selby smiled complacently.

"She can verify that?"

"She can. So can her brother and his wife, because we were having dinner together."

"Until when?" Robin might be flogging the proverbial dead horse, but he needed to ask.

"About midnight. We had to chuck them out of the door in the end. I need my beauty sleep," Selby added with another smug grin. "Why do you want to know?"

"We'll tell you when you've got your solicitor in," Robin replied, although he wasn't sure there would be any point going down that particular avenue again.

After the interview was properly concluded, the recording finished, and Selby taken away to make his call before being left to stew in his own juice in the cells, Robin remained at the interview room table, turning over things in his mind.

"Penny for them, sir."

"Eh?" Robin replied, once he'd twigged he was being spoken to.

"Penny for your thoughts." Anderson shifted in his chair, clearly uneasy at the uncharacteristic silence.

"Not sure I have any, to be honest. Only a nagging feeling that we've gone down a siding and away from the main track."

"I'm not sure I follow."

"I'm not sure I do, either." Robin shook his head. "For all that I'd put a tenner on us having cleared up the robberies, at one point it felt like the interview was going somewhere else before Selby realised quick enough to put the brakes on."

"I didn't really notice that. Maybe I should listen to the tape again."

"Why not?" Had Robin imagined Selby's reaction? Possibly he was seeing what he wanted to see, a nebulous appearance of relief in the suspect that the robberies were the only thing he was being fingered for. Perhaps they were hunting connections where no connections were to be made. "Leave it for now. If there's something to come to the surface, it'll come."

"Like cream to the top of the milk?"

Robin rolled his eyes. "More like scum to the top of the pond."

By the time they reached the afternoon, the search of Selby's rented flat had showed up a pair of knives, hidden in the bottom of a wardrobe, which fitted the description they'd had from the robberies and which the people from the garage and the bookie's shop could have a gander at once the forensics had been done. It also turned up a wodge of cash, stashed in one of those fake baked beans tins that always appeared in gadget catalogues, especially in the run-up to Christmas. Finally the police were getting close to having enough to satisfy even the most picky of Crown Prosecution Service staff.

Robin left Anderson to conduct the next interview with Selby, especially as he hadn't yet worked out what was bugging him about the previous interrogation, and an uncluttered mind might be more efficient for questioning. The sergeant could take Davis along for the experience. She deserved something more exciting than a continual diet of checking and cross-referencing.

He and Cowdrey were heading for Lindenshaw.

Adam had suggested he have a word with Chris in advance, so the headteacher would have wind of potential problems ahead, yet again, for the school. He'd texted Robin at lunchtime to say that Chris had taken the news pragmatically, although he'd asked if any initial interview could take place discreetly, off-site. It felt like a military operation, waiting in the car with Cowdrey in the lane outside the school but not in view of it, while Chris manoeuvred an unsuspecting Luke Brunning towards them. Strictly speaking, Robin wasn't supposed to be there, but his boss had insisted. The main active cases in the area were far too intertwined to allow for continued demarcation.

When the young teacher caught sight of Robin, he blanched, and a case of chasing a bolting witness looked like it might be on, but he managed to regain his composure.

"I'll leave you to it." The headteacher patted Luke's back before beating a tactful retreat.

"In the car or on the hoof?" Cowdrey asked Luke, exiting the passenger door.

"Out the car but down the road, please. Somewhere parents can't see us."

"I know the very place." Robin led the way to an old bus shelter, set back from the road and partly overgrown, unused for years since the service was stopped, but the location for many a bout of hijinks when he was a boy. He'd had his first puff of a cigarette here, and been violently sick afterwards. Kissed his first girl here, too, and felt just as ill.

"You said you were with your brother on Friday evening at the time Inspector Bright was attacked." Cowdrey asked the question while Robin, leaning against the shelter wall, had his pen poised to make notes.

"I did. I wasn't." Luke glanced at his hands, then crossed his arms to hide them. "I guess it's too late to hide it. Chris always tells the kids that honesty is the best policy."

"Chris is right." Cowdrey sighed. "I wish he could have told your brother that too."

"Sam's not the sharpest pencil in the box. He'd have owned up to that fight straight away if Hatton hadn't been killed. He wanted to buy himself some thinking time, but the longer you leave it, the harder it becomes to tell the truth."

Robin held his tongue. For the first time he felt a real sympathy for the young officer who'd found himself trapped in a web of his own making.

Cowdrey carried on. "He's learned the hard way, then. Now, if you weren't with Sam on Friday, where was he? Beating up the inspector?"

It was a good question, playing on Luke's sense of brotherly loyalty.

"No. He wouldn't do anything like that, the same way he wouldn't stab anybody." Luke uncrossed his arms, let his bruised knuckles come into view. "I'm the idiot who did that. I was angry—"

Cowdrey held up his hand. "If we're going to carry on this conversation, we need to give you the caution."

Luke turned even whiter, but nodded. Cowdrey used the proper words, so familiar to everyone now from the popular diet of television cop shows, then said, "You were angry. Who with?"

"Myself, as much as the police. I thought I'd let something slip to Adam and he'd passed it on to you." He gave Robin a sidelong glance.

"He hadn't. Not initially, anyway." Robin tried to keep his voice calm.

Luke shrugged. "Okay. Maybe I got that wrong. Maybe. But I wasn't thinking straight. I didn't mean to hurt you that much, honest."

"That's not what it feels like from my side. If you didn't want me to end up in hospital, what the hell *did* you mean to do?"

"I don't know. Frighten you. Deflect attention from Sam." The teacher stood, sulking like a surly teenager who'd been caught smoking behind the bike shed, a picture of injured pride, angry not at what he'd done but at getting caught. "I did ring 999 and get you help."

"For that small service I am eternally grateful." Robin's sarcastic tone earned him a dirty look from his boss. "Why didn't you finish me off while you had the chance?"

"I'm not a murderer, any more than Sam is." Luke kicked at a rotting post, then pulled his foot back sharply, perhaps worried that he'd get done for criminal damage as well as assault. "I remember telling myself I should take your mobile phone or something. Give the impression it had been a robbery. Then I decided that would be wrong, and what would the kids in my class think of me if they heard? I guess that was the only sensible thought I had the whole fucking evening."

"You're right." Cowdrey glanced at Robin, shaking his head. "We need to take you down to the station now and get a statement. You'll probably be charged and bailed."

"Can we go and tell Chris first?" Luke's tone was bleak, possibly seeing his potentially glittering career going straight down the plughole. "News of this is going to spread like wildfire, and he'll need to go into damage limitation."

"I'll come with you." Cowdrey motioned for Robin to wait for them. "My face isn't as well known here as Inspector Bright's. That might buy him some time."

Robin waited by his car. Despite the terrible things the school had done to him in his schoolboy days, it didn't deserve any further crap dumped on it. It was highly unlikely Luke would be allowed to return to his job for the moment, even if he was on bail, and chances were he'd end up losing that job altogether, and be thrown out of teaching to boot. Bringing the profession into disrepute was a big concern these days, and it cast a shadow on everyone, accused and their colleagues, guilty and innocent. It was just as well Adam was moving to pastures new; perhaps he and his lover would both get a clean break from the place and the bad luck that was currently dogging it.

Close by where they'd parked, there was a small fence, bounding a newish estate of houses that hadn't been there in his day and that would probably be beyond even his and Adam's combined income. The fence was exactly the right height for leaning on and thinking, and Robin had plenty to think about, not least the nagging sensation that he'd been given two vital clues to the jigsaw. It was simply a matter of linking them together. Or, to be accurate, linking them together when he'd worked out what they were.

An aspect of Selby's demeanour. A word or phrase Mrs. Williams had said, she of the serial-killer obsession. He remembered her reciting the list of women who'd been attacked. Mary Carpenter, Katie something or other who had died, Julie.

Julie. Wasn't that the name of Selby's sister? Selby who was so keen on an eye for an eye. Selby who'd apparently said he'd attacked the wrong man. Selby who wanted clarification about which Friday he was being asked about.

Robin got his phone out, but the mobile phone signal black spot centred on the school evidently extended up here. Perhaps it was as well, given that he shouldn't be rushing at this like a bull in a china shop. There were plenty of Julies, plenty of people who believed in taking an appropriate revenge. Robin's team would need to make sure the audit trail of facts worked out before they questioned Selby further.

Or until Root questioned him. Hatton's murder was still *his* case, no matter how persistent it was about making itself Robin's. He forced himself to hide his smug grin; how enjoyable would it be if the Stanebridge yokels cleared up yet another investigation for the Abbotston townies?

Chapter Twelve

Wednesday morning dawned sunny and clear. The day was made even brighter by the news that Selby, who had continued to maintain his innocence the day before, insisting that he'd been fitted up for the robberies, had decided that he wanted to amend his statement in an effort to come clean. Maybe this was part of a plan to head off the police sniffing around for any connection to the Slasher attacks, but if so, they were already wise to the possibility.

Robin explained his thinking to Anderson, who liked this new theory a lot, although Cowdrey had been circumspect when Robin had told him about it earlier. Which was fortunate, given the way the rest of the day progressed.

Ten o'clock, there was a decidedly tentative knock on Robin's office door. Davis's face, as she entered the office, appeared unusually hesitant.

"Why do I have the feeling you're bearing bad news?" It was a lie calling it only a feeling—Robin was certain things had gone tits up.

"Because I am. Probably." She took a seat. "I've checked the records, and the Julie who was the first of the Slasher's victims is Julie Flowers, maiden name Jones. Nothing to do with the Julie Pearson, maiden name Selby, who's our bloke's sister."

"Bugger." Thank God they hadn't gone with Anderson's madcap idea of dashing straight round to her house, because as far as the sergeant was concerned, that *had* to be the connection between the two cases. Sometimes it was too easy for the sergeant to get so caught up in his and his colleagues' theories—especially when he was on a roll of successful ones—that he forgot about the basic checking of facts beforehand.

"Indeed, sir." Davis grinned. "*Omelette sur la visage* narrowly avoided."

"What's that?" Anderson asked.

"Egg on your face." Robin thumped the desk with his fists a couple of times, but it didn't make him any happier.

"Lucky that we didn't tell Root anything," Anderson pointed out.

"You're telling me." At least damage limitation could be applied. The only people who knew they'd barked up the wrong tree were Davis and Cowdrey, and they'd both understand the thrill of the chase and how you ended up blinkered sometimes. Like Root appeared to be blinkered about the IRA; Anderson's mole was gleefully keeping them updated about the lack of progress in the Hatton investigations. Please God stories of their own shortcomings weren't making the reverse journey.

"Could be we're trying to make connections that aren't there." That was rich, coming from Anderson. "Perhaps these cases have overlapped as much as they're going to."

"Perhaps."

"There's one line we could go back over." Robin drummed his fingers along the desktop. "Phillips."

"Phillips?" Anderson's eyebrows shot up. "What's he got to say he hasn't already said?"

"I don't know. But even when he was taken ill, he was determined to tell me he'd help catch whoever did this." Robin recalled, with a shiver, the pallid grey tones of the chef's face, and his own worry that the bloke was about to peg out. "Perhaps now that he doesn't have to hide anything about the Slasher attacks, he'll be more use."

Anderson's expression suggested he didn't share that optimism, but he'd always back his boss up to the hilt. "How are you going to persuade Cowdrey to let you do that, given that it's not our bleeding case anymore and there's no useful connection to the one we do have?"

That was the million-pound question, wasn't it? The answer to which couldn't exist, because the chain of logic kept saying that they'd gone as far as they could, that they had no business pursuing this case any further.

Davis, who'd gathered her stuff but showed no sign of going as yet, suddenly chirped up. "Selby said he'd attacked the wrong bloke."

Robin wagged his finger at her. "I don't expect you to state the bleeding obvious. That's my sergeant's job."

She made a sarcastic face. "You know it wasn't you he hit in error, so we've assumed he thought he was attacking the Slasher. Won't the forensics on those knives show a connection?"

That was a very good point. "Only if we ask them to look for one. They weren't actually used on anybody during the robberies, so nobody's going to waste money ordering a set of tests unless they can be sure they'll find something on them that would help a conviction." Robin tried to form the right question to put to Cowdrey. "Everything's a bit chicken and egg. We need to have enough of a strong connection to justify asking for the tests, but we can't get that connection unless we're allowed to poke about in Root's sandpit."

"Black suede." Davis slammed her hand on the desk. "Sorry, sir. Got overexcited."

"You're forgiven." Robin would forgive her just about anything if this worked out. "The officers who searched Selby's place were after knives, money, whatever would link him to Porterfield and the robberies. What if we go back and have another shufti, only we'll keep more of an open mind?"

"Great idea." Anderson rubbed his hands together. "Want me to drive?"

"Not this time. Davis here deserves to get out and about. She needs to develop her skills for when she's a sergeant." He nodded at Davis, who beamed.

"What about me, then?" Anderson frowned.

"You can go and see the girlfriend. We need her statement—what he was doing when, including the Friday Hatton was attacked, if he's been flashing cash about, all the usual stuff."

"If he's got any black suede gloves? If he's been talking about duffing anyone over?"

"Yes, but only if you can ask about those things subtly. We don't want to risk his getting the wind up just yet." Robin fingered his lip; there was something else he'd meant to say too.

"Shall I go and interview his sister as well?"

That was it. "Absolutely. Especially given the fact that Porterfield mentioned her. Only, be careful with any questions concerning where he was and what he was doing that Friday—hide them in amongst a load of other stuff."

"I'm not wet behind the ears, sir." Anderson's grin belied his theatrically injured tone.

"Never said you were. I'm making sure we're singing from the same hymn sheet."

"Don't you mean the same charge sheet?"

Robin groaned. Hopefully Davis wouldn't be so fond of making bad jokes.

By the time they got to Selby's flat, Robin had discovered that Davis was a lot more interesting to chat with than Anderson, if less talkative generally. How little he actually knew about this woman, even though they'd been colleagues for the best part of two years. But then, how well did you generally get to know the people you worked with? Adam was Luke's mentor but hadn't noticed he had a violent streak.

"Do you think we will find something to link him to Hatton?" she asked as they turned into Selby's road.

"Who knows? Even if we do, black suede isn't that uncommon." And they were pursuing a long shot. Still, Robin was hopeful of finding proper evidence—just enough to keep pursuing the connection would do. They hadn't brought the full bunny-suit rig, but they had everything they needed in terms of gloves and evidence bags. Real life wasn't like the television shows, with detectives stomping over the crime scene and contaminating stuff left, right, and centre.

After ten minutes of turning everything out and over, it seemed likely that the evidence bags wouldn't get used. The only unusual thing they'd found had been some vile green writing paper, and all that suggested was a lack of taste. No sign of anything made of black suede, whether gloves or shoes or whatever. If Selby had ever had a pair and used them that night Hatton was attacked, they could be long gone, stuck in a convenient dustbin on the other side of town as soon as he noticed they'd got blood on them.

"No camel-coloured coat either, sir," Davis, who'd been rummaging through every cupboard she could find, said despondently.

Robin blew out his cheeks. Maybe that was long gone as well. He went into the kitchen to give the bin one more check, even though it must have been inspected half a dozen times.

"Bugger!" He jumped back as his shin hit something wooden that was sticking out from under a worktop.

"What's up?" Davis came bounding over.

"I whacked my leg. I'll have a bruise the size of Andorra tomorrow." As the pain subsided, he realised what he'd collided with. Even Campbell didn't have a basket as solidly made—or as sharply cornered—as this one. "Does Selby have a dog?"

"Not that I'm aware of. Why?" Davis had come to the kitchen door. "Oh, dog basket, right. Well, the place doesn't smell doggy. And I don't remember seeing any dog food in the cupboard. Could belong to the people he rents from." She stopped, brow wrinkling. "Okay. What am I missing?"

"Look in the basket. The blanket. Or what's being used as one."

Davis got out her disposable gloves, slipped them on, then gingerly lifted a corner up for inspection. "It appears to be a woollen coat with the buttons cut off. It's certainly camel coloured. Doesn't smell or look like a dog's used it, though."

"Perhaps he was planning to get a puppy. Or perhaps he's simply hiding this 'blanket' in plain sight?" Much harder to get rid of a coat than a pair of gloves, given the bulk of the thing, but they mustn't run before they could walk. "I'm ringing Cowdrey. I bet he'll let us get the forensics people here to do a proper job."

"Good luck, sir."

"Do I need it?" Cowdrey had always covered his back, but now Robin had momentary doubts. Only one way to tell; he got his phone and dialled.

"Cowdrey speaking." The boss's crisp tones came on the line.

"Got a development in the Selby case, sir." Robin told him what they'd found in the dog basket. "I know it's a bit of a long shot, but we can't leave it without knowing one way or the other."

"Hmm. I agree. Especially given your propensity for tripping over important bits of evidence."

Quite literally in this case, although Robin saved that quip for the time being. "So do we get the CSIs in?" Grace would jump at the chance of turning up things that even *they'd* missed.

Once Cowdrey had agreed to that, there was another question to ask, although Robin dreaded getting the wrong answer. "Should we mention this to Root?"

"Not at the moment. We've no proof as yet there *is* a connection to Hatton, and Root's far too busy with his IRA bloke. They've tracked him down at last, *and* found he was in England at the time Hatton was attacked. He flew back to Belfast two days later."

Robin swallowed hard. Was the IRA thread going to be the right one after all, and when Root pulled it, would the whole tapestry *he'd* woven come apart? "Has he got an alibi?"

"Yes, but Root's boasting that he can pull it to shreds. Whether this Irish bloke has black suede gloves or a camel-coloured anything, I don't know. I *do* know Root's going down the same forensics trail as you, so you might have to wait for your results."

"I'll be patient, sir. I can find plenty to occupy me."

"Like Phillips? I guess you want my permission to go and talk to him now?"

Robin almost heard the smile his boss must have been wearing. "You've read my mind. Selby himself can wait until the forensics return. He's not going anywhere."

"Okay. I've got your back on this."

"Thanks. Although I've got to ask you: are we barking up the wrong tree? Hello? Hell-o-o?" The line went dead—he'd lost the signal.

When he got through to Cowdrey again, the boss fumed about why it was their misfortune to live in what seemed like the most remote—or maybe the most old-fashioned—part of England, at least where the mobile phone network was concerned. "In answer to your question, no. I think both Root and his guv'nor *are*, and they're too blind to see. Or could be you're nothing but a stupidly lucky bugger."

"You know what they say, sir. The harder you work, the luckier you get."

Cowdrey snorted. "Get away with you. Go and put that hard work into action."

"Are we on?" Davis asked as Robin put his mobile back in his pocket.

"We? Are you slipping into Anderson's shoes?"

Davis rolled her eyes. "You know what I mean, sir."

He knew. And she'd earned as much right as anyone to be part of the team who were in at the kill. "Yep. I'll get Grace in here, and then

I'll arrange for us to visit Phillips, although that will probably have to wait until tomorrow. It won't hurt—I could do with time to get my thoughts together."

He had plenty of food for thought already, and that pile was added to when he met Anderson back at the station.

Selby's girlfriend had insisted he was with her the night Hatton was attacked. The trouble was she'd also insisted she was with him at the time of the two robberies.

"I think if I'd asked her where he was when we were interviewing him, she'd have sworn she'd had him right at her side for the whole time." Anderson rolled his eyes. "Loyal to a fault."

"Does she own a dog?" Robin enjoyed his sergeant's bemusement at the question.

Anderson frowned. "Not that I'm aware, but I interviewed her at her office, so there could have been one at home. Why?"

Robin related what he and Davis had found at Selby's place. "That old coat makes me think there's a connection, although I have no idea why he'd want to attack Hatton. Any corroboration for his alibis?"

"Only the Friday you were attacked. The family gathering. Which is interesting in itself, seeing as *that's* the crime we know he didn't commit."

"Indeed." If the girlfriend was covering for Selby, and potentially perjuring herself in the process—should she be called to appear at his trial—it suggested she was both besotted with him and would cover whatever he said. Did she believe he had been committing a robbery the night Hatton was attacked? Or had he actually been committing a robbery, one they didn't know of yet?

Were they barking up the wrong tree, and a tree in somebody else's forest while they were at it?

Chapter Thirteen

The evening was unseasonably warm, ideal for taking sandwiches, cakes, and a jug of Pimms into the garden and pretending to be on holiday somewhere exotic, rather than having dinner at home in Lindenshaw after a hard day's work. Adam had made the food, while Robin had got the table and chairs from the shed to give them their first airing of the year. As they ate and drank, Campbell gambolled about the garden like a puppy, making an ass of himself by chasing bumblebees and any other insects he happened to spot.

"Campbell!" Adam tried to distract the Newfoundland from his attempt to eat a bee. "We should let him get stung. Teach him a lesson."

"Would it really teach him a lesson?" Robin smiled ruefully.

Adam shrugged. "Probably not. For a dog who can demonstrate an almost human intelligence, that same dog can be incredibly dim at times."

"I know the feeling. It's been a bit like that at work today."

Adam topped up their glasses. "Tell Uncle Adam all about it."

Robin took a sip of drink. "You do make a good Pimms. It's an art."

"Thank you, but stop changing the subject."

Robin raised his right hand, the left being too occupied with his glass. "Guilty as charged. Anderson and I came close to making a major cock-up, because we'd got carried away with a great theory." He launched into a story of robbers and mystery men with posh accents and people hiding something and sisters called Julie who didn't turn out to be the correct Julie. Adam just about followed everything.

"That'll teach Anderson."

"He's as likely to learn from experience as Campbell." Robin took a deep breath, another drink, then said, "Did Mike Edwards have a girlfriend? You know, standing up in the box to give a character reference, or sitting wringing her hands in the gallery?"

"I can't remember. I think there was something about his wife having left him. More excuses for his behaviour. Why do you ask?"

"I'm trying to make connections between a group of men and they won't be made, so I'm returning to basics. One of which is starting with friends and family. I'll get Davis back on the legwork again."

The sun, which had hidden itself behind some high clouds, reappeared to bathe them in warmth. They sipped their Pimms in contented silence while Campbell kept up his pursuit of the inedible.

"Those clippings you kept." Robin's words jerked Adam out of a state of semi-somnolence.

"Yes? What about them?" Maybe he'd missed an important part of the conversation.

"I was wondering if you chucked them away in a fit of pique when I made a tit of myself last week." Robin smiled, the boyish grin that had been one of the factors in Adam first falling head over heels for him. The boyish grin that made a man turn to putty. Perhaps, after they'd done whatever Robin needed to do with the clippings, they could go and do what Adam needed to do in their bed. That micro-nap had supplied another burst of energy.

"I'm not that daft. I put them back in their box. Why?"

"I might check if they mention the rest of his family."

"They did. Don't you remember the family picture? Cosy little domestic scene in their garden or something." Adam put down his drink, left his chair, and was halfway through the door into the house when he had an attack of the bleeding obvious. "Is this another one of your wild geese?"

"I sincerely hope not. Promise you'll forgive me if it is."

"You're forgiven." Adam had no intention of falling out with Robin for the time being. His hormones were starting to run as rampant as they had back in his juror days; at least it would be easier to get the desired outlet for them now. He fetched the box and returned to the garden, where Campbell had at last given up his hunting and was settled at Robin's feet. After a few seconds of rummaging, he laid out on the crumb-ridden table a half spread from the local newspaper. "Here. That's the one. Does it help?"

"Might do." Robin picked it up to better read the faded caption. "Hold on. Got your iPad to hand?"

"Am I taking on Davis's role? Now I know what a rotten time that girl must have at your beck and call." However, he fetched it. "What do you want me find out?"

"The names of the Slasher's victims." Robin took another slow, thoughtful sip of his Pimms. "For starters."

"Okay. I've got the local newspaper site bookmarked, so that should be easy enough." Adam knew where this was going. "Julie, who wasn't the Julie you wanted. You know about her."

"Yep." Robin rubbed Campbell's ear.

"Then there's Mary Carpenter and poor Katie Russell. Ah, Katie." Adam looked up. "You're hoping that's Katie Russell née Edwards?"

"Yes. I don't suppose you can find that out for me?" Robin didn't sound hopeful.

"It's a long shot, but I'll put my google-fu onto it."

Fifteen minutes and another glass of Pimms later, the google-fu had failed, Adam unable to identify the magic combination of words that would bring them the right search results.

"Don't worry. It can wait until the morning." Robin drained his glass. "Would an early night be on the cards?"

Adam knew what "early night" implied; the sooner they could complete the pre-bed clearing up and getting Campbell sorted routine, the better. Unfortunately, inspiration put erotic plans on hold. "Sally might know."

"Sally?"

"Sally at school. She knows everything about the Slasher case."

"A lot of people seem to have been in the same position," Robin said drily. "But if the information about Katie Russell's maiden name isn't in the public domain, I'm not sure how much help she can be."

"Didn't you realise that Sally knows everything? Including a whole lot of inside stuff on the Slasher, because she knows one of the victims. Whatever she's got to say will be gold standard, I promise." Adam got up, heading to the kitchen to fetch his phone.

"I can't remember which, but with any luck, it'll be the one you're interested in."

Their luck was in. Sally's husband had been at school with Katie Russell, back when she was Katie Edwards. He also reckoned that Phillips had first targeted Katie during a birthday trip to the Florentine. At that point Adam had handed the phone over to Robin and let him make a note of anything that might be relevant.

"So what's all this about?" Adam asked when Robin was at last allowed to end the call.

"Remember I said Selby was hiding something? And that he was indebted to Edwards?"

"The Julie who wasn't the right Julie thing? Yep."

"I've got this mad idea come into my head that he might have attacked Hatton thinking *he* was the Slasher. Taking revenge, not on behalf of his own sister, but Edwards's." Robin picked up his glass, then drained it. "Didn't realise until later that he'd got the wrong guy."

"Whew." Adam whistled. "Just as well *we* didn't go to the Florentine that night. If Edwards is still your doppelganger, *you* might have been the one he picked on."

"Have you had too much Pimms?" Robin grinned. "It wasn't Edwards they were after, and I don't resemble Hatton."

Adam, feeling like a fool, pleaded tiredness and a bloody hard day trying to get the kids in his class to understand rotational symmetry. "It's amazing I can think at all."

"It's the doubles confusing you. They confused us as well, especially when we thought I was mistaken for somebody else. Bloody stupid to miss the most important mistaken identity of the lot. Touch wood." Robin caressed the arm of his chair.

Adam went over, leaned down, and kissed him—on the brow, his cheek, his nose. "You ring Cowdrey while I clear away and get Campbell settled for the night. To hell with the washing-up. Let's go to bed."

"Sounds good."

Adam was still waiting for Campbell to finish his last visit to his favourite tree when Robin reappeared. "Can't get Cowdrey's phone. His number's unavailable. I'll try again later."

"Maybe it's that." Adam pointed at a vast, iron-grey cloud creeping nearer. "Buggering up the signal." He ushered Campbell in as the first drops of rain appeared.

They'd no sooner reached the bedroom than the heavens opened in earnest, resulting in a dash to shut the window as the sudden deluge lashed against it.

"Bloody typical." Adam mopped spots of water off the windowsill with his handkerchief. "Did you know my grandfather served in Burma? He'd tell me tales about raindrops the size of old pennies swamping the soldiers when they were playing hockey or trying to parade. Never thought we'd get a monsoon in Lindenshaw."

"I like it." Robin wound his arms around him, nestling his head on Adam's. "Significant moments of our lives appear to be played out to an accompaniment of rain."

"I'd never thought of that." Adam flicked through his mental notebook, back to the first time they'd made love. They'd watched the weather turning foul through these very bedroom windows as they bridged the gulf of space and expectation between them. It had been no simple thing to move beyond rozzer and witness. What they'd done since had been part of an unhurried progression, slowly venturing into a deeper understanding of each other's needs and desires. A sudden flash of lightning forked down through the clouds, followed swiftly by a deafening rumble of thunder. "I do hope that's not a sign of celestial displeasure."

Robin chuckled softly, sending shivers up Adam's neck. "If I thought you believed that, I'd be out of here like a shot. How can something that feels so right be in any way wrong?"

"True." Adam turned round to start the kisses where they'd left off. Thank God that through the challenges of life—being in and coming out of the closet, dealing with sympathetic people and rampant bigots, let alone dealing with a proper, grown-up relationship—they'd both managed to keep some degree of faith. "Possibly He'll send a rainbow afterwards, to show how pleased He is we've made up again."

"Afterwards?" Robin chuckled once more. "After what?"

"Don't play dim. You know what."

"Ah. A bit of the old 'you know what.'" Robin was laughing full pelt now, shoulders heaving. Adam pushed him backwards two strides, then onto the bed.

"How I put up with you beats me." Adam needed to add to his thoughts about keeping faith, something about needing to keep a sense of humour.

"It's because you love my magnificent body." Robin struck a caricature of a seductive pose on the bed.

"Modest with it." Adam pounced, pinning his partner down. "I certainly love you, you great pudding."

"You say the nicest things."

"I do the nicest things, too," Adam said, before setting about proving it.

Next morning, Robin headed off to the station with a distinct spring in his step. The residual romantic glow, and his boss's delight at what he'd reported when the storm had passed over, even saw him through the car journey from Stanebridge later with a noticeably grumpy sergeant at his side.

With Cowdrey's connivance, they'd managed to keep their visit to Phillips sufficiently under wraps that Root hadn't got wind of it, or so Anderson's spy reckoned. Robin suspected he—or she, he'd never quite established who was feeding them this stuff—must have reckoned right. Otherwise they'd have heard about it, in the form of a ton of bricks coming their way from Abbotston. Anyway, they still didn't have enough evidence to incontrovertibly link the two crimes, so for the moment they were free agents.

"I hate coming here." Anderson shivered as they drew up outside Highwood Prison, the nearest maximum security unit to Abbotston. A good forty minutes' drive from Stanebridge in the general direction of London, it held a motley collection of murderers, terrorists, and sex offenders.

"You've made that plain. You're as irritable as when you had an ingrowing toenail."

"This is worse." The sergeant screwed up his face. "There's something incongruous about finding a place like this, accommodating inmates like these, in such a nice setting."

He had a point. The rolling countryside seemed incompatible with an establishment housing lifers. "Wasn't it Sherlock Holmes who talked about more evil being committed in the country than in the city? He said something like that, anyway."

Anderson, whose reading tastes didn't get beyond conspiracy-theory thrillers, shrugged. "I don't know. I can't see rural England being as ridden with crime as the telly makes out."

Robin nodded. "And long may that remain true." They'd had enough knives and assaults and other atypical Stanebridge crimes to last them the rest of the year. He could do with a month or so of low-level drug dealing and joyriding.

Anderson took a deep breath and, with a weary "Shall we get this over and done with?" opened the passenger-side door.

"Yep. Dawdling will only make it worse."

Waiting in the interview room didn't appear to improve Anderson's mood. He prowled around, muttering about "decor in the style of institutional cheer" until Robin ordered him to sit down and behave.

Phillips, as he came into the interview room under guard, looked content enough with life on remand, even though signs of his recent injuries were plain. Staying in the hospital wing must have made him more comfortable. Robin's chat with the prison governor on arrival had revealed that the guy was apparently showing genuine remorse for what he'd done. The governor said that, according to the psychologist's initial assessment, it was likely that twenty-nine or thirty days of the month, Phillips would seem to be a real gentleman, and on the other day he might be unable to prevent his monstrous side coming out. Clearly that could only be verified over the next few weeks, but Phillips had given the explanation and stated he hated himself for the fact. Robin was going to take that with a pinch of salt, but Anderson—who'd been having a quiet word with one of the warders at the same time—suggested that the theory might be true.

"I hoped you'd be back," Phillips said as he took a seat. "Didn't reckon you'd take so long."

"It's not officially our case anymore. Not so far as Hatton or the attacks on women are concerned." Robin chose his words carefully. They couldn't pussyfoot around the reason that Phillips was on remand, but Robin didn't want the conversation to get waylaid by the witness going into sackcloth-and-ashes mode. "We've been up to our armpits in armed robberies."

"Oh." Phillips frowned. "You didn't get my message, then?"

"Sorry?" Robin glanced at Anderson, who shrugged.

"Ah. Clearly not. I asked Laughing Boy to tell you that I wanted to talk to you."

"Laughing Boy?" Robin felt as confused as his sergeant appeared.

"Yes. My pet name for Inspector Root, as he never cracks a smile. And is that Root as in 'filling,' because he's that painful?"

Robin stifled a snigger more successfully than Anderson managed to. Funny how the message hadn't filtered back to them. Did Root not consider it relevant? "He didn't pass on any communication like that. Although if he thought you wanted to talk about Hatton, he'd not necessarily have felt the need to. As I said, that's his case now." Robin's words stuck in his craw; Root's sheer bloody-mindedness was beyond a joke.

Phillips snorted. "Maybe he'll need you to solve that for him too." He glanced from Robin to Anderson, then back again, a satisfied smile breaking out. "Well, that was a lucky guess, wasn't it?"

"Lucky guess?"

"I've been wondering if you were the bloke who'd connected the accident I had and the lack of an attack that night." Phillips's face contorted at the word "attack."

"Not me who made the connection. You have to thank Sergeant Anderson for that."

"Then I will. Thank you for saving me from myself." Phillips inclined his head at Anderson, flushed at what appeared to be genuine gratitude. "You've no idea what it's like to live in a soul divided, half of you wanting it to stop and half of you desperate for it to go on."

"You had a message for me." Robin, speaking quietly and authoritatively, returned to the matter in hand.

"I did. I do. It relates to that day in the hospital when you came to question me. I thought I'd breathed my last. Came over all peculiar."

"We remember. Gave us a hell of a shock, but not as much as it must have given you."

Phillips grinned. "Funny thing was I'd not been too concerned about the injuries I got in the car crash—I was simply glad to be alive—but it appears the shock of hearing about Tom was the last straw." He shuddered. "I thought I was having a heart attack."

"*Was* it your ticker?" Anderson asked him.

"No, thank God. Just the effect of anxiety or jolt to the system or something, the doctors reckoned, but they tested me to high heaven because it could have been anything, given the state I was in. I was so doped up to the eyeballs, I had no idea how bad my injuries really were."

Anxiety. With the evidence of the blood and fibres in his car, and a pair of rozzers sitting at his bedside, he'd have had a lot to be anxious about.

"Go on," Robin urged him.

"There was something else. I couldn't talk about this at the time, because I was still a free man. Once I was arrested, the case was altered." Phillips sat silent for a moment, fingers nervously tracing figures on the table. "I received threatening letters, soon after . . . soon after the last attack I made. And don't ask, as your colleague Laughing Boy Root did, why I didn't report the threats to the police."

"We won't. I suspect the answer to the question would be stating the bleeding obvious." Trust Root to miss the point. Robin steepled his hands to his chin. "Is that what you wanted to tell me?"

"That's where it all starts. It's where it goes that might be more important."

"Wait a minute. Before we go anywhere else, can we focus on the threats for a moment?" Anderson tapped his pen against his notepad. "How many? How did they come?"

"Three letters. Each one addressed to me, by name, at the restaurant. Discreetly done so they looked like a business mailing."

"Hold on," Robin cut in. "If S . . . he . . . whoever it was, knew your identity, why the hell didn't he shop you to us?" He stopped himself using Selby's name, wanting to keep that as a surprise. "Why risk that you'd attack someone else?"

"I guess he—and I'm assuming from the fact you said 'he' you've got a name in the frame—wanted to play the 'vengeance is mine' card. He wasn't going to be satisfied with an arrest and me getting banged up in jail; I know that from what he said in the letters. He made it very plain what he wanted to do. Letting the punishment fit the crime, he said."

Robin and his sergeant shared a knowing glance. "You could guess what that punishment might mean. Did you expect to receive your retribution before you had the chance to attack again? Before the next new moon?"

"Of course. So I made sure I took care going to and from my car. Locked the door when I was driving, all that malarkey."

"And how had he worked out you were the Slasher when the police hadn't yet made the connection?"

"A hunch, he said. Bloody stupid, isn't it? Same stroke of luck you had, I guess. He talked about it in his letter, although he didn't specify exactly what it was." Phillips closed his eyes and shuddered. Revulsion at what he'd done or anger at getting found out? Robin couldn't tell.

Anderson, who seemed less edgy now that they were down to proper police work, asked, "This is probably going to go straight onto your list of pointless questions, but did you keep any of those letters?"

"What do you think?" Phillips spread his hands on the table. "I put them through the shredder. I wish I *had* kept them now, if it would help convict whoever attacked Tom. I'm assuming you believe the person who stabbed him mistook him for me? Right time, right night, right location, wrong victim?"

"We think it's a possibility. Possible that it was the same person who wrote those letters too."

"Then I'll do everything I can to help you. Not for me: I don't want to cut some sort of a deal. I may have deserved getting done over, I admit that, but Tom didn't. I probably won't be the most credible witness in the box, either, but I'm at your disposal."

Maybe there was some honour left among criminals. "Okay, if that's so, we can start with one of the women you attacked."

"Ye-es." Phillips sounded less confident, as though his guard had come up.

"Did the letters mention any of them?"

Phillips shook his head. "Not that I recall, and it would have been a clue to who may have sent them. Is one of them the connection, then?"

"Possibly." Best not to lead the witness by specifying Katie. "Did Tom Hatton know any of the victims? Or their families?"

"That I *can* tell you. We'd discussed the Slasher before. Me and him and the nice girl. Beryl. Neither of them knew any of the women I attacked. Thank God."

Robin resisted saying they were better thanking God for the car crash that had prevented another assault. "Might Hatton have suspected your involvement?"

Phillips shook his head again. "If he did, he'd have told me, and he never so much as dropped a hint."

"I'm going to show you some pictures." Robin opened the large envelope he had laid on the table. "Do you recognise any of these people?"

Phillips studied each photograph as he came to it, picking out both Beryl and Zandra, but drawing a blank on the others, including Selby, although he returned to Mike Edwards. "This bloke. I don't remember meeting him, but he's vaguely familiar." He glanced up to study Robin. "Resembles you a bit, but that's not what I'm thinking of."

"Perhaps this will help remind you." Anderson produced another collection of photos, this time of his victims.

Phillips turned white at the sight of them, but he compared them carefully with that Edwards. He stopped when he came to the one of Katie Russell. "They have to be related."

"They are. Brother and sister."

"I see." Phillips picked up the photo of Edwards. "Is he the one who threatened me? She ate at the Florentine, you know. I remember seeing her there, although I didn't recognise her until after . . . afterwards."

Robin narrowed his eyes. "You didn't target her especially?"

"No. I swear to God. I always chose them at random. It was nothing more than coincidence. And I didn't mean to kill her."

Robin, who'd heard plenty of liars in his time, was pretty sure that was the truth. The randomness of the attacks had been a factor that had made them so hard to investigate.

"He did time for assault," Anderson cut in. "Although we're not sure he did the threatening. He's supposed to have turned over a new leaf."

"Don't look so dubious. Some of us do, you know." Phillips paled. "So if not him, then who?"

"Somebody else. You can't expect us to tell you who, but we might be able to link them to Hatton's death, and if we can match them up to the letters, that could seal the deal. By 'we' I mean the police in general," Robin added hastily, even if he couldn't shake off the feeling it was *their* case, his and Anderson's.

"There was something about the paper the letters were on," Phillips said, suddenly. "Thick, good quality. Distinctive green colour."

"Can you be more specific?" Robin remembered the unusual writing paper he'd seen when searching Selby's flat.

"Imagine a washed-out version of British racing green. Like that."

Robin nodded at Anderson to make a note. The fact that matched what he'd seen wasn't conclusive, but it would be another piece of circumstantial evidence that might get Selby to come clean.

"One final question. Does the name Selby mean anything to you?"

Phillips shrugged. "Not a thing. Unless it's that snooker player. It wasn't him who wrote those letters, was it?"

"I doubt it." Robin couldn't help grinning. Selby, Hatton, Sergeant Anderson himself—it was starting to sound like an episode of *A Question of Sport*. If somebody called Sue Barker turned up, it would be no surprise at all.

As soon as they were through the door and outside the prison, Anderson visibly relaxed. "Free at last."

"Positive incentive not to ever end up locked away. Maybe Adam should suggest it would make a good school trip. Discouraging bad behaviour." Robin imagined how horrified Adam would be at the notion.

"That would work for me. Now, the hunch Phillips talked about. The one the letter writer, who I assume we're thinking is Selby, referred to. Any idea what it might be?"

"Yes, I do, actually." It was satisfying to have made a logical connection before his sergeant had. "That meal Katie Russell had at the Florentine, before she was attacked. Possibly Selby had his suspicions about the place. Knives, chefs, simple."

"But Phillips said he didn't target her then."

"Selby wouldn't be able to read Phillips's mind, would he? Katie's friends were discussing that meal at the Florentine after his arrest. What if they were already speculating about a connection to where she'd been?"

"Hm." Anderson rolled his eyes. "That's a real long shot, sir."

"Not much more of a long shot than we took when we searched Phillips's car." Anderson was right, though. They had little better to go on than a coat, some writing paper, and what might be a false alibi. As a case, it was pathetically thin. "Or either Selby or Edwards has a snout, like you. I can imagine the criminal underworld intelligence network wanting to hand down their own sentence for this type of crime, rather than put it into our hands."

"Let's go back in. Talk to Phillips again."

"And ask him what?"

"If there's anything else that might have given him away. Something that Root and his team were too thick to follow up." Anderson clearly relished any dig at the Abbotston team; his loathing for the place knew no bounds. "Okay. I'm willing to swallow my pride if it means we make a connection."

Both the prison authorities and Phillips himself were surprised to see them.

"Back so soon?" the prisoner asked once they were ensconced in the interview room again.

"Got to eat a slice of humble pie on behalf of my colleagues." Robin forced a smile. "You said that whoever wrote the letters said they'd acted on a hunch in identifying you as the attacker. But there has to be more than that, surely. Where did we go wrong?"

Phillips took a long, deep breath. "I've been mulling that over since you went. I've come up with an idea."

"Go on." Robin glanced at Anderson; the sergeant was making his usual efficient notes.

"I told somebody. Wanted to get it off my chest. Deathbed confession, only not my deathbed. Guy that used to come into the restaurant, who I got friendly with."

"Why choose him? Because your secret would go straight to the grave?" Anderson asked. "What if he'd lasted longer than you expected?"

"Then I'd have made an error of judgement." Phillips shrugged. He kept his eyes on the table, doodling with his fingers. "Thing is, I don't believe he'd have given me away. He was an old lag himself, done time for attacking women."

"And he simply happened to visit your restaurant? Then confess to his past?" Anderson rolled his eyes.

"Coincidences happen. And I got to hear about him from the waitresses. They didn't like serving him. He didn't have any friends left, and his family had disowned him. So there he was, riddled with cancer, and I took pity on him." Phillips looked up. "I understood, you see. So I knew he'd understand *me*."

An old lag. Might have had time to pass the information on, once Phillips had left him. It would only take a phone call. "What was his name? Where did he serve his sentence?"

"No idea about the second, but his name was Jeff Pringle. You should be able to follow him up."

"We will, I promise."

Once they were outside once more, it didn't take long to make the necessary phone calls. Pringle had been in prison with Edwards and Selby, but had been released early because of his medical condition.

Robin took a deep breath of clean, non-prison air. "We've got to have enough to take this on to the next step."

"You genuinely reckon Selby killed Hatton?"

"I think there's every chance, if the forensics line up."

Anderson nodded. "In that case, why have you got a face like you've lost a tenner?"

"If I knew that, I'd tell you. Pricking of my thumbs or something."

"Well, at least it seems you were right about this being simple. A variation on the old domestic theme, if not exactly being done in by your loved one." Anderson wrinkled his nose. "On behalf of your friend's loved one. Does that get included as a domestic?"

"Only if it turns out to be a fact. I'm not counting any chickens until the forensics have hatched. And don't you laugh at my mixed metaphors." Although once they had the forensics back, they could . . . what, exactly? Confront Selby? Surely Cowdrey wouldn't let them do that, because it wasn't their case. Would he make them pass their information over to Root? That would hurt like hell.

"You're at it again, sir. Lost in your thoughts."

"It's called employing one's logical faculties." Robin talked through what he'd been thinking.

"We could hand everything over to Cowdrey himself and make it his problem."

"True." They couldn't tilt at every windmill. "I'd love to know why Root's being so obstructive, though. Seems like he's getting in our way at every turn."

Anderson nodded. "I hear he was spitting nails when we proved it *was* Sam Brunning in that fight."

"Because he got egg on his face for sticking up for someone who turned out to be at fault?" Robin snorted. "I can understand him sticking up for one of his own, the old 'all for one and one for all' mentality. I even, just about, get that when the loyalty turns out to be misguided, so long as people don't knowingly cover up for scrotes."

"Perhaps that's why he's been so determined to go down the IRA line. Consciously or subconsciously trying to deflect attention from Brunning."

"Then he's a bloody idiot. I thought we'd gone past the days of having bent coppers." A bus pulled up outside, discharging a couple of old ladies. Visiting time? Coming out here to visit a husband or son who'd done something awful—it had to be a particularly nasty crime for them to end up here—to whom they were still devoted? "*Quis custodiet ipsos custodes.*"

"Sorry?"

"Who guards the guardians. Or mentors the mentors. Whatever. I was thinking of those old dears." Robin gave the women a smile. "I hope nobody twisted the facts to suit their own purposes when their nearest and dearest got sent down. They deserve better."

"Don't go soppy on me, sir." Anderson looked alarmed.

"Don't worry, I won't. There are simply lots of little things about Root that keep nagging me. Why didn't he pass on the message from Phillips?"

"You should ask him."

"I'll do better than that. I'll get Cowdrey to ask him. I bet the boss will put on his best 'put the fear of God into God' face." Robin smirked. "If Root's got more to hide than sticking up for a pal, we need to go through the proper channels. Though even I'm going to fancy working the guy over if it turns out he's deliberately made things murky."

When they got back to Stanebridge station, Cowdrey told Robin he'd take over the questioning of Selby where it concerned Hatton. Root's possible obstructive behaviour was enough for the boss to keep the matter in Stanebridge's house for the moment. Caesar's wife—and all her relatives—had to be above suspicion. On the same basis, he'd take another officer with him, one who hadn't been directly involved with any of the cases so far: an independent eye and ear, and one who couldn't be accused of tainting. Cowdrey could always ring Robin to clarify points arising that weren't in the case notes.

Robin and his sergeant could look forward to a busy afternoon making sure everything was up to date for Cowdrey when he conducted the interview the next day. By then they'd have the full forensics back, and they could turn out that green notepaper from Selby's house for Phillips to have a shufti at beforehand.

The best outcome would be to produce so much circumstantial evidence that Selby would simply break down and confess, although given the convolutions of the last few days, Robin doubted things would be that simple.

Chapter Fourteen

As usual, Campbell heard the phone going long before his owner did, alerting Adam to the fact by jumping up and down. Adam, who'd managed to get home early with a stack of planning to do, had been at the table, hard at work with Classic FM in the background.

"Thanks, boy. Bet it's your other dad." He prayed it wouldn't be Robin ringing to say there'd been yet another murder to prevent his getting home at a decent time.

He picked the phone up, giving his usual "Hello?" without saying his name. That dated back to pre-Robin times, the point where he'd got his first teaching job and had gone ex-directory, so that the parents of his pupils couldn't get hold of him. The anonymity aspect was doubly imperative now there was a rozzer in the house.

"Adam? Sorry to ring you at home like this. I wouldn't do it if it weren't important." The voice sounded vaguely familiar, but not enough for him to put a name to. Not one of the Lindenshaw school parents, though. It didn't sound like a cold caller either, but they were developing a savvy line of chat these days, so who could tell?

He kept his tone clipped and businesslike. "What's it in connection with?"

"Your Robin."

A wave of nausea flooded Adam. Had there been another attack? Luke Brunning was on bail, so the idiot might have decided to have a second pop. It wasn't Anderson on the line, though. Surely he'd be the logical one to deliver bad news?

"Hello?"

"Sorry." Time to stop panicking—he didn't yet know if there was anything to panic about. "Is that Superintendent Cowdrey?"

"No. He's tied up at the moment. Is Robin there?"

"No. He's still at work. Isn't he at the station?"

"Not that we're aware of. Hence the call."

The wave of nausea worsened into a tsunami. "Isn't he answering his mobile?"

"We tried. We assumed he was in one of those signal dead zones we get round here."

Adam winced at the word "dead," his riot-running imagination barely in check.

"Can you come in and help us with some stuff? I wouldn't ask normally, but in the circumstances . . . We'll send a car," the caller added. "We're putting you to enough trouble without expecting you to drive over here."

"No trouble at all."

"Thanks. I'm sure there's nothing to panic about, but given everything that's been going on, better safe than sorry."

"I'll be ready."

Adam rang Robin's phone, but only got the number-unavailable message as the caller had done. He tried to keep his mind off things, concentrating on making sure Campbell had emptied his bladder and had a full bowl of water with which to refill it again. He was already watching from the window when the car drew up outside, the driver waving and flashing his warrant card.

"Don't worry, boy," he shouted over his shoulder as he opened the front door. "It'll be okay."

He wasn't sure he believed that.

Robin hummed along to the car stereo, glad to have got a flier. Shingles was no laughing matter, but a colleague coming down with it meant a cancelled meeting and an early finish. As he pulled onto the drive, the house appeared strangely dark. Had Adam got a parents' evening or school governors' meeting booked? Normally he'd mention anything like that over breakfast, but perhaps Robin had been so preoccupied by thoughts of vengeful knifemen that he'd not heard.

Once indoors, he checked the calendar, but there was nothing scrawled on there.

"Where's your master, boy?" he asked a whimpering Campbell. "Did they get the Ofsted call at the school?"

It was only when he went into the lounge—finding the pile of work strewn over the coffee table—that the worry kicked in. Adam's keys were gone from the place he normally left them, but his car was in the garage, as was his bike, so where the hell was their owner? Robin got his mobile and checked for a message or a missed call, noting that Adam had tried to ring but missed him. He rang Adam's number, but the phone was either turned off or in a signal black spot, the officious automated voice informing him that his call couldn't be taken. On ringing the school, he got the fractionally less officious voice of Jennifer Shepherd on the answerphone.

Time, as it so often did in a crisis, expanded out of measure. His mind whirred with images of Adam lying under the wheels of a lorry somewhere, Adam with a knife in his back because he'd got too close to the man masterminding the armed robberies or some friend of Selby's. The last few months, Robin had come to understand why the Superman of the original comics had been so loath to get involved with Lois Lane; it was bad enough to put your own life at risk, but when the people you loved became a target, it could break your heart. This time there wouldn't be Campbell present to save the day and save a life in the process, as there had been before.

He called Mrs. Matthews, trying not to alarm her and failing miserably, and as soon as he'd got off the phone to her he dialled Anderson, because he'd lost the capacity to think straight and needed somebody to employ common sense on his behalf.

"Anderson? Are you free?"

"What's up? You sound like you've seen a ghost."

"Worse than that. Got home and can't locate Adam anywhere." Robin apprised him of what he'd found. "Can't be anything to do with the dog, because he's here and fine. But there's a half-drunk mug of tea in the lounge, and that bothers me."

"Okay, don't panic." Anderson used the voice he employed on distressed witnesses. "Have you rung round the obvious places?"

"I've tried the school, but I got the answerphone. Then I tried his mother, and all I managed to do was get her into a panic as well."

"Right. There might be a simple explanation." The degree of kindness in the sergeant's voice was growing by the moment. "Have you tried the 1471 service? Could be he got a call from somebody who had the sense not to block their number."

"I haven't. Good thinking." Robin didn't feel as bullish as his words implied. What if he found that the number *had* been deliberately withheld? That wasn't going to make him any less panicky. *Grow a pair, because you're acting like a great wet lettuce.*

"While you do that, I'll ring the station, in case they've heard anything. You know, road accident or incident at the school or whatever." Anderson sounded too deliberately casual for comfort. "Then I'm coming round."

Robin thought about arguing, before deciding that he honestly would benefit from having his sergeant here, not least for the comfort of the familiar. "I'll ask around the neighbours too."

"Yeah. Probably he's gone to lend some poor old dear a bag of sugar and been delayed while she tells him about her latest operation."

"Could be." Common sense, as desired. It would turn out to be something as mundane as that. The relief waned when dialling 1471 produced the result he'd dreaded. There *had* been a phone call, some twenty minutes before Robin got home, which was around the time the mug of tea might have been abandoned, given how warm it felt. And the number had been withheld.

He pressed his forehead against the cool glass of the front door. *Think clearly; go and talk to the neighbours.* And if it turned out that Adam was sitting having a glass of sherry as a reward for changing a light bulb for Mrs. Wotsit at the thatched cottage, he'd give the guy an earful for not leaving a note. He'd take him home, drag him upstairs, and roger him stupid, but not until after he'd delivered the bollocking.

The neighbours to the left were clearly not in. Robin vaguely remembered a conversation over the garden hedge about their having booked a week's holiday, so gave up ringing the doorbell and headed for the neighbours on the other side of Adam's house. *Of our house,* he reminded himself.

The chap who lived there said they hadn't seen or heard anything suspicious, although given that he'd been having dinner with his family—or chimps' feeding time at the zoo, as he called it—an alien spacecraft could have touched down in the road and he'd not have twigged. His wife, appropriately concerned that something might have happened to Adam—whom Robin suspected she secretly fancied—suggested, waspishly, that they try the woman who lived across the road and who had nothing better to do with her time than watch the local comings and goings.

Robin thanked them, turned on his heel, and then took a deep breath. Sylvia would have been the most logical person to visit in the first place, but she put the wind up him a bit. Actually, more than a bit, given that she tended to stare disapprovingly at him and probably thought his relationship with Adam was the depths of depravity. She had, however, a well-deserved reputation for knowing everything that went on, so he'd simply have to man up.

Naturally, it turned out that Sylvia *had* seen something, and was extremely worried about it.

"I'm so pleased you knocked, because I was wondering whether to ring the police, and I didn't want them thinking I was an old fusspot."

"Nobody would think that." Robin mentally crossed his fingers at the obvious lie. At least it couldn't have been something horrendous, like Adam being beaten up on the pavement, as she'd have been in no doubt about reporting that. "What worried you?"

"A strange car pulled up outside your house, with a man driving it who I didn't recognise. Then Adam came haring out, white as a sheet, and got in. They set off that way." She pointed left, towards the village centre.

"When was this?"

"Oh, not long before you got in. I was going to make a note of the time, then the phone went. One of those annoying cold calls. When I got rid of them, I saw you pulling up." She laid her hand on Robin's arm, much to his surprise. "I hope he's all right."

"I'm sure he will be. Thank you, you've been very helpful." Robin patted her hand before extricating himself from her grip. He'd evidently underestimated her. "Any idea what make of car it was?"

"Oh yes, an Audi A6. Silver. New looking, although I didn't catch the number plate. My husband used to be mad about cars, so I know them all."

"Thank God for that." Robin grabbed her hand back, pumping it up and down. "When this is sorted, would you like to come over for a meal? We can talk cars the whole evening."

"I'd love that, thank you."

He'd not been long back in the house, checking his phone every ninety seconds in case there was a message from Adam, when Anderson drew up outside. Robin was on the drive before his sergeant could get out of the car.

"Heard anything?" Anderson asked.

"Not directly. But he went off in a car, according to my new friend across the road. In a hurry too, and looking upset."

"Any idea who he might have gone with?"

Robin shrugged. "Description of the car didn't ring a bell."

"Have you contacted Cowdrey?"

"Not yet. I'd make a right idiot of myself if there's an innocent explanation."

"Okay, there is that, but can you come up with an innocent explanation offhand? One that would involve your Adam not sending a message or leaving a note?"

It was a good point; the lack of contact was entirely out of character. A cold spike of fear shot up his spine. This wasn't a case of worrying unnecessarily—he knew, both in his brain and in his bones, that something was amiss.

"Right. I'm officially panicking now. What the hell do you think has happened? And what do I do next?"

"No bleeding idea on the first count, and have a cup of tea on the second. You need to get your brain in gear." Anderson got out of the car, then led him into the house and through to the kitchen, where he put the kettle on.

Campbell, whining, rubbed his head against Robin's leg. He stroked the dog's back. "It'll be all right, boy."

"Shame he's not a bloodhound."

"Shame he can't *talk*. Eh, Campbell?" Robin smoothed the dog's ears. "Where's your dad gone? Who rang him?"

Campbell gave him a sympathetic look and put his head back into prime petting position. The regular, gentle movement of his hand along silky fur helped Robin to calm down a bit—pet therapy, who'd have thought he'd end up using it—while Anderson made and poured the tea.

"It couldn't have been a friend or a member of the family, come round to show off their new motor or anything as stupid as that?"

Robin shut his eyes and rubbed an increasingly achy brow. "Perhaps, but I doubt it. Not unless Aunt Clare's taken to dressing as a bloke and splashed out part of her pension settlement on an Audi A6."

Anderson thrust a mug in front of him. "Drink that, and don't grumble about the taste. You need the sugar."

Robin didn't complain, even though he hadn't taken sweeteners in his tea since he was a child. This was the standard British treatment for shock, and he'd give it a chance to work.

Eventually, Anderson asked, "So who could the man in the car be? We have to consider the possibility that Adam's been caught up in some scheme to get at you."

"I've been considering that ever since I found the abandoned mug of tea." Robin stared into his own mug, but the answer didn't seem to be in there. "Phillips is banged up, and he didn't give the impression of being the vengeful type, so I wouldn't have thought he'd have asked somebody to do the job for him."

"He'd have had to be damn quick to get it arranged, too. Unless he called in one of those old ladies to help him. Sorry." Anderson held up his hand. "Not a joking matter."

"It isn't. Remember that." Robin took another swig of tea. "Selby *is* vengeful, but he's banged up as well. Who else has got it in for me? The mystery man at the Wig? One of the Brunning boys?"

"That might make sense, especially with the school connection. The brother would either already know where you live and what your number is or he'd be able to find out." Anderson set down his mug. "Somebody else knows where you live, too. Worsley. Although why the hell he should want to hurt Adam . . ."

Not hurt him, Robin wanted to say. Snog the face off him, probably. He shut his eyes and shook his head, trying to put his brains straight. Could Adam have been made a romantic offer he couldn't refuse? No. No on every count.

"Can't be Worsley. He doesn't drive."

"Doesn't he? How do you know?"

"He told us. Medical reasons. He has fits or something and never learned to."

"Hm." Anderson's brows wrinkled. "How do you know he wasn't lying? I mean, even if he never passed a test, it doesn't mean he hasn't picked up how to."

Robin nodded. It was a good point, one that he'd have made himself, surely, if he hadn't felt so addle-witted.

"And your Adam isn't an idiot. Don't tell me he'd get into a car with some total stranger?"

"I'd hope not. Especially after the rollicking he gave me after I was attacked. Great long lecture about locking the front door and the rest of it."

"So would he have gone off somewhere with Worsley? He could have been strung a story about being needed."

Robin's thoughts had already travelled, reluctantly, down that line. A sob story about Campbell would have got Adam's knickers in such a twist he'd have hared off after any wild goose. Considering that Campbell was tucked up safe—at present snuggled on Robin's feet— could the sob story have been about *him*? "Given what happened to me in that alley, I can imagine he'd easily believe I was in danger if somebody told him so."

"So he'd trust Worsley. Possibly. Who else? I doubt he'd be inclined to go with one of the Brunnings, despite what I said earlier."

Robin remembered the time Adam had been doing a "people we trust and why we trust them" topic with his pupils. Who else would you go along with unthinkingly? A doctor, a priest, a member of the emergency services, a policeman . . .

"What if it was one of us?" He shuddered.

Anderson's eyes opened wider. "Police? Well, it wasn't me, and I doubt it was Cowdrey."

"I know you're trying to keep my pecker up, but don't be an idiot. It wouldn't even have to be a real policeman, I suppose, just somebody flashing something that resembled a warrant card." He finished the last of his tea, then pushed the mug away. "Back to Sam Brunning, again."

"My mate at Abbotston is on duty tonight. I'll ring him and find out if he knows where Brunning is. Not a lot goes on he doesn't know about."

"Ask him if he knows whether Brunning has a silver Audi, as well."

"I will. I—" Anderson suddenly slammed his hand on the breakfast bar, making such a bang that Campbell jumped six inches in the air. "I know who has a car like that, but you won't like it. Inspector Root."

"Root?"

"Yeah, he got it brand new a few months back. It's been a running joke at Abbotston." Anderson screwed his face up, in envy or disgust. "People wondering how many blind eyes he'd have had to turn to get a bribe as big as that."

"And who would the bribe come from?" Robin's icy words wiped the expression off Anderson's face.

"Hell. You don't believe he really *has* been taking backhanders, sir? No wonder he got uppity when they were ribbing him."

"I wouldn't rule out anything at the moment." Some light on things at last, although it might not be the sort of light he wanted. "You get on to Abbotston and find a number for him. If he's snug at home with the wife and kids and has been all evening, then we're barking up the wrong tree. I'll ring Cowdrey and do the 'I'm simply covering every base' act."

For once, Robin hoped that he'd end up with egg on his face, that it would turn out to be as simple as Adam having gone off somewhere with Chris to deal with a child protection case, because the thought of Root and bribes and that car with Adam in it made his flesh crawl.

When the Audi had got a hundred yards down the road, the logical part of Adam's brain, which had been kept at bay by sheer panic, started to kick in. What the hell was going on?

He studied the driver, who certainly had that rozzer air about him, but Adam hadn't seen this guy's warrant card close up, and he couldn't exactly ask for a second glance at it now. The voice matched the person he'd spoken to on the phone, though. "I don't think I caught your name?"

"Barry. I work at Abbotston."

Barry what? And was it just the strange atmosphere in the vehicle that made Adam so reluctant to ask the question? He settled for what they'd discussed on the phone.

"Right. So what do you reckon's going on with Robin? And what do you want me to do?"

"We're not sure anything *has* happened. We're having trouble contacting him, which is unusual." Barry smiled, probably in an attempt to be reassuring.

Adam wasn't comforted. If they weren't pretty sure something disastrous had occurred, why send a car for *him*?

"We want you to go over some pictures at the station. There are a couple of blokes who might have a grudge against Robin, and it would be useful to know if they'd been hanging around here anyway. As Jonesy says, 'Don't panic!'"

"If you say so." The fact Barry didn't appear to be taking the right route for either Abbotston or Stanebridge didn't do anything to reassure Adam. Was Barry simply lulling him into a false sense of security, with the intention of taking him along somewhere to identify a burned body? Or was that manner of thinking simply ridiculous?

"Relax. It'll be fine."

"I'll try." Adam stared out of the car window. Where was he being taken? The sight of a group of Brownies, out with their Brown Owl, doing whatever Brownies did to stop them getting into mischief, brought his thoughts up short.

Didn't he spend hours warning his pupils about "stranger danger" and how you should never get into a car with somebody you didn't know? Or even somebody you *did* know, unless you'd made sure with your parents it was all right to do so? Back to that old thing about being more at risk with people you knew than those you didn't.

Why on earth hadn't he listened to his own advice rather than get in a car with God knew who, going who bloody well knew where?

He did a quick calculation about how much damage he would do to himself if he opened the passenger door and rolled out as they went along. *Too much.* Better to wait until they came to a red light or a level crossing, although there was little traffic around and they'd not had to do more than slow down at any of the junctions so far.

How could he admit to his class he'd been a complete idiot, in an effort to hammer the lesson about safety home? *If I ever see my class again.* His stomach jolted. It wasn't only children who ended up dead.

Time to start using some common sense.

"I'm sure you gave me your surname, but I can't remember what you said." His voice came out surprisingly shakily.

Barry glanced at him, then back at the road, mouth hardening into a thin line. "Root. Inspector Root. The bloke your boyfriend wants to get one over on."

"Right." That's why the voice was familiar—he'd heard the guy talking on the radio when the Slasher case first broke. Adam took a deep breath; what to say now that wouldn't sound bloody stupid or make the situation worse? Because he was eighty percent certain he'd been sold a dummy here. "Strikes me he's not your favourite colleague."

"You're telling me. He—" Root suddenly appeared to remember where he was and what he was supposed to be doing. "He's too bloody lucky, I reckon."

"Something like that." *Not to mention better at his job than you are, but I'm not going there.* If he kept Root talking, could he surreptitiously text Robin, signal black spots allowing? "Do you think his luck ran out today?"

Root's head turned towards him. "What do you mean?"

"Just that, if somebody has a grudge, perhaps it's the day they thought they'd cash it in." Not that Adam now believed in the load of nonsense he'd been told. If Robin were in trouble, wouldn't Cowdrey have been the one to contact him? Why the bloody hell hadn't he thought of that when he was back home?

"Yeah." Root's shoulders visibly relaxed. "Could be it's along those lines."

"This is clearly pretty serious." Adam, despite his clammy palms, had managed to get his mobile phone into his hand without Root noticing.

"I've got my suspicions about that Worsley bloke. There's something dodgy about him."

"Honestly?" Adam's thoughts became jumbled up again. Had he been too quick to assume he'd been hoodwinked, or was Root just good at telling a credible story? "What's he done?"

"We believe Robin might have been picked up by a bloke in a car, earlier. We've got a good description of the driver, and it fits Worsley."

The driver was Worsley? Had Root given one detail too many in search of authenticity? Unless Worsley had lied about not driving, of course. Adam kept his trap shut; his gut told him that he'd rather trust Worsley than Root, but that might be those lustful days back in court talking. "What on earth has he got against Robin?"

Adam continued to blindly fiddle with his phone, waiting for Root to reply. Thank God it was on silent, as was standard practice within the school. A probably pointless practice, given that there were only two places within the building where you got a signal, one of which was the ladies' toilets. And thank goodness as well that the last time he'd used it was to read a message from Robin, earlier that day, so it would be less complicated to try to reply rather than start afresh. Especially as his shaking fingers could be pressing anything.

"It's to do with the Hatton case." Root said eventually, his airy tone suggesting he might have gone on to say something like "Don't you worry your pretty head about it" if he'd had a woman passenger. "As they say, it's complicated."

"Right. I won't ask." He took a furtive glance at his phone, alarmed to find out that he wasn't as efficient at messaging like this as he'd hoped. Hopefully it would make some sense, if he could get the bloody thing sent.

"What's up?" The car jolted to one side as Root turned to him.

"Nothing. Unless you count the great big hole I've just found in my trouser seam. I hope I haven't been walking around with it all afternoon. Maybe it isn't my day." He tried to sound convincing, but the fear in his voice must have been obvious.

Root's sneer sent a cold shiver up his spine, chillier than any hole in his trousers would have produced. The car pulled round a corner and almost ploughed into a herd of cows, which were crossing the road post-milking.

"Bloody yokels," Root fumed, hands tight on the wheel.

"Relax, we could be stuck here ages. At least two of them have gone walkabouts down the lane." Enough time for Adam to get out and leg it into the field? Although the increasing proximity of a large Friesian would soon make opening the door a challenge in itself. "So these pictures you want me to go over." He kept his tone casual, slowly manoeuvring his hand towards the door handle. "Why do I need to have a gander if you're pretty sure it's Worsley you're after?"

Root didn't respond at first, apart from giving Adam a malevolent look. It clearly was a question too many. "That's for me to know and you to find out," he said at last, centrally locking the car doors as he did so. "Sit still, shut up, and don't let any of those bloody things lick the windows."

Adam nodded, keeping his eyes trained on the cows, willing more of them to misbehave and both delay this journey further and distract Root's attention. With his left hand he pressed a series of keys, desperately hoping that he'd managed to find the correct sequence to send the message to Robin.

And was within range of enough signal not to end up with only the dreaded "failed to send" message.

When Anderson got off the phone, he wasn't exuding optimism. "Root's not at home and he's not at the station. Nobody's sure where he is."

"Why doesn't that surprise me?" Robin shut his eyes, then exhaled loudly. "Cowdrey's going to ring Root's boss in case *he's* got an inkling of what's up."

"Want me to get Root's registration number?"

Robin shook his head. "No point, I'd have thought. I suspect Mrs. Doings over the road would have told me if she'd got a note of it."

"Yeah, but that would let us put out a call to for all units to keep an eye out for him. And generally for a silver A6 with two blokes in it."

"Cowdrey's one step ahead of you on that bit. He's already on the case, and he wants *us* to stay off it." Robin made a sour face. "Says I won't be able to remain objective."

"*I* can remain objective."

"Yeah. But he wants you to keep an eye on me. Make sure I don't go maverick."

Anderson snorted. "Does he reckon that you'll go haring round the countryside chasing Root, then beat the crap out of him if it turns out he's got Adam?"

"Something like that. Although at the moment I'd settle for finding Adam alive and well." He stopped, took a deep breath. "Am I overreacting? Seeing danger that isn't there?"

"Not so far as I can tell. If it were my Helen in the same situation, I'd be mental with worry." Anderson knitted his brows. "You heard Cowdrey's voice, as well as his words. The way he reacted, do you think he had suspicions about Root already?"

"It wouldn't surprise me. Think about the last few weeks. At every turn, Root's been getting in the way or going off down the wrong road. We've been assuming it's a case of sheer incompetence, or covering for his mates, but what if it's more than that?"

Anderson nodded slowly. "Okay, but who would he be doing it for? It's a pretty big risk to run, because if you're found out, that's the end. Goodbye career."

"Hello Audi A6, though."

"Could he really have been bribed?"

"I don't know. But you have to be given a big incentive to cross the line." Robin remembered the nineteen-sixties bribery scandals that had done so much harm to the police force's reputation. "Who's involved with any of our recent cases who'd have the clout? I can't imagine Phillips or Selby having a tame policeman in his pocket."

"Does it have to be connected with one of those cases?"

"I'd have thought the answer to that was obvious, given that the obstruction and misdirection are all apparently linked to Hatton's death." But the point was a good one. Who would most benefit from having their part in that crime covered over?

"Do you think we might have got it wrong about Selby? That somebody else was culpable, and that's who Root was covering for? Somebody like Edwards himself?"

"Cowdrey doesn't believe so, not after his interview with him. He didn't extract a confession, but Selby was very cagey when confronted with the story about the threatening letters. The boss reckons if we can get Phillips to identify the paper and work on getting Selby's girlfriend to tell us everything she knows, he'll break."

Anderson drummed his fingers on the side of his mug. "And none of this answers the question of why Root should want to abdu—talk to Adam."

"You might as well say 'abduct,' because that's what we've both got in mind. He wants to put the frighteners on me for some reason, is my guess. He's never met Adam, as far as I know, so I can't think there's a personal connection."

"Unless it's through the Brunnings. Sam tells him that Adam lost his brother his job or some sob story along those lines."

"Luke Brunning hasn't lost his job. Yet. And if he does, it's his own damn fault." Robin slammed down his mug. "This isn't getting anywhere. Where the hell can they have gone? What if—"

His mobile phone beeped, making both of them jump. He hesitated for a second, worried that this was the worst of news, then reassured himself that nobody in their right mind would deliver that information with a text. The message itself looked like it had been written by a lunatic, given the eccentric spelling, but it came from Adam's mobile.

"It's him." Robin had never believed in guardian angels, but perhaps somebody *was* watching over them that day. With shaking hands, he passed the phone to Anderson.

"This gives the impression it was written in the dark. Without looking at the screen, anyway." Anderson handed it back. "Does that say he's on the Roman road?"

"Yeah. That's what we call the *B* road that goes through Tythebarn. It's one of the old network, which is why it's straight as a die." Why the hell were they talking about road construction? "It connects with the motorway link road."

"Are they going to London?"

"Or down to Southampton. Or crossing the motorway and heading into the wilds." Robin checked the time it arrived, trying to fathom if it had been sent immediately or if Adam's whizzy new phone had the capacity to hold messages until it connected with a signal. He'd never had the need to find out.

"I'll ring Cowdrey and update him. At least we can narrow the area we're keeping an eye on."

"I'll message Adam back and say we've received it." He dithered for a moment, wondering if that would make matters worse, but they could guess and second-guess until the cows came home. They couldn't even be sure that Adam *was* with Root, for God's sake, but they couldn't simply sit on their hands and do nothing.

Anderson was clearly thinking along the same lines. As soon as he finished talking to Cowdrey, he fished in his pocket for his car keys. "We're no use here. The boss can get us on our mobiles if we're needed."

"He'll have your guts for garters." Despite his words, Robin was out of his seat and ready.

"He can't stop us going down to the fish and chip shop to get some tea, can he? And if the fish and chip shop happened to be in the vicinity of wherever that silver Audi is, then we couldn't help it if we had another lucky break, could we?"

"Talking of breaks, we should let Campbell out to relieve himself."

"Bring him with us. He'd be good corroboration that we weren't out on police business."

"We should set him on Root, or whoever's got Adam. You or I would be in trouble for belting a suspect, but nobody could put Campbell in the dock for protecting his master." Robin stopped.

"What's up?"

"In the dock. Court cases. Hang on." He let Campbell into the garden, then went through to the lounge to fish out the newspaper cuttings from Edwards's court case, bringing them back into the kitchen. He found the picture of the Edwards family, pointing out the brother. "Who does he remind you of?"

Anderson held the picture up to the light and squinted. "Those ears look just like Sam Brunning's. What's this about?"

"The Brunnings boys were adopted."

"Blimey. You're never saying they might be related to the Edwards family? This bloke would be too young, given the date on the photo, unless he got started early?"

"Adam says he died when he wasn't that old, so I think he's out of the frame entirely." Robin pointed to the figure in the middle of the photo. "Shame this picture's so fuzzy. What are the chances that Edwards himself was their father?"

"Fucking hell. I suppose it's possible." The sergeant turned the photo once more, as if another angle might give him the answer. "It's a bit of a long shot, though, and I'm not sure we'd be able to get the information verified any time soon."

"Not through the official channels, but somebody's got to be able to tell us."

The reappearance of Campbell at the kitchen door spurred them into action again. Within minutes the three were bundled into Anderson's car and were heading off in the direction of the motorway. The sergeant reminded Robin that Edwards's business was on the industrial estate by the motorway junction, so that might be a sensible place to go. He knew a back way that would cut minutes— potentially vital minutes—off the journey time. Meanwhile, Robin contacted the station to suggest a team get out to the industrial estate, and got hold of a contact number for Sam Brunning's parents while he was at it.

Mr. and Mrs. Brunning were reluctant to talk to him, and even more reluctant to discuss the background of their boys, but Robin insisted that somebody's life might be at risk, a phrase that stung as he uttered it.

The persuasion worked. "The family were called Edwards," Mrs. Brunning explained. "The mother's long gone. She ditched the boys when Sam was hardly out of nappies. Went abroad with her fancy man. The father did time, more than once, but he's back in the area now."

"Mike Edwards?"

"Yes. That's him. Why do you need to know?"

"We're simply checking something he might be involved in." Best to keep as vague as possible. "Did he ever try to get in touch with Luke or Sam?"

"In the early days, yes. We had to get social services to warn him off, which worked for a while, although after he went to prison, we didn't hear from him again."

"Might he have been in contact with your sons recently?"

Mrs. Brunning's voice, which had been full of ire at Edwards, turned cold. "If he has, they haven't told us."

Robin made sympathetic noises, then said his goodbyes. That last response had held a wealth of unspoken detail, stuff he didn't want to get into at present. He updated Anderson, whose mind careered along the same path. "If he's been in touch with them, it might explain why they're suddenly running off the rails. It can't be easy to discover your old man's got previous."

"Even if he's supposed to be going straight now?" Robin asked.

"Do you reckon Edwards *is* going straight? Despite what Selby said?"

Robin shrugged. "I've no bloody idea. I'm not sure I believe in 'once a villain, always a villain,' but I'd have thought it was like the urge to smoke. You have to keep fighting it."

"And it would be handy to have a friend in the force to help you keep your nose clean." Anderson's voice had a snarky edge.

"Do you really mean it would be handy to have somebody covering up for you? So it *appeared* you were keeping your nose clean? A tame copper onside." Robin didn't wait for a response; his sergeant's grin displayed his thoughts. "Like Sam Brunning?"

"Nah. He doesn't have enough clout. I just remembered what Selby said. About the officer who picked Edwards up feeling sorry for him."

"Pike said much the same." Robin nodded. "How did we pass over the fact that the arresting officer was Root?"

"I wonder if they kept the connection up."

"It's possible. Might explain why he was so keen to cover up for Brunning as well. Did it ever occur to you that Root was a bit quick off the mark ringing up Pike? What if he already knew that Brunning had blotted his copybook?"

"Before we did?"

"Yes. Maybe he was already set up to be Brunning's agony aunt." Robin leaned over to glance at the speedometer. "I know I normally dread you putting your foot down, but once we get up onto the straight bit of the road, feel free to let it rip. I'll keep my eyes shut."

"Bloody hell, you must be worried, sir." Anderson kept his eye firmly on the road and eased up through the gears.

Campbell, who enjoyed rides in fast cars, made a delighted little doggy noise while Robin gritted his teeth and thought of Adam.

When they reached the roundabout where the *B* road met the main arterial routes, Adam expected Root to guide the car down the motorway slip road, but he took the next exit, heading for the industrial estate. They couldn't keep on pretending that nothing unusual was happening, not least because Root must have sensed the state Adam was in.

"I know it's a daft question, but why are we here, exactly?"

"There's somebody you need to meet." Root turned the car into a car park in front of an office building, one that must have been seeing a load of renovations, given the debris piled up by the wall. As they pulled into a space, the front door opened, and a large fifty-something man emerged, one who bore a horribly familiar face, even if Adam was struggling to put a name or a context to him.

"Am I supposed to know who that is?"

Root gave Adam a hostile glance. "Don't you recognise him? That's Mike Edwards."

"Bloody hell." Adam watched the man approaching the car. "Why do you want me to meet him?"

"I don't. *He* wants to meet you. Don't keep him waiting." Root's expression suggested doing what Edwards wanted was the sensible— safe—thing.

Adam weighed his options between arguing, insisting he'd stay in the car, and getting out to face the music. What would Robin have done? Not been so bloody stupid as to get himself in such a situation in the first place, probably. It was small comfort to Adam that Edwards wasn't obviously toting a firearm with him, and there must be security guards doing regular rounds of the estate, so surely there was nothing as dramatic as a shooting planned? He could easily be carrying a knife, though.

Adam got out of the car and busked it. "Mr. Edwards. I believe you wanted to see me about something?"

"Too right I do," Edwards snarled. "You've made a lot of trouble for my boys."

"Sorry?" Which boys? Adam racked his brains in case he'd ever had a child called Edwards in his class, although they'd be too old for him to have taught, unless they were the offspring of a late marriage.

"Sam and Luke. Luke who works in that school with you. They're still mine, no matter that they got taken from me. A man has to protect his own, especially when they're pretty well all the family left to him."

Adam, with a sickening jolt to his stomach, remembered the details of Luke's background, the violent family he'd been removed from. "You're Luke's biological father?"

"I'm Luke and Sam's *real* father, yes."

Shit. Why did such a big world have a habit of turning out to be so small? Adam gave Root a glance, but he seemed fascinated by the state of his nails. There'd be no support from that quarter. "Luke's a good bloke and he's got the potential to be a great teacher. I enjoyed being his mentor."

"Yeah. You enjoyed it so much, you've probably lost him his job." Edwards snorted. "They should give Luke a second chance. He'd be a fucking sight better teacher than Kenneth Vince ever was."

"Kenneth Vince?" Who the hell was that? The name rang a bell, but not a loud one.

"He was a paedophile. Taught at the boys' school. They never officially caught him at it—whatever he did was covered up—but I wasn't going to risk him laying his dirty hands on my lads." Edwards glanced sidelong at Root, but the policeman kept his gaze directed at his fingers. "Sometimes you have to take things into your own hands. I gave Vince a lesson he wouldn't forget. I hope you're going to be more reasonable."

Vince. Yes. How could he have forgotten that timid little bloke who'd been beaten up at the Rings? The paedophilia aspect hadn't been exploited in court, although it must have been mentioned because Adam remembered noting that you couldn't judge an abuser by appearances. He wished he had his trial notes with him now, in case they contained a clue to getting him out of this bloody mess.

Adam took in Edwards's rugby-player build, his massive hands. The clenching and unclenching of those powerful fists implied he was a ticking bomb. "More reasonable about what?"

"Getting Luke his job back, for a start." Edwards looked up as a car went along the main service road to the estate, frowned, and ignored it.

"He hasn't actually lost his job yet. The headteacher has got him on leave until we know what's happening."

"You can put in a word for him, though. You must have some influence." Edwards's words were those of a reasonable man, but the angry tone belied them.

"You don't need to ask me to do that. I've already said everything I can to our headteacher on Luke's behalf." Adam took a deep breath. He couldn't promise more than that and wasn't sure Edwards would be satisfied with a word put in. "But these matters end up out of the school's hands. We can't influence things if his case goes to a disciplinary panel. And if he gets convicted for assault, it probably will."

That was a red rag to the bull. "Don't talk to me about disciplinary panels. Shame they didn't have them when Vince was touching up little boys. He wasn't a great advert for the profession, was he?"

"No. I agree with you there."

Edwards ignored the mollifying remark. "Anyway, Barry here will make sure it doesn't get to court, won't you, Inspector?"

Root smiled sheepishly but didn't respond one way or the other.

"Will he?"

"Of course. He's always been a good friend to me. I asked him to help take care of my lads, and he's done a proper job. I've made it worth his while to do it." Edwards grinned at Root's evident discomfort. "Carrot and stick. He gets carrots—which one do you want?"

Adam weighed the odds on grabbing a lump of wood from the pile of rubbish to defend himself should Edwards decide on "stick" and make a lunge for him, as he must have lunged at his victim up at the Rings. Vince's attacker might be brawnier than Adam, but *he* had to be quicker, surely?

Edwards continued, flexing those enormous hands again. "What *would* it take for you to be so helpful? I understand your bloke, the copper, got himself beaten up by persons unknown." He appeared to deliberately ignore Root's little nervous laugh at the "persons unknown" bit. Possibly Root hadn't yet worked out how he was going to ensure any assault charge against Luke Brunning could be dropped. He wouldn't want to disappoint the paymaster.

Adam bit back on saying *We all know who beat Robin up*, settling instead for "Go on, I'm listening."

"Well, I'd hate to see anything else happen to him. Dangerous job, policing. Your lads do a great job, don't they, Barry? And nobody gives a toss if one of them finds himself the wrong end of a knife." Edwards turned to face Adam once more. "You'd give a toss, though, wouldn't you?"

"You leave Robin alone. You're not going to take him up the Rings and belt him one."

"How did you know I followed Vince to the Rings?" Edwards glowered, edging forward to stare at Adam's face. "And why do I reckon I recognise you?"

"I was on the jury when you were convicted." Adam kicked himself—yet again—for being such an idiot. Why the hell couldn't he keep his big gob shut? Evidently Root hadn't passed that bit of information on—maybe he didn't know it.

Edwards took another step forward, then checked himself. "You had me put away?"

"You were guilty. You've just admitted that, even if you didn't at the time. We had to bring that verdict in." Adam glanced at Root, but there was no point appealing to him. He clearly wanted to be somewhere—anywhere—else.

"Yeah, well, he deserved it, didn't he? Like Hatton did. Like your bloke did. Nobody messes with our family and gets away with it."

"Does that list include getting somebody to take revenge on your sister's behalf?"

"Wouldn't you do the same?" Edwards might have been cultivating an image as a respectable businessman, but standing there, he looked and sounded every bit the thug, as he'd done in the dock. Chances were he'd never gone straight, like he was supposed to have done. Root's patch. Root's blind eye. "Hm? Or don't you hold with family, because you're queer? Hm? Don't I deserve an answer?"

Ignore the insult. Keep him talking.

Adam glanced at Root again, but he was keeping his head down, finding his shoes fascinating now. Adam didn't look at the pile of lumber this time, but he'd got it clear in his mind's eye. He needed a distraction.

"Of course you deserve an answer. And of course I believe in family values. I'm as old-fashioned as they come." He forced a smile.

"Yeah, well." Edwards narrowed his eyes. "All I want is for Luke to keep his job, and your bloke off Sam's back. Or is that too difficult for you?"

"Difficult?" Adam had managed to inch a bit closer to the pile of debris. Slowly did it. "Of course it is. I can't change the government rules about teachers' misconduct. And it'll be just as hard to change Robin's mind."

"Maybe you need some help with that last one. Or a positive incentive." Edwards's face contorted with derision. "It would be such a shame if your handsome copper wasn't quite as handsome, wouldn't it? Just do what you're asked."

"Asked? Should that be 'told'? Like you told that guy to stab Hatton?"

Edwards made a theatrically innocent face, all wide eyes and open mouth, but those eyes were cold and those massive hands were still flexing. "*I* wouldn't tell anyone to break the law. I simply asked a pal of mine to have a polite chat with Selby. I'm no thug. I'm being a good father and a good brother."

Was that pal the man who'd been in the Wig, the one Robin couldn't identify? Although that question was less important at present than the increasingly wild look in Edwards's eye and the unpleasant nervous twitch that the guy had developed. The level of tension was almost palpable, and that pile of debris wasn't yet within reach. "A good friend to Selby too?"

"Maybe. But he'll have to look after himself from now on. Here, what are you up to?"

"Nothing," Adam squeaked, instinctively backing away from the heap of potential weapons.

"Nothing, my arse. You think you can take me on, eh?" Edwards's friendly veneer had now completely slipped, revealing the deep anger behind it. The guy might have started off sounding reasonable, but maybe that was just part of an act, like he'd put on in the dock. Adam's impression that Edwards only understood violence as the solution to his problems was reinforced as he made a fist and jabbed at Adam with it. "Eh?"

Adam, heart pounding in his chest and legs turning into jelly, held his tongue. He couldn't have got a word out, even if he'd wanted to.

"I offered you the carrot, but you wouldn't take it. Fancy the stick? It's got to be one or the other. I'm not going to just let you go home, do what I asked, and then forget we had this conversation."

"But," Root cut in, "that's what you said you'd do, once you'd told him what you wanted."

"It's too late for that!" Edwards shouted, ignoring the policeman. "He had me put away. That changes things." He bent down to pick up an ugly, hefty lump of wood, one spiked with three-inch nails where it had been prized off something, then weighed it in his hands. "Is this what you were looking for? Because you're going to get it. And my mate Barry here will help clear away the mess." Cars went along the road, although none of them showed any sign of pulling up.

Adam tried to swallow, finding his mouth dry as a bone and his tongue cleaving to his palate. He should make a run for it, but his bloody legs were still on strike. Edwards meant business, Root was too scared to interfere, so how the hell was he going to get out of this alive?

Anderson swung the car into the industrial estate, screeching to a halt by a notice board that showed the names and locations of the various businesses. With a mumbled "Got it," he revved up again, guiding the car along a service road that circuited the offices and industrial units. Once they'd reached a quarter of the way round, the need for directions disappeared, the presence of an incongruous silver Audi among the vans and lorries that populated the estate signalling they'd found Edwards's business. The three blokes involved in some kind of standoff confirmed they'd reached the right place.

"Drive past. Simply ignore them. Hopefully backup will get here in time."

Anderson frowned, but he complied with Robin's order, pulling up round the corner. "I don't think they spotted us," he confided, once Robin had finished his call.

"I hope not. Root wasn't facing us, anyway."

"If Edwards did observe us, having old slobber chops in the back makes sure we don't scream out that we're cops."

"You could be right. I'm glad *you* resisted the temptation to swing into the car park. Squealing tyres have never appealed to me."

"Softly does it, eh?" Anderson eyed up the buildings. "We should be able to sneak round the other side. Or splitting up could be better, one each side."

"I assume you're not interested in waiting for backup?" Robin wasn't either, but he'd welcome reassurance that he wasn't being a macho idiot for wanting to barge in.

"Not unless we have to. Did Edwards appear to be armed?"

"I couldn't see anything, but he could be carrying in his jacket pockets. And he's built like a barn door—he wouldn't need more than a lump of wood to do a lot of damage. And there was a pile of that next to the unit door. Hey, steady, boy." Robin pushed Campbell away as the dog tried to force his way into the front of the car.

"He doesn't want to wait for backup either. Hey, get off me too." Anderson took his turn to ease the dog onto his proper seat. "Whose idea was it to bring him?"

Campbell, thwarted, scrabbled at the car window, whimpering. He'd saved Robin's bacon before, and he was clearly keen to do the same for Adam. If he'd had an opposable thumb, he'd have had the door open and been heading round the building to get at Edwards's throat by now.

"You stay here," Robin hissed at the Newfoundland. "No heroics."

"Does that order include me?" Anderson already had his hand on the door handle.

"He's more biddable than you are." Robin's voice caught at the words; Adam had used similar ones to describe Campbell when they'd first met. "Come on." He opened the passenger door but was too slow in closing it again, unable to prevent the dog, who'd managed to wiggle himself between the front seats, from leaping out and bounding off.

"Campbell!" Robin whispered loudly, reluctant to shout and alert the group the other side of the unit, but the dog was having none of it. His tail disappeared round the corner before Robin had barely got ten yards from the car.

"That idiot dog's got the taste for action." Anderson, hard at Robin's heels, followed Campbell's route. They came round the second corner in time to observe a big black lump of fur and muscle launch itself at Edwards, but unlike the previous time Campbell had saved the day, the dog was faced with a tough opponent. Edwards lashed out before the Newfoundland's teeth could connect, swinging the lump of wood to whack the animal on the head. Campbell fell to the ground, stunned—or worse—and lay without moving.

"You bastard!" Adam flung himself forward, grabbed a wooden spar from the pile, then lashed out at Edwards's arm. Root, who'd been keeping his distance, tried to seize him, but a shout from Robin made the inspector turn round, swear, then back off.

"Car!" Robin shouted at Anderson, who immediately made a dash for the Audi, seeing the need to grab the keys before Root made a getaway. Robin had other fish to fry. Edwards had dropped his own weapon and grasped the spar, twisting it out of Adam's hands, then pulling it back like a six-iron pre-shot. "Put it down!"

Edwards ignored his shout, lunging wildly at Adam's head but missing as Adam ducked out of the way, snatching up another lump of wood in the process.

"You talked about retaliation for your own. This is for Campbell." Adam smacked the board against the side of Edwards's head, sending him reeling.

"Steady on." Robin grabbed Adam's arm as he was about to get another blow in. "First one counts as self-defence. Any more than that and you'll be in trouble."

"Get *him* away from me, then." Adam flopped down beside Campbell, ear to the dog's mouth. "He's not dead." He scowled at Edwards, who'd landed on his backside, dazed. "You're bloody lucky. If you'd killed him—"

"No!" Robin was getting a pair of handcuffs on Edwards while Anderson pursued Root, who was heading for the main road but wasn't likely to make it before being overtaken. "Don't say any more. Look after our boy."

Adam forced a teary smile, then began an examination of the Newfoundland. "He's breathing steadily enough. Just out for the count, I hope."

"You want to keep him under control. Bleeding vicious mutt. Ow!" Edwards winced as Robin tightened his grip.

"You can keep your gob shut." Robin jerked on the handcuffs. "Root won't be able to help you this time."

"I don't know what you're talking about. You've got nothing on me. I was defending myself from that mutt and then this lunatic." Edwards gave Adam another dirty look. "He took a swing at me because he's got it in for me and my boys."

"I haven't got it in for you. But I *have* got an app on my phone. I've been recording everything since the car crossed the motorway." Adam, holding Campbell, extracted his phone with the other—shaking—hand. "Here—it's still going. The audio may not be too clear, but it'll back up everything I say."

Anderson, pitching up with Root in tow, sounded impressed as he said, "Keep that safe for when the cavalry arrives. They can take it in for evidence."

Root's breathless, slightly winded tones cut in. "They can have my statement to go with it. I've had enough of playing all ends against the middle."

"Seems like your number's come up, Edwards." Robin should have been ecstatic, but the great, shuddering sigh sweeping through Campbell's body as he remained out for the count took the shine off everything.

"Just—" Any argument from Edwards was cut short as a muted whimper emerged from Campbell. They waited anxiously as the dog opened an eye, lifted his head, snarled at Edwards, licked Adam's hand, then lay down again, thumping his tail against the concrete.

"You should thank your lucky stars that he's okay." Adam scowled at Edwards again before returning his attention to the casualty. "Otherwise—"

The loud screech of tyres that Robin had wanted to avoid earlier signalled the arrival of an unmarked police car and a highly visible police van, both of which pulled up not ten yards from Root's Audi. The door of the car flew open to reveal a flustered Cowdrey, who was clearly fighting between amusement and anger.

He gave Root a filthy look, then turned his attention to Robin. "I thought you were staying put at home?"

"There were developments." Robin, both arms free now that Edwards was being bundled into the police van, used one of them to make a sweep of the scene. "Time was of the essence. Fortunate I got here when I did."

"And other clichés." Cowdrey rolled his eyes, but Robin guessed he was trying to cover up the fact he was troubled.

"Now listen to me!" Adam clearly wasn't standing for any nonsense. "It's as well he and Anderson *were* here, or there might have been more murders to clear up by the time you'd arrived."

Cowdrey's eyes narrowed, as though he was about to argue, but then he sniffed, nodded, and said, "Right. Time to get this pair back to the station."

"You'll need to take my phone, too. Get a copy of what's on there. But I'll need it back as soon as you can. Unless the police want to buy me a new one," Adam added defiantly, waggling the device concerned.

If Adam had offered Cowdrey a duck-billed platypus, he couldn't have appeared more confused. "Phone?"

"I'll explain on the way to the station, sir." Anderson took the iPhone, grinning as he examined it in the fading light. "Blimey, it *is* lucky we got here when we did. The battery's pretty well run out."

Cowdrey rolled his eyes. "Come on. We've got a lot of work to do, and the Independent Police Complaints lot are going to be having a field day."

"I'll have to go with them. Sorry." Robin jerked his thumb over his shoulder at the police van.

"That's okay, honest." Adam smiled. "I'm alive, Campbell's alive; we can't expect routine to be thrown out of the window on our account. You've got a job to do."

Robin squeezed Adam's arm and smiled. "I'll take your phone. Anderson can run you home. He can take your statement there."

"We could go to the vet, first, if you want." Anderson cast a concerned glance at Campbell, although the dog was looking less bothered about his adventures by the minute.

"That's no bad idea." Adam gently stroked Campbell's paw again, avoiding contact with his head. "I'd ring her en route, but I've no phone and no idea of the number."

"Take mine." Robin got out his mobile. "Her number's stored in contacts."

"Is it?" Adam's expression of surprise, quickly turning to both relief and pride, took Robin's breath away.

"Of course." He ruffled his lover's hair. "Family, right?"

"Yeah. Thanks. I know they say that where's there's no sense there's no feeling, but I'd like the old boy checked over." Adam patted the dog's paw. "Sorry. *Young* boy."

"He wouldn't have stood up for me like that," Robin joked to Anderson, the tremble in his own voice shocking him.

"You get going." The sergeant slapped him on the shoulder. "Sooner you get this lot processed, the sooner you'll be home."

Home. Yep. How could he have doubted that Adam's house was exactly that?

A weekend on their own, at last, with no chance of the phone ringing. Cowdrey had insisted Robin get a proper break, saying that even if aliens landed, he wasn't going to be called in to work. Anderson could cover, and Davis would benefit from any extra practice that came her way, given how close her sergeant's exams were. Blackstone's may have got plenty of people through the test, but you couldn't beat hands-on experience.

Beer, packet of tortilla chips, sport on the television, Campbell lying across the carpet snoring so loud that they could hardly hear the commentary: bliss. Adam admired the bottle of Peroni beer on the table—perfectly chilled and with condensation running down it. Drips of water on green glass, a sight to well and truly whet the appetite.

Or it would have been if Adam's thoughts hadn't kept returning to unanswered questions.

"Relax." Robin patted his thigh. "What's bugging you now?"

"Nothing. Ow. Don't pinch."

Robin poked the spot he'd made sore. "I'll keep pinching until you tell me the truth."

"I keep coming back to Root. How could he have known that you weren't at home with me when he rang?"

"I'm guessing he's got spies at Stanebridge, who'll have told him I was due to be in a meeting and didn't want to be disturbed. It got cancelled, thank God."

"Yeah. Although he was still chancing his arm."

"That's no surprise. Seems he's been living on his wits the last few years, so it's no shock if he made things up as he went along. The more success he had, the more he'll have thought he could get away with."

Hubris. It asked for comeuppance. "I suppose if you'd been here, he'd have probably just hung up."

"Yeah. You wouldn't have known who it was, there was no number to go trace, and it would have left us worried, which was the whole point." Robin rubbed his knuckles together. "He'd have kept his powder dry for another day."

"And it *was* nothing but chance? You don't imagine Root might have been keeping an eye—or getting somebody else to keep an eye—on when you left the station, so he'd know he had a window of opportunity?" Adam shuddered. Worsley, Brunning, now this; the thought of people stalking the pair of them was horrific. "I wish Campbell had gone for *him* instead."

"*I* wish I'd put that spar of wood you got hold of into the boot. If it wasn't a career ruiner, I'd go round and smack both Root and Edwards with it a couple of times. Just to make me feel better."

"Says you. You're far too well behaved to do any such thing. You always play by the book. *Usually* play by the book, I should say. Or maybe even *sometimes* play by it, given the poking about in other people's cases. Whatever it is, I love you for it."

"Smoothie." Robin snuggled his head against Adam's shoulder. "I never meant you to get hurt."

"I know that, you daft bugger." Trust Robin to apologise for something that couldn't have been his fault.

"No, listen, I'm serious. I'd hate for you to ever be threatened again. Or him." Robin nudged the dog with his toe. "I'd rather get another job, out of the force entirely. I'm sure I'm a mass of transferable skills."

Adam turned Robin's face up; eye to eye, there couldn't be anything hidden. "You won't, not on that account. You love what you do."

"Do I?" Robin rolled his eyes. "I'm not so sure."

"Okay, you may have times you want to throw the whole lot up, but everyone gets like that at some point. I've seen your face when you make connections, when the light dawns on a case and a nasty little scrote ends up getting caught." Adam grazed his fingers down his lover's face, across his chin. "You'd be struggling to get that sort of job satisfaction anywhere else. And if you gave up, you'd be giving in to intimidation. We'd both hate that."

"Yeah, I suppose you're right. As usual. Teacher knows best." Robin brought Adam's fingers to his lips.

"Of course he does. He's thought long and hard about it." Adam stroked his lover's face. "The most dangerous thing you do—any of us do—is get in the car and drive. Yet we're not going to worry every time we get behind the wheel, are we? You simply take the best care you can and get on with life."

"You *do* know best." Robin shared a long kiss with him.

"Perhaps you need a change of scene," Adam murmured when he came up for air. "Get some perspective, well away from the Brunning family and the crew at Abbotston nick and all the other annoying buggers. What about applying for another district?"

Robin's face revealed his thoughts, the sudden realisation that he was at risk of throwing the baby out with the bathwater. "But I like living round here. And what about travelling distance to your new school? And . . . Oh, I get it. You called my bluff."

"Didn't I just?" And didn't it need calling? "This is no time to be making decisions. Act in haste, repent at leisure or something. Things will be different on Monday, when you're back in the office and can think about Root with a smug grin on your face. You're a born policeman."

Adam leaned down, then breathed softly on Robin's neck, at the very spot that drove the bloke wild.

"I suppose you're right." Robin squirmed happily. "Being a policeman's appropriate right now, to tell the truth. To use the old cliché, I have means of getting my hands on you, motive a-plenty, and adequate, legitimate opportunity."

Adam groaned. "You've used that line on me before. It doesn't get any better."

"I'll try a new one." Robin smirked. "What about if I said that a policeman's always got the time if you ask him nicely?"

Adam groaned again, so loudly that Campbell raised his head and gave them both a dirty look. "I suppose I'll have to keep kissing you. It's the only way to get you to shut up."

Which it did.

Explore more of the Lindenshaw Mysteries:
riptidepublishing.com/titles/series/lindenshaw-mysteries

The
Best Corpse
for the Job

Charlie Cochrane

Dear Reader,

Thank you for reading Charlie Cochrane's *Jury of One*!

We know your time is precious and you have many, many entertainment options, so it means a lot that you've chosen to spend your time reading. We really hope you enjoyed it.

We'd be honored if you'd consider posting a review—good or bad—on sites like **Amazon, Barnes & Noble, Kobo, Goodreads, Twitter, Facebook**, **Tumblr,** and your blog or website. We'd also be honored if you told your friends and family about this book. Word of mouth is a book's lifeblood!

For more information on upcoming releases, author interviews, blog tours, contests, giveaways, and more, please sign up for our weekly, spam-free newsletter and visit us around the web:

Newsletter: tinyurl.com/RiptideSignup
Twitter: twitter.com/RiptideBooks
Facebook: facebook.com/RiptidePublishing
Goodreads: tinyurl.com/RiptideOnGoodreads
Tumblr: riptidepublishing.tumblr.com

Thank you so much for Reading the Rainbow!

RiptidePublishing.com

Also by
Charlie Cochrane

Novels:
The Best Corpse for the Job
Lessons in Love
Lessons in Desire
Lessons in Discovery
Lessons in Power
Lessons in Temptation
Lessons in Seduction
Lessons in Trust
All Lessons Learned
Lessons for Survivors
Lessons for Suspicious Minds
Lessons for Idle Tongues
Lessons for Sleeping Dogs

Anthologies (contributing author)
Lashings of Sauce
Tea and Crumpet
British Flash
Encore Encore
I Do
I Do Two
Past Shadows

Standalone short stories:
Second Helpings
Awfully Glad
Don't Kiss the Vicar
Promises Made Under Fire
Tumble Turn
The Angel in the Window
Dreams of a Hero
Wolves of the West
Music in the Midst of
Desolation
All That Jazz
The Shade on a Fine Day
Sand

Paired novellas:
Home Fires Burning

About the Author

As Charlie Cochrane couldn't be trusted to do any of her jobs of choice—like managing a rugby team—she writes. Her favourite genre is gay fiction, predominantly romances/mysteries, often historical, sometimes hysterical.

Charlie's Cambridge Fellows series, set in Edwardian England, was instrumental in her being named Author of the Year 2009 by the review site Speak Its Name. She's a member of the Romantic Novelists' Association, Mystery People, and International Thriller Writers, Inc., with titles published by Carina, Samhain, Bold Strokes Books, MLR, and Riptide. She regularly appears with the Deadly Dames.

Social media links:
Facebook: facebook.com/charlie.cochrane.18
Twitter: twitter.com/charliecochrane
Goodreads: goodreads.com/author/show/2727135.Charlie_Cochrane
Blog: charliecochrane.livejournal.com
Website: charliecochrane.co.uk